AN EXCERPT FROM *TAUNT ME (ROUGH LOVE PART TWO)*

"Don't scream," said a voice against my ear.

I knew that voice. I knew the body, the height, the strength, the scent of his cologne. I knew the scratch of his stubble against my jaw and the feel of his hand over my mouth. He'd stifled me that way so many times. I lifted my eyes and looked into the mirror across my apartment and saw him behind me, holding me.

I couldn't believe for a moment that it was him, but his body curved around mine the way it used to. He looked the same, like he'd left the note for me just last week. *Good luck, starshine.* His eyes were half closed in the dim light. He took a slow breath.

"Jesus," he said. "Chere."

He was here. He was in my apartment.

Two and a half years. It had been *two and a half years.*

Motherfucker.

I started to struggle, snarling and yanking at his hand. He moved his fingers up to cover my nose. Motherfucker. Not today. I drove my elbow into his ribs and was rewarded with a grunt. He released me and I spun on him. I didn't understand why he was here. I didn't understand his dark expression. All I understood was that W was in my apartment after *two and a half years.*

I flew at him, to hurt him, not embrace him. "Motherfucker," I cried, my voice breaking. "Tell me your fucking name."

Cover art by Bad Star Media
www.badstarmedia.com

"A Chorus Girl" by E.E. Cummings was originally published in *Eight Harvard Poets*, New York, Laurence J. Gomme, 1917. It and the following poems are used in this work by rights of public domain:
"Choice" by Angela Morgan was originally published in *The Second Book of Modern Verse*, Boston, Jessie B. Rittenhouse, 1920.
"In a Boat" by D.H. Lawrence was originally published in *Amores*, London, Duckworth and Company, 1916.

Taunt Me

Rough Love Part Two

Annabel Joseph

Other Books by Annabel Joseph

Mercy
Cait and the Devil
Firebird
Owning Wednesday
Lily Mine
Disciplining the Duchess

Fortune series:

Deep in the Woods
Fortune

Comfort series:

Comfort Object
Caressa's Knees
Odalisque
Command Performance

Cirque Masters series:

Cirque de Minuit
Bound in Blue
Master's Flame

Mephisto series:

Club Mephisto
Molly's Lips: Club Mephisto Retold
Burn For You

BDSM Ballet series:

Waking Kiss
Fever Dream

Properly Spanked series:

Training Lady Townsend
To Tame A Countess
My Naughty Minette
Under A Duke's Hand

CHERE

I turned my head in the pulsating dark room, caught by a flash of blond and the hint of a white, tailored shirt. My heart rate accelerated as I looked past spanking benches and web racks to a cluster of clubgoers in the corner. By the time I filtered out the leather vests and silk bustiers, the white shirt was gone. A trick of the light, or that girl flitting across the room with the white collar.

It had been two and a half years, but I still thought I saw W sometimes. I'd catch a glimpse of him out of the corner of my eye, but then I'd look closer and realize he wasn't there.

Random things reminded me of him. A dominant stance, a hint of cologne, a man's ironic look or sneer. I stayed on the subway an extra hour once to watch this guy smile down at his device the way W used to smile down at me when he was torturing me in one of his depraved sex games. Sometimes I followed tall, muscular men down the street because they moved the way he moved or looked the way he looked. I hated myself for doing these things, because it meant I was still as weak and stupid as I'd been the first day I met him at the W Hotel.

I despised W for what he'd done to me in the course of our escort-client relationship, the way he'd humiliated me and turned me inside out, and made me love him when he'd never wanted more than a sex toy. Two months. He had fucked me up completely within the space of two months. Years later, the wounds still lingered, festering emotion and unsettled angst.

Now I watched for him at places like this, in slick, exclusive BDSM clubs in Manhattan, in hopes I might get to confront him one day. I stood on the outskirts, in all the dark corners, thinking of the things I'd tell him, the things he hadn't let me say. *I hate that you left me. I hate that you pretended to care.*

The last and only time I'd heard anything from W was a little over a year ago, when I'd received my apartment deed and title in the mail. It had come from the legal offices of Klein and Dunsingbush, containing my full legal name and address, and the name and address of the conveying party. W's real name? Of course not. The property came to me from "Taunt, Incorporated," his dummy corporation. I remembered the poetic allusion at once, as I'm sure he meant me to:

I'd rather have the want of you
The rich, elusive taunt of you

He was an asshole. A generous asshole, but still. His taunts were all around me and he knew it. Living in his apartment was a taunt, visiting these BDSM clubs was a taunt, my memories of him were a taunt I wished I could forget. He'd left me, deserted me, knowing full well I'd never be able to get over him. Taunt, Incorporated? Fuck you very much.

Since then, there'd been no other W-related contact, which was probably for the best. I wanted my heart to be free, and I'd kept it free of other entanglements since I'd walked out of the Gramercy Park Hotel with W's glib dismissal in my hand. *Good luck, starshine*, he'd written.

I repeated that to myself whenever I started to feel too much, or care too much about someone who attracted me. It had become my mantra of self-awareness. *Good luck, starshine. You're just going to get fucked again.* I didn't even want to try. Love hurt too much, and I was clearly bad at it, based on my past and the selfish, harmful jerks I'd fallen for.

Instead I prowled the kink clubs in search of W, in search of closure, as if there could ever be closure for our fucked-up thing. I'd try to resist, stay home and watch TV instead, but then I'd think, *what if this is the day he shows up? What if I miss him?* I was a design major, not a math major. I chose not to think about the insurmountable odds of running into one soul-destructing pervert amidst the thousands in attendance at fetish clubs in New York City on any given night.

Forget the odds of running into him in New York—a rich guy like him might play in a different city every weekend. Vegas, London, Manila, Hong Kong, Berlin, the fucking Bahamas... By the time you added up those odds, running into him again seemed pretty impossible.

Good luck, starshine.

Ugh.

I watched a nearby couple whispering to each other, a thin, blond submissive male and his bear of a Dominant. The sub wore a black leather harness that accentuated cut muscles while simultaneously making him seem lithe and petite. Directly across from me, a woman moaned under her Domme's whip. I couldn't see anything of W in that statuesque and businesslike dominatrix. She was restrained elegance, and he was...

He was passion and violence, and all the fucked-up things.

Beyond the Domme and her sub, a well-known rigger decorated a woman in webs of robe. She was gone, utterly blissed out as he manipulated her body. He was tender and attentive, nuzzling her as he worked at the pattern of knots. I could see a little bit of W in him, in the control he exerted over the woman, but any similarity ended there. It bothered me that I still compared all men to W. It bothered me that I remembered so clearly the dread and adrenaline of being under his power.

The Domme laughed, a mocking, joyful crowing, as her submissive victim waggled her bottom. There was appreciative laughter, a round of applause. The gay couple beside me remained in a world of their own. The bear unzipped, never breaking eye contact, as he played with his sub's wild, blond curly hair. A moment later he grabbed a handful of those curls, and the harnessed plaything melted to his knees.

I tried not to watch, but I listened. W used to do that, grab my hair like that, and I used to melt for him in the same way. The young man made such beautiful moans and noises. Had I made noises like that? W used to choke me and slap my face, and drive into my throat until I couldn't breathe.

The bear was growing more passionate—rougher—by the moment, not that his sub seemed to mind. I felt like an interloper. I hid my furtive glances beneath the dark curtain of my hair. Right after I stopped escorting, I'd gone back to my natural hair color, because brunettes blended in more easily than peroxide blondes. I'd also stopped straightening it. I'd basically changed everything about myself in an effort to become someone new and better, and indestructible. Not that I felt indestructible on any given day.

The scene with the Domme ended and another scene began. The characters took their places with their props: the top, the bottom, the bondage, the implements. I'd learned a lot about BDSM in the past couple years, since I'd been coming to the clubs. I learned that most people do BDSM in a relaxed and civilized way, protected by strict rules of consent. Within that consent, a whole array of activities might happen, some of them even wilder than the things W had done to me. We had never really negotiated, though, like these people. Everything he did to me was a trauma or a surprise.

And you loved that, Chere. You lived for those sessions.

Once the new Dom had his sub arranged on the spanking bench, he leaned down and whispered to her as he stroked her shoulder. So relaxed. So *civilized*. Sometimes I tried to convince myself that my "thing" with W had superseded such niceties as consent and civility, that we were *that* passionately connected, but then I remembered that our connection was pure illusion, and that he'd never even told me his name. To this day, I didn't know his name. I'd bet that submissive knew her Dominant's name, knew where he lived, knew his phone number.

I retreated farther into the shadows. The blond sub beside me was still on his knees, giving an incredible blowjob, if his Master's drawn-out groans and grunts were any indication. The massive, muscular man was twice his size, and he wasn't being gentle as he rammed his cock into the sub's throat. I stood behind another couple so I could full-on stare at the blowjob without being noticed.

Watching them brought everything back: W's force, his scent, even the hardness of his cock against my tongue and lips. This Master wasn't as tall and handsome as W, but the aura of command was there. He finished with a roar, rearing deep into the sub's throat, and the sub knelt there and took it in graceful surrender. Tears filled my eyes from the memories, or maybe the knowledge that I had never been that good. I'd always fought. W told me that he liked it that I fought. It didn't matter now.

He'd left me.

The Master stepped back and disengaged from the sub's mouth with a clumsy, awkward pat to his shoulders. The younger man looked up at him with a clear offer of continued availability. The Master wove a hand through the sub's blond curls and then, to my shock, turned and walked away. I watched the sub, expecting him to crumble. Instead, he sat against the wall, took an elastic off his wrist, and used it to pull back his shoulder-length hair.

Wow. Not crushed at all. Apparently he didn't care much about the man he'd just submitted to. After a longer look, I realized I knew the guy from Norton Art and Design. Now that his hair was pulled back, I recognized his face from the cafeteria, and the subway station where we often waited for the same trains on the way to class. While I stared at him like an idiot, he gave a little wave, then reached to adjust the straps of his harness.

I turned away, embarrassed. His act of submission had brought back so many uneasy memories. A moment later, I felt a brush of contact on my shoulder.

"You okay?" he asked.

"Yeah. I'm sorry if I was staring."

"I don't care if you stare." He grinned at me. "I like when people stare. I'm an exhibitionist. Well, I'm a lot of things, but 'exhibitionist' is near the top of the list."

I ran my eyes over his very impressive physique. Since he was an exhibitionist, he probably didn't mind.

"I think I know you," he said.

"I go to Norton."

"That's it." He snapped his fingers. "Digital art?"

"No. Commercial design. Metals. But I think we shared a drawing class first year."

"Yeah, we did. I remember now."

The sub tinkered with his harness again. He seemed nice, maybe a little shy for all his bold subservience. I thought he would leave, even though I kind of wanted him to stay. It had been so long since I felt anything in common with someone. "Are *you* in digital art?" I asked, to keep the conversation going.

"Fine Arts," he said. "Painting."

Painting, like my ex-boyfriend Simon. I wondered if he was moody and precious in the studio, the way Simon used to be. I wondered if he used drugs.

"I had a boyfriend once who was a painter," I said. "Things didn't end well."

"Painters make shitty boyfriends," he joked.

"I agree. Let's not talk about it." I was trying to joke back. Probably failing. My lips wobbled and my voice wobbled and all I really wanted to know was how he could be so happy when his Master had just finished with him and walked away.

"Are you okay, really?" he asked.

"I'm okay. It's just that…things get intense here sometimes."

"Yeah. When I'm here I like to let my hair down, in more ways than one. But it's good, don't you think? I like that dude," he said, gesturing in the direction the bear had gone. "He really gets into it. We hook up now and again."

"Oh. And you like that?"

He shrugged. The chains on his harness tinkled with the movement. "I don't dislike it. I'm looking for The One like everyone else, but in the meantime, I might as well have a little fun. Stay in practice and all that," he added with a wink.

"When you were with him... The intensity...it reminded me of someone I used to know."

"Really?" His eyes were dark like mine, and he had straight, white teeth. "And did you sub to this 'someone you used to know'?"

"Yeah. I was the sub in our relationship, I guess."

"If you're guessing, honey, he wasn't doing it right."

I sucked in a breath. "He definitely wasn't doing it right, but I was for sure the sub within our...thing."

"Your *thing*?" He put a hand on my arm and gave me a sympathetic look. "I love a girl who'll refer to a relationship as a 'thing.' I've had a few 'things' myself. That sounds like the beginning of a painful and fucked-up story."

"You have no idea."

He threw a look around the room, at laughter and perversity and lust. Like everyone else, he knew I didn't belong here. Unlike everyone else, he was friendly to me anyway.

"You want to go get some coffee somewhere, and tell me your painful, fucked-up story?"

I looked around too, everywhere but his dark, earnest gaze. "I don't know. It's possibly too painful and fucked-up to tell."

"Then I'll tell you some painful, fucked-up stories instead. Most of them are good for a laugh."

I hesitated. I'd been living as a closed-off, emotionally unavailable hermit for so long, rejecting even the kindest advances of my classmates. But here was someone who might understand my dark inner world.

But...

"Will you tell me your name?" I asked.

He laughed. "Of course I will. I should have before. It's Andrew." He held up a hand just out of reach. "I'd shake, but you know where this hand has been. Let me clean up and put on some real clothes..." He trailed off, expectantly waiting for my name.

"Chere," I said. "Like the French word for dear.'"

"Okay, Chere, my dear. Wait here, all right? And we'll go get some coffee and something to eat. We Norton *artistes* have to stick together, especially when one of us looks so fucking bleak."

That was me, the bleak one, and him? He seemed kind and bright, so different from Simon's tortured level of painter-*artiste.* "I'll wait here, Andrew," I promised.

And silently, to myself I added, *Thank you for telling me your name.*

PRICE

There's a difference between being private and being an asshole. I never told Chere my name because I was an asshole.

For the record, my name is Price Thomas Eriksen. I'm forty years old and I live on Bleecker Street, across from the apartment I gave her. Never been married, no kids. I work a lot, more than anyone should, and I travel a lot, to China, the Middle East, Europe, Russia, more places than I can remember.

I'm known professionally as P.T. Eriksen, sort of the way Edward Estlin Cummings was known as E.E. Cummings. I can't defend the fact that I never revealed any of this to her, except that I was an asshole, and I thought secrecy and privacy might maintain some barriers between us. When they didn't, I got uncomfortable and left.

I didn't leave her with nothing. To atone for my crimes against her body and her psyche, I gave her an apartment. I got her into my alma mater, the prestigious Norton School of Art and Design, by arranging a fake scholarship in my grandmother's name. You could do that kind of shit when you had money and influence, even if you were an asshole. I'd watched from across the street as she arrived for class the first day, nervous, newly dark-haired, clutching a large leather portfolio. She didn't see me, although I was sitting in front of a coffee shop not fifty yards away. In the beginning I'd watched her a lot, watched her in her apartment, watched her on the subway. It wasn't stalking.

Well, yeah. It was stalking, but only with benevolent intent. I had to be sure she'd swim instead of sink. I had to be sure she wouldn't go running back to her drug-addicted boyfriend or her smooth-talking pimp as soon as I was out of the picture. I had to be sure she was as strong as I thought she was, and she'd impressed me by being even stronger than I thought she was.

Once she'd settled into her new life, I tried to settle back into mine. There was always work to do, a skyscraper to design in Jordan, and then a suspension bridge to consult on in Brussels. I stressed about her when I was away, but then I'd return and look through my binoculars into her sixth floor apartment, and find her completely safe. She was secure and busy, if not happy.

She hadn't been happy in a while now.

I'm sorry I left you, Chere. It was better that way.

Now I was just back from Edinburgh, skulking around the same coffee shop, watching her leave Norton with her curly-haired buddy. They'd been hanging out for a couple weeks now, but he wasn't her boyfriend. I'd checked. No, he was gay as fuck, and steady and well-adjusted, so I approved. He smiled at her and seemed to care about her. She needed that, all those things I could never give her. Kindness. Nurturing. Love.

I preferred hurting and mindfucking to love. I liked rough, encompassing control and sexual mayhem. Unfortunately, Chere didn't need another asshole taking over her life and jerking her around. Oh, I would have treated her better than Simon, but I wasn't sure it would feel better to *her*, because she was looking for romantic, caring love, and I had none of that to give.

I have nothing against romantic love. I don't care if other people want to believe in it, but I personally think it's shit. I think it's fake, imaginary, stupid, a fairy tale made up for the weak and needy people of the world. It's a construct created to sell roses on Valentine's Day, and seats at fantasy-fulfillment chick-flicks. I avoided romance as a rule, even if I'd written out a few lovey-dovey poems for a bleach-blonde prostitute. Momentary weakness, nothing more.

Now Chere had dark hair and spiral curls she tugged on while she sat at her computer working on her design projects. I wanted to fuck those curls. I wanted to fuck Chere, but I couldn't, because I wasn't what she was looking for. She'd taken so many positive steps to turn around her life. She was in school. She was kicking ass. I had to leave her alone. She was serious about becoming a designer, and she'd be happier as a designer than an escort. As much as I enjoyed fucking her, she wasn't for me.

But sometimes I wished she was for me. Sometimes I sat in the dungeon next to my bedroom and imagined her bound to the rack, or manacled to the chains anchored in the ceiling. Sometimes when I stared at her through my binoculars, I imagined knocking on her door and inviting her to my place, and taking her in that dungeon and keeping her there, even against her will.

Chere thought the worst thing between us was the leaving. She was wrong. The worst thing was what I had started wanting from her by the end, what I still wanted from her with inappropriate intensity: her tears and misery, her trembling surrender, and my selfish perversity unhinging her soul.

Chere

Andrew half-skipped, half-walked me down a silent hallway, past office doors and faint fluorescent lights. It was almost midnight and the studio wing was closed, but Andrew knew the night guard and managed to get us in.

"Are you sure we're allowed to do this?" I asked.

He turned back to me. "You heard what I told Grayson. I have a project to finish. I might have lied when I said it was due tomorrow, but I want you to see it."

"I thought we were going to do something fun, not hang out in the paint lab. I don't make you hang out in the metals lab."

Andrew rolled his eyes. "Because the metals lab is horrifically boring. Spoons and drain grates and thermostat covers. Kill me."

I designed spoons and drain grates and thermostat covers, and I knew Andrew was only kidding. When he got out of Norton, he'd probably take some workaday design job too until he caught a break with his painting.

"It's called the Norton School of *Art* and Design," he went on. "Notice which one they put first? Art. We're the acknowledged badasses of this place." He pumped a paint-stained fist, pretending not to notice when I muttered something about asses. "Besides, it's fun hanging out in the studio at night."

"How is it fun?"

"It's fun, Chere. It's peaceful and super cool, and you can look up at the night sky."

I followed him a few steps farther, and then the smell reached me, the odor of stripper, primer, and oil paint. It transported me right back in time to my ex's art studio.

"Jesus." I stopped in the hall. I wanted to see Andrew's work, but that smell triggered too many memories.

"I know." Andrew wrinkled his nose. "The stench of creation. You get used to it."

"It's not that."

He looked at me a moment, then understanding dawned. He reached for my hand.

"Are you thinking about Simon? Don't think about Simon."

The first night, over coffee, Andrew had wanted my "painful and fucked-up story" and it had been easier to talk about Simon than W, so that was the fucked-up story I told. Andrew had already known who Simon Baldwin was, because Simon was the current darling of the New York art scene. Since we'd broken up, Simon's career had gone stellar, his drug-fueled mania and erratic craziness driving his burgeoning talent to unforeseeable heights. Critics dubbed him the *Tribeca Train Wreck*, tsking at his narcotic shenanigans while they crowed about the genius of his work.

And they were right, his paintings were genius. Since I'd left Simon, the art had come at a frenetic pace, the paintings and murals, the packed galleries and sold-out shows. He'd attracted a major following, not just in New York, but also in the international art world. I tried to be happy for him. It was hard.

When Andrew learned how abusive Simon had been to me, he looked like he'd been stabbed by a unicorn. But Andrew was faithful to our friendship and immediately demoted his hero from "best artist of all time" to asshole. He'd done that for me, because he was that kind of person.

"Maybe this will be good for you," he said, tugging me forward. The smell was getting worse. "It'll be good for you to be around painters who aren't psychotic, abusive assholes."

"But no one else is here."

"I'm here! And you know what I mean. It'll be good for you to be around art stuff. To be in a messy, creative place with good energy. You need good energy, girl."

"I need to go to bed. It's late."

We reached a heavy door marked *PAINTING STUDIO*. Andrew swiped his student ID and the lock clicked open.

The smell inside turned out to be ten times worse than the smell in Simon's studio, I suppose because this room was ten times bigger, with easels, canvases, and paint-strewn tables and work benches arranged in a mish-mash pattern.

"Come on," he said, guiding me toward the center of the studio. We wove around corners, past half-finished paintings that looked ghostly under weak work lamps.

"Why is it so dim in here?" I asked.

"It's best to paint by natural light." He pointed at the ceiling, at rectangular skylights. "The lighting's designed to complement, not illuminate. This studio's not meant to be used at night."

"It's freaking creepy."

"I know." He grinned. "I love it."

He left me and darted between two workstations, disappearing from sight. "Andrew?" I peered into the dark corners. "Come back."

"Just a sec," he called from a few rows over.

I hugged myself, trying to figure out if it was the ghostly lights or the reminders of Simon that made me so uneasy. I remembered all of this: the paintbrushes, the cans, the palettes and color-streaked towels, the thick, enveloping smell...

I jumped as music blasted through a speaker a few feet away. Andrew said "Oops" and turned it down a dozen decibels or so. Trippy 60's music wafted from all four corners of the room, and Andrew reappeared, brushing an errant blond curl back into the mop barely contained by his furry fuchsia scrunchie.

"*Evermore*," he said, pointing to the nearest speaker.

"This band is Evermore?"

"The band is Led Zeppelin. The song's called *The Battle of Evermore.* Geez, you're in art school. Why don't you know stuff?"

Andrew's insults were always delivered with a smirk that made it impossible to feel pissed. He grabbed my hand again. "My carrel's over here. I've been working on some paintings for my senior exhibit. Come see."

I've been working on some paintings. Come see. Simon used to say that to me, at least until he got strung out on drugs and turned into another person. Andrew's workspace was near the back corner, a disorganized but joyful explosion of color. Unlike Simon, Andrew painted real things, people who drew you in, and everyday objects that made you look twice. I'd seen some of his work at his apartment, but I'd never seen it in progress, spread around makeshift walls.

"This looks so...creative," I said. "You hang out here every day?"

"Whenever I can. We're old school in the paint lab. We can't do our projects on computers like you design nerds."

"I'm not a nerd, thank you."

"You are, but that's okay."

Andrew's work was like his personality, clear and fresh and unaffected. You couldn't not look, and one look was all it took to fall in love.

"You're going to be famous someday," I said. "How could anyone not want to own this?" I pointed to a work in progress, a young child in rough brush strokes. Boy or girl, it was hard to tell, but the features glowed. "Who is that?"

"The daughter of a friend. She's adorbs."

"It's the most beautiful portrait I've ever seen."

He blushed. One of his curls had broken loose again, a corkscrew of energy, like Andrew's soul. I smoothed it back behind his ear.

"You're too nice to me," he said. "Why are you so nice to me?"

I looked into his eyes and didn't answer. We'd been hanging out a lot since we struck up our unlikely friendship at the fetish club. We'd grown really close, even though we were different in so many ways. I was a decade older than him, and hetero, and an ex-prostitute, although I hadn't been brave enough to reveal that to him yet.

I sat on the edge of his carrel, a rolling workstation that doubled as an art pedestal. The music had changed to a quieter, more contemplative song, and I thought how fortunate I was to have Andrew in my life. Before him, I'd pretty much forgotten how to feel things. Or maybe I'd decided not to feel things. Now a bunch of feelings caught me by surprise.

Hope, wonder, maybe...happiness? The kind of happiness that felt sad at the same time.

Andrew lay back across the platform, knocking over a can of brushes. We scooped them up together, and he placed the can on a nearby desk. By the time he returned, I was lying back on the platform too. I could see gray clouds through the skylights, and the looming shadows of nearby buildings.

"I come here for the peace," he murmured. "It's very peaceful, to be in a place full of art. Maybe you don't feel that way, after Simon…"

He touched my side. It was a friendly touch, a comforting touch. That was the nice thing about gay friends. You didn't have to worry about them making some kind of uncomfortable move during an emotional moment.

"I'm sorry," he said. "I'm sorry if being here is bringing back bad memories, and I'm sorry your ex was an abusive prick. Why isn't he in prison or something? With the drugs, and the stuff he did to you?"

"I guess because he's good at surrounding himself with enablers. I stayed with him for years, and explained away all his shit. Somehow I turned 'He's abusing me' into 'He needs me.' How sick is that?"

I stared up at the sky, like it might have answers. Even Andrew didn't have answers.

"I want to meet someone well-adjusted," he said. "Someone nice. I want to love someone."

"I don't have the Y-chromosome you need, or I'd beg you to fall in love with me. You're handsome and kind, and you have beautiful hair."

"Aw, Chere."

"You'll find someone. You're the easiest person in the world to talk to. You're considerate. You're vivacious."

"I'm anxious. I'm obsessive. I'm clingy in relationships. I put up with total bullshit just to spend the night with someone. Most of the time, I'm like a starving stray dog, grateful for scraps."

That was my cue to say something reassuring and uplifting, but I had nothing. I'd lost faith in happily ever afters long ago. "The problem with love is that there's only a one in a hundred chance it'll work out," I said. "I mean, that's just science."

"Really? That's been scientifically proven?" Andrew wasn't buying it. He formed his fingers into the shape of a heart and held it above us. "I believe in love. I just have to find it. That's your one-in-a-hundred chance: not just finding that person the universe has set aside for you, but recognizing that he's the one. I understand your issues since you got burned so bad in your last relationship, but there's someone out there for you."

"I don't want anyone."

He made an impatient noise and let his fingers drop. Our heads touched as we stared up at the same patch of wispy clouds. The music swirled around us, wistful, slow, melodious, as complex as our feelings and the general screwiness of life. *Don't think about him.*

Not Simon. It wasn't Simon haunting me.

I'd rather have the want of you, the rich, elusive taunt of you...

"You know what I want?" said Andrew, breaking into my thoughts.

"What do you want?" I replied in a soft voice.

"I want someone to love me for me. With all my faults and shortcomings, with my skinny body, my personality flaws. I'm tired of trying to be someone better, someone worthy. I just want to be me. I want someone I can be honest with, someone who'll accept me as I am."

Tears gathered in my eyes at the tortured longing in his voice. He was so innocent, so sweet, so sure that his true love was out there. It made me sad.

"The thing is, people are so shitty," I said, my voice trembling. "No one loves. No one cares. No one is faithful. Everyone is cruel and fucking awful."

The song changed to a rock anthem. My face ached with the effort not to cry, but some tears squeezed out anyway. Andrew scooted closer to me, until his head rested against my shoulder. His hair tickled my cheek but I didn't move my head. I realized he was crying too. The music was rough and hypnotic, twanging guitars and words I couldn't understand. Maybe the paint fumes were making both of us a little high. I stared at the black night through the windows as Andrew lay beside me, my partner in misery, my stalwart friend.

"I'm sorry I'm so down on love," I said. "It's just difficult for me. I could tell you things about my past..."

"What kind of things?"

"Nothing. Stupid things I want to forget. I'm sorry I made you cry."

"I'm crying because you're crying." He wiped my eyes with the edge of his sleeve, a gesture that was so gentle and normal it made me start bawling again. "No one should be down on love, Chere. Our purpose in life is to love."

Was it? Maybe that was why my heart felt so black and dead and decrepit, and so numb. I felt so numb I thought I might disappear completely, without touching anyone or anything. That was disappearance, pure and simple, the opposite of being alive. Which meant I was dead.

His hand touched mine and I gathered my courage, and closed my fingers around his. In the dim fluorescent light, with our shoulders touching, I decided to tell him everything.

"You want to know a secret about me? I used to be a prostitute," I said. "A high-class escort. I used to see three or four clients a week." I paused for him to freak out, but he didn't. The lack of reaction gave me the fortitude to forge ahead. "And just before I got out of the business, there was this guy..."

Price

When I first met Chere, I was pissed. I'd told her pimp—excuse me, her *agent*—that I wanted a beautiful, natural blonde. Chere was beautiful, yes, but as far from a natural blonde as you could get. Her hair was fake on purpose, the kind of sex-kitten, Marilyn-Monroe blonde that broadcast "I'm a sex object." Beneath her fake-blonde hair and Lanvin suit, she was pure guttersnipe, with old New Orleans features, dusky skin and freckles. Her body was strong, not elegant. She wasn't what I wanted at all.

I almost sent her away, but there was something about the tilt of her chin that compelled me. I'd bound her instead, with cheap hardware-store zip ties. I did everything bad to her that first session. I insulted her, I called her a bitch. I slapped her face and made her call me Sir. Worst of all, I didn't let her see me or know my name. All these awful things were done to her by a nameless, faceless stranger who had complete control.

She was hysterical and fake that day, but something clicked for me by the end of our date, clicked as it had never clicked before. I wanted to fuck her so hard and so rough by the end that I probably could have fuck-killed her if I was that kind of guy. But I wasn't. I didn't harbor any psychopathic desires to maim or kill women. I only wanted to feel something honest, and there was nothing more honest than a woman going batshit crazy because of the shit you were doing to her. I throat-fucked her—hard—and I pussy-fucked her—hard—and she submitted to it with such delicious ambivalence. She didn't want it, but she *did.*

I can't explain my fetishes...why I need women to want it and not want it. I can't pinpoint where my force-driven fantasies came from, or recall the moment sex and suffering crystallized, for me, as a necessary combination. I'll only say this: I never met a woman who wanted it and didn't want it with the same intensity as Chere Rouzier. The second time I slapped her, the hardest time I slapped her, it triggered a monumental orgasm for her.

I almost let her go, I thought as I watched her tremble through the climax. *I almost let this one go.*

I'd been rough with a lot of women through the years. I sought out self-identified masochists so as not to waste anyone's time, and when I slapped them during sex, I got two responses. They either liked it too much, which I hated, or they pretended to like it, which I also hated. But Chere neither liked it nor pretended to like it. She hated it, and came anyway like a fucking madwoman.

I'd gazed down at her on the bed, watched her squirm, blindfolded, shivering, so overcome by my sexual demands that she couldn't speak. Her nipples had been red and sore, and her hands had been bound behind her, and I thought, *this is the most fulfilling intimate encounter I've ever had.* I'd grabbed her face and kissed her, overwhelmed in my own way. I felt angry that it had taken so long to find this amazing partner, and crazed that I'd almost rejected her, and anxious that she wouldn't see me again.

The first thing she said to me after she came was *Please let me look at you.* And I knew I would let her look at me eventually, which was really unsettling. I knew if she kept giving herself to me with so much spirit and so much fight, and so much goddamned intensity, things would get out of hand. It didn't take long for things to get batshit crazy, although I suppose it was worth it.

Every time I saw her, I thought, *I want to hurt you. I have to hurt you. Please let me hurt you.*

And she let me. Every single time.

Chere

Fall semester wound down, dreary winter days in the dreary metals lab. Andrew was right, the labs were awful, but metals were my thing. I loved the shine, I loved the solidity. This lab was my second home, and I was probably one of the more obsessive students. I maintained a prickly, love-hate relationship with my metals professor, a hawk-nosed hardass named Martin Cantor.

From first year onward, Cantor picked on me more than anyone else. It was irritating, but it also meant he paid more attention to me, so I put up with his constant criticisms. I figured maybe it was because I was older, or because he wasn't able to ruffle me the way he ruffled some of the other female students. When Andrew dropped by the labs once, he decided Professor Cantor was in love with me, and renamed him Professor Predator.

"This is your last semester before your internships," Cantor said as he dispersed us to our various stations. "You may think your vision is everything, that you know enough, that you're prepared to get out there and do spectacular things, but I have news for you. You're not."

Some of my classmates shifted uncomfortably. His gaze landed on each of us in turn, judging, measuring. When his eyes fell on me, I stared back.

His gaze lingered, betraying a hint of irritation before moving on. It reminded me a little of W, that gaze. I wondered if the man was secretly into rough, perverted sex, if he choked his wife every night after he finished preparing his lesson plans. I knew he was married—he wore an obtrusively large, ornate gold wedding ring that he'd doubtless designed himself.

Once the threatening lecture was over, we moved to our sections around the room. I knew everyone in the class, even if we weren't close friends. They were my metal peeps, drawn to the same tools, the blowtorches and solders, hammers, punches, bits, and picks. Most of us were in our final year, and would soon be paired with some successful Norton graduate in the field.

The professor moved around the room as we worked, asking students what they hoped to accomplish during their upcoming internships. When he arrived at my workspace, I kept my eyes on my project, a miniature silver-plated spoon with filigree of my own design.

"Tableware," he scoffed. "How original."

"Everyone uses it. There's a market for it." I straightened and met his eyes. Depending on the light—and his mood—they were either dark brown or satanic black.

"Is that important to you?" he asked. "Creating for a market?"

"I don't usually make silverware, Dr. Cantor. It was just something to try."

"Trying things is good. Catering to the market is bad. That's not artistry, Chere. It smacks of cowardice."

"I'm not a coward." It came out too loud, too defensive.

He studied me. "Have I touched on a nerve?"

I turned my electric engraver over in my hand. I didn't like the low, taunting way he said it, like he knew me or something. No one knew me. I worked hard to keep it that way.

"What did you do before?" he asked.

"Before?"

"Before you came to Norton. Did you have another career?"

A flush burned over my cheeks. Did he *know*? I studied his face, but there was no hint of lurid insinuation in his gaze.

"Shall I guess?" he said when I didn't answer. His eyes flicked to my tiny silver spoon. "Food service, perhaps?"

He still wore that underdeveloped, insincere smile. A lot of the students here found him attractive, but to me, he was Professor Predator through and through. "I was in the customer service industry," I finally said.

"Ah, service."

He said "service" like it was something sexy. Ugh. *Eww.* Dom, I thought. He had to be a Dom. Maybe he'd noticed me in one of my numerous forays to Manhattan's BDSM clubs. Maybe he'd stared at me from some hidden corner. I remembered, with a sudden, intense prickling on the back of my neck, all those times that I'd felt watched, not that I ever did anything besides skulk in the corner.

"Why is it so small?" he asked. He picked up my spoon, squinting at the half-finished etching. "The design's nicely wrought, if a little pedestrian." He turned to my case, looking over some of my recent work. He studied the rings and earrings and chains, the simple pins and streamlined hair clips.

"You make such delicate things," he said, touching a pair of very tiny, very spare hoop earrings. "Why do you make everything so small and simple?"

"I don't know."

"You should know. You should know why you design the things you design. Until you know, I'm not sure we can find you the internship you need."

His gaze raked over me, and I had the weirdest feeling he wanted to punish me. I felt like I'd just been verbally spanked. But this wasn't a BDSM club, it was a design lab, and he was my professor.

"Well, think about it," he said, moving away.

I took a deep breath and shook off the icky feeling of his closeness as he turned to inspect another student's work. Dark hair curled at his nape, shot through with a few strands of gray. Early forties? Cantor was W's age, probably.

Stop it, Chere. Stop thinking about him.

I'd had too much W on the brain lately. I blamed it on Andrew and his obsession with our history. I'd only told him the basics of what transpired between us, but then I made the mistake of showing him W's poetry. Now he insisted I *had* to find him, if only to demand what all that poetry meant. To that end, he'd bullied me into inviting Henry to lunch, since he was the one who'd set up my dates when I was escorting. I'd already pumped Henry for info many times, but that didn't discourage my friend.

Andrew was waiting for me at the Big Apple Diner with a huge smile. His hair looked especially curly and cute.

"Hi, beautiful," he said, giving me a hug and kiss in welcome. "Is Henry here yet?"

I scanned the half-empty, hole-in-the-wall restaurant. "Not yet. You'll know him when you see him. He shines."

"How was your lab?" he asked as we slid into a booth against a mirrored wall. "You had metals today, yes?"

"It's all metals for me this semester, and class was okay. Cantor was exuding his usual creepy presence."

"For God's sake, tell me all the details."

"His voice, his manner, his eyes, his lecture. All of it was creepy today." I suppressed a shudder, recalling the way he'd said *service* to me.

"Ah, good old Professor Predator. He wants you, I swear. The day I saw him, he looked like he wanted to take out his cock and rub it all over your face."

"You're making that up to gross me out."

"Maybe. But he was definitely, *definitely* staring at your breasts."

"He didn't stare at my breasts today. He stared at my eyes like he was trying to Dom me."

"Ooh, how exciting."

We gave our drink order to the waitress and Andrew filled me in on his day, his time in the studio and his preparations for his senior exhibit.

"I don't get it," he said, rolling his eyes. "We still have a semester to go, and I feel like they're trying to push us out into the world early. The whole class is all about *What are your goals? Where are you going? What are you doing next?* They want us to network, to intern, to find galleries where we can do shows. How the fuck are we supposed to do shows with the senior exhibit coming up?" He dropped his voice. "A couple students left."

"Left the class?"

"No, left Norton. Left to start their careers. Or give up. No one knows. They just stopped showing up."

"Maybe they're sick."

"No, their carrels are empty. They left. Not in the class anymore."

Andrew's fingers tapped restlessly on the laminate tabletop. The painting group wasn't very big to begin with. It was one of those super risky careers.

"You're gonna do great," I said. "Don't freak yourself out. You have a really fresh style, a vision—"

He interrupted me with a frantic hand motion. "I see a vision. He *shines.*"

I turned, and sure enough, there was Henry in all his golden-haired, sexy-pimp glory. He was wearing a current season Armani suit and a purple tie, and he walked like he'd just left a limo full of fawning beauties. He probably had. I grinned as he pulled me out of the booth and hugged me.

"Chere, love. You look great. How are you?"

It said a lot about Henry, that we were still friends even though I'd stopped escorting for him. He hugged me nice and tight, a real hug, and then turned to Andrew.

I performed the introductions as Andrew ogled him worshipfully. Henry had it going on, in more than just the looks department. If he wasn't constantly involved in illegal enterprises, I might have developed a crush on him myself.

Henry cast a bemused glance around the place. "Nice shithole you picked."

"The food's good. We eat here all the time."

He rolled his eyes. "Students. Anyway, it was great to hear from you. What's up? Is everything okay? You must be nearing graduation."

"Yes. Andrew is too," I said, gesturing across the table. My friend preened. "One more semester to go."

"You like it?"

"Yeah, I do. The tedious classes are over. Most of our classes now involve making actual stuff, which is fun."

"Still into the shiny things?"

Andrew smothered a laugh, since we'd called Henry "shiny" twice.

"I love shiny things," I said effusively, which made Andrew giggle harder. "So how's business with you?"

The waitress came to take our order, and then Henry pitched into a very candid recitation of the most recent client contacts, and new hires, omitting names of course. He caught me up on some of my old coworkers, all of whom were doing well. His pride in his business was evident. I guess that was why I'd always enjoyed working for him, at least until the end. Andrew followed our conversation with goggle-eyed interest.

"How often do you hire new people?" he interrupted at one point. "Or, more specifically, do you ever get requests for really submissive, really obedient gay male subs?"

Henry looked Andrew up and down with interest. "As a matter of fact, we do."

I held up a hand. "No. We're not here for that."

"I have some clients who'd love to get a hold of that hair," Henry said, eyeing Andrew's crowning mop of curls.

"I said no." I waved a finger at Andrew. "You're about to graduate. You're going to be an artist, not a rent boy."

Henry and Andrew exchanged a look that made me want to slap them both.

"This isn't a recruitment lunch," I said to Henry. "We're here to ask for information about someone. One of my old clients."

"You know I can't give out personal information, Chere. People trust us to protect their privacy."

We paused as the waitress arrived with our sandwiches and greasy fries. Henry gave his plate a doubtful glance and sighed. "You're talking about your final client, I assume?"

I didn't want to ask it, but the question burst out anyway. "Did he continue using Sublime Services after I left? Did he start seeing anyone else?"

"I can't talk about that kind of thing," he said, reaching for the ketchup, "but if I could, I'd probably answer no."

Henry looked at me a little too closely as he wielded the ketchup bottle. I busied myself scraping mustard off my sandwich and dripping it onto my plate. I didn't want to care if W had seen one or a thousand escorts after me, but I did care. Maybe he'd simply gone to another agency. I felt a flush rise in my neck and cheeks, because I knew Henry would see right through my façade of disinterest.

"We were wondering if you ever noticed anything about him that might indicate where he was from," Andrew asked. "Or what he did for a living."

"I'm sorry. I've told you everything I can about Mr. Cumming. It's not unusual in this business for clients to guard their privacy. If he never told Chere anything about himself, I'm sure that was intentional." He tossed down a greasy French fry and turned to me, crossing his arms on the table. "I believe he stopped seeing you because he felt too embroiled in your life. I should never have allowed the two of you to go exclusive. If he started to care for you...even a little..."

"He loved her," Andrew said, ignoring my quelling look. "He adored her. He gave her poetry."

"We don't encourage love in our escort-client relationships," Henry replied sharply. "In fact, we discourage it."

Andrew looked chastened, like Henry was already his boss. I wanted to yell at him to wise up. He didn't have the makings of an escort. He was too bright, too sensitive. I had a panicked feeling, like I'd better cut our lunch date short.

"I'm sorry we bothered you with this," I said to Henry. "It's just that I have no closure. I hate that I don't have a name."

"Why do you need a name?"

"I don't know. We had some pretty intense dates, and then he disappeared with no goodbye and no explanation. I thought...if you had any information..."

"What? You'd go track Mr. Cumming down? For what purpose? To complain? To question him? To tell him off? I think you should drop this right now. It's not wise to pursue him. You're better than this."

I knew Henry's sharp words were true. "I don't want to track him down," I insisted, like a big liar. "I just want to understand—"

"Here's some advice for you, from someone who's spent years in the escorting business. Don't try to understand people." His gaze softened, and he reached to touch my cheek. "Look at you. You've moved on." He tugged a lock of my dark hair. "You're real now, and beautiful. Don't dwell on the past."

Henry firmly changed the subject. We talked about Norton, and the Manhattan art world, deftly maneuvering around the subject of Simon and his continuing success. We talked about the early snow and the construction in lower Manhattan, and the more we talked, the more I realized how pathetic I must look. It had been two and a half years. *You're better than this.*

Maybe I wasn't better than this. Maybe I still wished W would reappear in my life.

And then what, Chere?

I excused myself to go to the restroom to take some deep breaths, to fix my lipstick and pull myself together. When I returned, Henry and Andrew were on their feet. I clearly saw Henry slip Andrew a card, and just as clearly saw Andrew shove it into his pocket when he saw me.

"Henry's got to head out," he said, in too bright a voice.

"Yes, I'm sure he's got business to attend to. He's *always working.*" My caustic comments were answered by Henry's California-golden smile.

"It was good to see you again, love. And thanks for introducing me to your friend. I wish I could say the restaurant was a pleasure, but the sandwich is sitting in my stomach like a brick."

"You're a snob."

"And you're a goddess. Take care, and call me if you need anything." He gave me a hug and then he was out the door in a swish of tailored coat and designer shoes.

I turned to Andrew with a scowl. "Give it to me."

"What?" he asked innocently.

"The card. Henry's card. You're not allowed to work for him."

"Don't get all bitchy and angry just because you didn't get the information you wanted."

"The information *I* wanted? You're the one who wanted information. I told you he wouldn't be able to help us, but you insisted we meet with him anyway." I glared at him with narrowed eyes. "Was this all part of some intricate plan? Did you push me to meet with Henry so you could pitch yourself to him as an escort?"

He was silent a second too long. His face betrayed an iota too much outrage. "No, of course not," he insisted. "I was trying to help you."

"You were trying to meet my agent so you could get his information." I looked down at his unusually nice—and matching—jeans and sweater, and his fluffed up, adorable hair. "That's shitty, Andrew. That's just shitty."

He threw up his hands. "So maybe I wanted to do both. I wanted to help you find out about W, though. That was always part of it."

"Not the main part."

Andrew was the one person I'd let into my heart in the last two and half years, and he was already using me. I felt betrayed. It took me back to that Gramercy Park hotel room, to the envelope on the bed with my name on the outside. *Good luck, starshine. You gullible idiot.*

"Don't be mad at me," he said. "I just wanted to talk to him. I'm graduating soon, and I don't have a fucking idea what I'm going to do."

"You're going to paint!"

"With what money? Working as an escort will get me some short term funds, and probably provide a lot of inspiration too."

"Inspiration?" I pushed away my plate. "You don't get it. You think it's fun, romantic, sexy to be an escort? It's not."

"I know that."

"Not every client writes poetry on your back. A lot of them are assholes. Total assholes. They're entitled and demanding and they only care about themselves."

"Even one good client, one client like W—"

"W wasn't a good client. He was an asshole." The couple at the next table scowled at my language. I lowered my voice and glared at Andrew. "Look, W was handsome and kinky and mysterious, but he wasn't a good person. He did crazy shit to me."

Andrew crossed his arms over his chest. "You told me how hard you fell in love with him. If he did crazy shit to you, you liked it."

Yes, I'd liked it. Why was I so angry at the thought of Andrew becoming an escort? I guess because I'd gotten so lost in the business, or maybe because I'd fallen in love with a client, and had my feelings betrayed.

"W manhandled me and terrified me," I said. "He called me a whore and a slut. He choked me—more than once—until I passed out. He—he raped me."

The R-word was so ugly. Andrew went still, his dark eyes full of confusion and dismay. "How... But... How could that happen? I thought he paid you for sex."

I sighed. "It's hard to explain. He was weird."

"Explain it to me."

I didn't think I owed him any explanations, but the story came spilling out. "The first time he let me meet him without a blindfold, I was supposed to watch for him in the Empire Hotel lobby."

"How were you supposed to watch for him when you'd never seen him?"

"That's just it. I was supposed to guess who he was, and follow him to the elevators. And I did. I guessed correctly, and I followed him, but he pretended to be someone else, and when I followed him into the room, he went all psychopath on me. He ripped off my panties and stuffed them in my mouth, and gagged me with his tie."

Andrew's mouth sagged open. "Holy shit. That's fucked up."

"It was very fucked up."

"You thought he was a psycho stranger, but it was him?"

"I didn't know what to think. Meanwhile he's suffocating me, raping me, threatening to kill me."

Andrew swallowed hard, and spoke very quietly. "Is it wrong of me to say that sounds really hot?"

I glowered at him. "It wasn't hot in the moment. I thought I was going to die."

"I know. I'm sorry. But, God, I would love to feel that kind of intensity, that excitement. I'd love to experience it just once."

"You think so, but escorting isn't as sexy as it sounds. I promise you, there are a lot of times you'll wish you were anywhere else. And you still have to be there, and cooperate, and earn your money. Andrew, please don't get into escorting. Please think before you act."

"I will, I promise. I'm sorry. Don't be mad at me. I thought I might enjoy the work." He gazed at me in concern. "Are you mad at me?"

"Fuck yeah, I'm mad at you."

My emotions were in an uproar, from seeing Henry and talking about W, and thinking about Andrew meeting some rich, horny john.

"What did you say to W when you realized...when you realized it was him?" he asked. "Did you fucking kill him? Did you try to cut off his dick?"

"I wanted to. I was pretty freaked out. I cried really hard, and yelled, and he apologized. Then I tried to leave, and he asked me to go swimming with him."

"The old swimming trick."

I gave Andrew a look. "What old swimming trick?"

"The swimming trick. You can't stay angry in water. It's soothing. It worked, didn't it? You forgave him. You saw him again."

"I saw him again," I admitted. "That same night, I let him take me back down to the room, and you know what he did?"

He got a wistful look. "He made it up to you with gentle, apologetic lovemaking?"

"No. He gagged me again, same as the first time, and fucked me just as hard. Somewhere along the line he also spanked the shit out of me." *And I liked it. I wanted more. That's the worst part, I still want more...*

Andrew whimpered. "I'm horny now. I'm sorry, babes, but that's so hot. I want that. I want to be someone's plaything. I'm a masochist, and a sub. You might not have enjoyed it, but I think I would."

"Why don't you try it then?" I said bitterly. "I'm not going to be able to talk you out of it. But don't say I didn't warn you when you eventually get hurt."

"Love always hurts." He shrugged. I could already feel him drawing away from me, and it was so sad, but so expected.

"No," I said. "Love always lies."

PRICE

Let me explain about the day I raped Chere. I never really meant to do it.

Okay, yes, I raped her. In hindsight I realize it was a very bad, very wrong thing to do. It was reprehensible. It's also reprehensible that the frantic terror of that rape is still my go-to fantasy when I'm rubbing one out.

I guess the best thing I can say in my defense is that it was not premeditated. When I busted out with the Texan accent—that was the moment I decided to deceive her. Up until that point, I had only meant to mock her for her uncertainty. I mean, she'd known right away who I was. But then she lost her nerve, and I saw a chance, and I took it.

At the beginning, still, I thought things would fall apart. I thought she wouldn't believe, that she would confront me and say, "I know it's you." When she didn't, when she started to fight me so violently, it was too exciting to stop. She thought it was life and death. I could see it in her eyes, hear it in her panting breaths, feel it in the spasms of her body.

I have to live with the knowledge that I caused those terrified spasms. I have to live with the fact that I choked her out, pretending to kill her, and then gagged her while she was out so she'd wake up in even more fear. She was so small, so easy to overpower, and I had a psyche full of force and rape fantasies, the fairy tales of my childhood gone screwy and off the map. I knew I was way off the map but I couldn't stop, because I knew I'd never have such an authentic chance again. Such an authentic chance to rape someone.

But I raped her. I did. I told myself everything would be fine afterward, when she realized it was me all along, but that wasn't what happened. I hadn't realized how badly I'd fucked her up until the thing was done and she was cowering on the floor. She shook and cried and shrieked and shrank away from me. The shaking was the worst part. I worried she was in shock, and maybe she was. I'd always prided myself on my ability to take things to a certain edge, take them as far as they could go without really harming my partner, and I knew, for the first time, that I'd crossed that line. Not just crossed it, but blown way past it.

Of course, I pretended I hadn't, which was probably the worst thing I did that day besides rape her. I pretended that it was merely a scene gone wrong, and everything would be okay now that it was over. I pretended that maybe we just needed to do a little more negotiating going forward. What else could I do? I didn't want to stop fucking her, and I knew she'd never agree to see me again after what had transpired.

I took her swimming, just to get her out of the hotel room, away from the scene of my crime. I took her up to the pool and we talked. Or didn't talk, because she was still pretty mad. I wanted to fuck her. I wanted to kiss her. That was the first day I saw Simon's abuse on her, his marks. His bruises. There was a bruise on her collarbone, and another one near her temple that she'd covered with makeup. I slapped her face sometimes because it got me off, but I never slapped her hard enough to bruise her.

Imagine me there, wanting to blow a fucking gasket at this bruise on her face, knowing full well I'd just stranger-raped the shit out of her. I was glad I was in the water. I needed it to calm me. We both needed peace. I knew how to give her peace. I took her back to the room and did the same brutal shit I'd done to her when I raped her, only this time she knew it was me, and I got her off even harder than I'd gotten her off at the Park Hyatt. I made her come and come and come.

I had to. I wanted to see her again.

I wanted to keep exploring this heightened intensity between us. I had no idea then where I'd end up, alone in my place on Bleecker, with a pair of hunting binoculars clutched in my sweaty hands, trained on her window across the street.

Stalking is fucking exhausting, because you can only know so much. Even private investigators can only learn so much. I knew about her classwork, I knew about her grades, I knew about her friends. I knew her habits, I knew her moods, or at least the moods she carried on her face. I knew when she met with her former pimp Henry at the Big Apple Diner, but I didn't know why.

They'd had a fight, her and her gay friend Andrew, just after she met with Henry. All I could think about was the resurrection of Miss Kitty, and Chere going back to escorting for Sublime Services. Why else would she have met with Henry? Why would she fight with her friend, when they'd gotten along so well for so many weeks?

Why was she pensive and anxious when she ought to be looking forward to her final semester, and graduation?

I thought about befriending Andrew and offering him money in exchange for information. He had access. He could have told me everything, told me what they fought about, what was going on with her, but it was too risky, so I was reduced to calling Henry myself. After all this time, I still carried his card in my wallet, because Henry was my one and only personal connection to Chere.

He answered on the second ring. "Sublime Services. How may I help you?"

Such a cultured greeting. He'd always run a classy show, even if he was a pimp who'd bled more money out of me than any decent person would. "Henry, it's Price Eriksen."

There was a pause, maybe the softest sigh. "Mr. Eriksen. This is a surprise."

"I'm not calling to make a date."

"Oh. Just calling to chat, then?"

"I need to know if she still works for you," I said. "If she's going back to work for you."

Again, the pause, because he had all the power here. "You mean Chere, I assume?" he said after a moment.

"Yes, Chere. Is she coming back to work at Sublime?"

"I can't really talk about that kind of thing," Henry said in a fuck-you tone. "But if I could, I'd probably answer no."

I let out a slow breath. What would I have done if she'd gone back to work for Henry? I would've lost my fucking shit.

"You met with her," I said.

"How do you know that?"

"I just know. How is she? Is she okay?" I pressed my fist against my forehead. If I was in the same room with Henry I would have grabbed him and shaken him like an addict looking for blow.

"It's been two years," Henry said. "More than two years."

It had been two years, five months, and a week, but who the fuck was counting? "I'd just like to know if she's okay."

"If you care, you should contact her yourse—"

"Just tell me. Give me one of your non-answers that's really an answer, if you have to. If you're going to keep up this charade of privacy."

A chair creaked over the line. Maybe he sat up straighter. I imagined him bristling, his color reddening beneath his golden tan.

"It's not a charade," the man snapped. "I've kept your secrets. It wasn't easy."

"I imagine the fee I paid for your silence made it easier."

"Your fucking 'fee.' I wish I'd never taken your money. Do you know how hard it is to keep your mouth shut when someone you care about is sitting across a table from you begging for some kind of closure? For the courtesy of a goddamned name?" His tirade cut off. "You know what? You don't get any information. You want to know if she's okay? Then call her. I'm sure she'd like to hear from you, if only to tell you to go fuck yourself."

He hung up on me. I rubbed my forehead, trying to construct her state of mind from his angry stream of vitriol. I dismissed the "fuck yourself" part of things. Of course she felt that way. But she still thought about me. She still wanted to know my name.

She'd met with Henry to *find closure.*

I let that sink into my system for a moment. Two and a half years later, she was looking for closure, which meant…

Fuck, did that mean she was ready to move on?

Shit. Why now? Who had come into her life? All this time I'd felt like she was still under my control, still under my protection. She'd seemed willing to stay under my protection, even if she didn't know it was there.

But now she was looking for *closure.* I should have been happy for her. I wasn't. There were too many fucking assholes out there, and she was so raw and trusting and vulnerable.

I tossed down the phone and grabbed the binoculars. She was at her computer, studying the screen, shifting, tracing an eyebrow. So dark, those eyebrows. She used to tint them blonde.

You want to know if she's okay? Then call her.

I didn't need temptation like that, because damn it, I wanted to call. Every night, I wanted to call her. I threw the binoculars on the couch and picked up the phone, thought wildly of smashing it so I wouldn't fucking use it. After a few deep breaths, reason prevailed. *If you care*, Henry had said. *If you care...*

If I cared about her, I'd leave her alone. She'd come so far in her new life, and I would only hurt her.

"Damn it," I roared in the silence of my apartment, so loudly I was surprised she couldn't hear it all the way across the street. But I didn't dial her number in a desperate frenzy. I stayed calm. I had to remember why...

After the Empire, there'd been the Gansevoort session. I was miserable at the Gansevoort. I was horrible to her at the Gansevoort. The Gansevoort was when I understood that I saw her as more than a whore, more than a sex toy. It's when I understood, clearly, that I cared about her as a person.

This was after I'd done some poking into her life, and learned about her abusive fucktard painter boyfriend. What I found out wasn't flattering to either of them. I wanted to despise her for loving him, for living with him and letting him use her money—my money!—for drugs. But I couldn't despise her and I couldn't stop thinking about her. I wanted to protect her. I wanted to rescue her like some goddamned knight in shining armor.

But I couldn't, so I showed up at the Gansevoort seething with frustration. I'd called her a bitch and a whore, and lied and told her, *All I care about is what's between your legs.* I mocked and belittled her, fucked her in the ass just to hurt her. I told her she wasn't allowed to come, and then I beat the shit out of her when she did. I used an orchid stake to do it. It must have hurt like hell, that piece of bamboo, but she never stopped fighting. She was amazing like that. I could hurt her and hurt her and hurt her, and she was still there, fighting back at me, tipping up her stubborn chin.

It was hard to remember that now. She deserved someone better, and I deserved to be alone. I deserved to be taunted by memories of her closeness and her scent, and that blazing rebellion in her eyes. I lay back on my bed, opened my hand and let the phone fall from my fingertips. I had work to do, buildings and bridges to design. A life to stumble through without her.

Closure. Fuck.

CHERE

It was the last Saturday night before the end of the semester, and I was alone. I felt Andrew's loss keenly, not that I'd really lost him. We were still technically "friends," but we weren't friends like we were before, because I didn't trust him as much as I used to. He'd decided to go into escorting even after my warnings. Henry had just called him.

Andrew was going on his first date.

He wanted me to be happy for him. I think he actually wanted me to come over and help him get ready, and dish with him about escorting, and watch him shave and manscape. He sent a flurry of texts, five or six for every one of mine. I felt guilty, like maybe I should have been over there helping him primp, but I couldn't do it.

Henry told Andrew he'd set him up with a Dominant client, one who had not yet found his perfect combination of servile and sexy. Maybe he would find it in Andrew, but probably not. Andrew seemed a mere baby in escort terms, with his mop of hair, his twink body and little-boy grin. I was so worried for him I cried, not that I told him that. Andrew would need his fluttery excitement and overconfidence to get through this first date.

As for me, I had no plans for the evening, no dates to go on, paid or otherwise. I didn't know how to get rid of my restlessness and guilt at being a bad friend. I debated whether to go out to one of the BDSM clubs in my current mood. I wanted to get beaten on. I wanted to feel something, but I hadn't played at any of the clubs before, and tonight probably wasn't the best night to dip my toe in.

Also, if I went to the clubs, I would think about W the whole time like I always did, about his roughness and cruel brutality. About his kindness. His kisses. His poetry. *Mine also, little painted poem of God.*

Ugh. Not anymore.

It was snowing, and bitterly cold, but in the end, I made the decision to go out. I painted my lips a deep red and painted my nails to match, and put on a fitted black dress, tights, and boots. The dress was some off-the-rack thing, and I'd found the boots in a thrift store. I used to wear designer everything, but my current scholarship didn't allow for that kind of extravagance, and I didn't want to touch my escort savings until I was out of school. This dress was fine for dark clubs where I didn't plan to play anyway.

Why are you going if you're not going to play? Why do you do this to yourself?

I silenced the voice in my brain, or maybe the cold, sharp air silenced it for me. I put my head down and crunched over the snow to the subway entrance across from the school. I rode to the Meatpacking District, to the biggest, noisiest, busiest fetish club in Manhattan: Evolution City. The bouncers welcomed me with big smiles. Single female patrons were always admitted with no cover charge, but Evolution was too smothering, too loud for my mood today.

I was back out on the sidewalk fifteen minutes later. I stood by the curb and blew condensation into the cold air, then turned and headed for Studio Valiant instead. It was smaller and less in-your-face, a casual, kinky hideaway with painted concrete walls. Instead of pounding club music, Valiant played an erratic mix of classical music, torch songs, and decades-old Top 40. The music lightened the mood and kept the club from feeling too full of itself. The equipment wasn't as luxe as Evolution's top-tier spread, but a dedicated pervert could find plenty of workable racks, tables, and spanking benches distributed throughout the dungeon floor.

I left my coat at the door and skirted around the scenes in progress, and shared a smile with one of the dungeon masters, an older gentleman I sometimes saw at Evolution too. There were four balconies upstairs, half-hidden by curtains, where voyeurs could look down on the action. I felt most comfortable there, where I could watch other people suffer and play.

By now, I felt at home with the accoutrements of these BDSM clubs: the rope, the chains, the cuffs, and the intermittent cracks of a whip. It wasn't very busy tonight, perhaps because of the weather. For once, I had a balcony all to myself, and from that private, elevated space, I watched intense, quiet scenes and fun, raucous scenes, watched duos and trios and quartets of people act out their freaky sides.

There was very little sex. Some heavy petting, some commanded blowjobs. I couldn't help remembering how W used to shove his cock down my throat. It could hardly have been called "giving him a blowjob" since I hadn't given anything, only had everything taken from me. My control, my dignity, my ability to breathe. None of the blowjobs here were like that.

I closed my eyes, overtaken by the past. It was so long ago now, but I could still remember the scent of his maleness, his fingers yanking at my hair. The thick, hard, driving flesh... His cock had ruled my life. His force and passion had ruled my life during our frenetic sessions. I still remembered how he used to slap my face and bark orders. I remembered the feel of it, the shock and the sting. Why had I enjoyed having my face slapped? I had no idea, but it got me in the mood every time.

I heard a step behind me, and a creak as someone sat on one of the balcony's bleacher-like benches. Just one person. A man? The image of W was so strong in my mind, because of the memories and the fantasies, that my hair stood on end. What if it was W sitting behind me, watching me watch the others?

I slid a look over my shoulder, my whole body cycling through hot and cold. Why was I experiencing this prickle, this sense of recognition? I saw dark jeans, the hem of a black tee. It wasn't W, because the man wasn't big enough, and W wouldn't wear jeans and a tee shirt to a club. He'd wear a suit and tie, and cuff links. I screwed up my courage and looked into the interloper's face.

It wasn't W.

It was Professor Cantor from my metals lab, looking more predatory than ever.

I turned back around. My face was steaming red. Maybe he hadn't recognized me. Shit, of course he'd recognized me. He probably recognized me from seeing me here before. All those assessing looks explained, and his comment about *service*. Ugh. I shot to my feet, determined to leave before things got any more awkward.

"Don't go," he said. He didn't touch me, but his authoritative voice arrested me in the act of motion. "You don't have to leave."

I tried to think of something to reply. *Of course I have to leave. This is embarrassing. You're my teacher.* But nothing came. When he gestured to the bench beside him, I sat.

"I've seen you around the clubs before," he said, without insinuation or judgment. "I apologize that I've never said hi."

"That would have been kind of awkward."

"Why? Because we know each other from Norton?" The corners of his mouth tilted up. I understood why some of the students found him handsome. In that sensual smile, I understood, but I didn't want to think about it.

"Trust me when I tell you we're not the only kinky people roaming Norton's halls," he said. His dark eyes took in my black dress, then lingered at my bare throat. "So what are you? Dom or sub? Or switch?"

I touched my neck. "Nothing, right now. I don't know."

"Just curious?"

I didn't want him to think I was some gawker, that I hadn't paid my dues—hellish dues—under a Dominant's hand. "I have experience. I was in a really intense relationship. I was a sub, I guess, but I...I wanted to take a break. I mean, I have been taking a break."

"Sometimes you need a break."

I looked at his gold wedding ring, maybe too obviously. He looked at it too and wiggled his ring finger. "She knows I'm here," he said. "She's okay with it. She's not into submission, or playing around with pain."

"Oh. Okay. I mean, whatever. I guess that's your business."

"But you wanted to know." He shrugged. "I don't come out to these places looking for attachment. I love my wife very much. It's more to do the things I like, that she doesn't like."

It seemed alien to me, that someone could do these things without a deep and complicated emotional attachment. That someone could come here and leave a wife at home.

"Doesn't she get jealous?" I asked.

He chuckled, stretching one of his legs to rest on the bench in front of us. "She has her own lovers, loads of them. We have an open marriage.

But our most *intense* relationship," he said, borrowing my word from earlier, "is the relationship we have with each other."

I kind of hated him for throwing his happy, open marriage in my face. I had nothing, no one, just a bunch of depressing memories. Out of the last two people I'd loved, one had taken my money and abused me, while the other had dumped me without sharing anything of substance except a whole lot of sex.

"You're lucky," I said, hunching over and resting my elbows on my knees. "I've never had a good relationship. I'm done with them."

"You're too young to be done with relationships." I could hear the soft, chiding mockery in his voice.

"What does it matter to you?" I muttered.

"You're one of my favorite students. It matters to me."

I was surprised by his forthright reply. I guess in some part of my brain I'd known he felt some favor toward me, even if he rode me harder than everyone else. But to hear it here, in this situation...it made me uncomfortable.

I scuffed the toe of my shoe against the opposite bench. "It's going to be weird now to see you in class."

"We only have a couple more weeks as professor and student."

The way he said *professor and student* sounded porn-y, or maybe it was my inappropriate mind. I wasn't attracted to him. I didn't want anything to do with him or his dark jeans or his hipster open marriage.

"Are you looking forward to your internship?" he asked as the silence went on too long.

"Can we not talk about school, since you're my teacher?"

He blinked, once, twice. Now it was the satanic gaze. "What do you want to talk about?"

"I don't know. Nothing, really. Why are you sitting up here with me? Why aren't you down there?" I jerked a thumb toward the concrete dungeon. An 80's hair band song blared over the sounds of thudding implements, laughter, and cries.

"I just wanted to say hello," he said. "You looked lonely sitting up here." When I didn't reply to that comment, he stood. "I think I will go down." Then he paused, and looked at me. "Would you like to come?"

"No, thanks. I'm more of a watcher."

"Nothing wrong with that." He again made as if to go, then stopped. "If you want to be less of a watcher in the future, and you're looking for a no-strings-attached partner, I'm experienced and safe."

Wow, that was a ballsy offer. At least he didn't say it in a skeevy, entitled way, like some of the Dominants who hit on me. He sounded sincere. I appreciated that, even if the answer was *no, no, no, no.*

"Is it the professor thing?" he asked when I failed to respond. "That's understandable." He turned to go, then stopped again. "You're sure you're okay?"

"I'm fine," I said too quickly.

He nodded. "I'll see you in class."

There was too much of a seductive edge to those five words. I'm ashamed to say I stuck around through my embarrassment and trauma to watch my predatory professor in action. It didn't take him long to find a willing partner, a statuesque blonde with short, aqua-tipped hair. From the way they interacted, I thought they'd probably played together before. I peered down from the balcony, trying to look disinterested, trying not to focus on him too long in case he looked up at me.

But he didn't look up at me, and I was soon absorbed in watching him play. He had an expertness about him, a confidence he also had in the classroom. His movements were slow as he bound and teased his partner, fixing her to a St. Andrews cross. He was unfailingly attentive, leaning his head close when she talked to him, and checking her bonds to make sure they weren't too tight. I couldn't help contrasting his smooth, calm mode of operation to W's heightened grasping. His *violence.*

Even now, engrossed in someone else's scene, I couldn't stop thinking about my lost lover. I squeezed my eyes shut and willed him out of my thoughts. The girl Cantor had picked was pretty. Very young. Reckless. I wondered if W would have liked to play with her. Probably.

Stop. Just stop.

Cantor warmed up the girl with some spanking, some caresses. A little bit of massage. He reached around his play partner to caress her breasts, and she very audibly liked it. His hand moved lower, playing over her panties. She arched her hips and smiled at him, and he gave her a little slap there. Her expression said, *do it again.*

I also wanted him to do it again, but he didn't. He unbuttoned his shirt, shrugged it off and leaned down to stow it in his bag. It wasn't until he stood again that I appreciated his impressive set of muscles. He was no W, but for a middle-aged professor, he had a good body. He had a great ass.

Just a couple more weeks. In a couple more weeks, he wouldn't be my teacher. Maybe...

Jesus God, no. Had I learned nothing over the past few years? I was terrible at picking guys. *Really, Chere? A married, polyamorous, ex-professor of yours? Just because he has a decent ass?*

But it was more than that. It was his capability, his control. He drew a flogger out of his bag and went to work on the pretty blonde. She made great noises, adorable noises. I wondered how much she turned him on. I wondered if he ever thought of his wife at moments like these.

From where I sat, I had a view of his back, of muscles bunching, and the practiced swing of his arm. There was no protocol here, no collars or commands or anything besides casual impact play, but he was unmistakably Dom. Other girls in the room watched him too. I wondered why I'd never noticed him at any of the other clubs, but then I realized it was probably because I was too busy watching for W.

But W was gone...and I could have this...

He'd offered. I was afraid if I watched him for very much longer, I'd accept. He flogged his moaning victim, fast, slow, soft, hard, teasing her curves and walloping her back, striping her legs because she especially seemed to like that. W had never asked what I liked. He just grabbed and forced and took, and gave me soul-crushing orgasms.

There was nothing soul-crushing in what Cantor was doing, and I knew—sorry, Professor Predator—that he wouldn't be able to give me the kind of orgasms W did. But he might be able to take the edge off my loneliness, and give me a little pleasure.

No, no, no. Idiot. He's married. He's your professor. Don't make another stupid choice, and fall in love with another undeserving person.

This was why I had to be alone, because I wanted things I shouldn't want. I forced my gaze away from Cantor, forced myself to stop thinking about the playful way he'd spanked her pussy. Tried not to remember the time W beat the shit out of my pussy with his belt, and made my eyes roll back in my head from the pleasure of it.

Stupid of me, to even imagine being with someone else. W had ruined me forever for other lovers before he left, and I hated him for it. I needed to move on, yes. But not to someone else.

Fortunately, my phone lit up with a text from Andrew, and I had something else to think about. I turned away from the scene downstairs to read his message.

OMG. Chere.

That was not enough information. I texted back, *What? Date's over? Are you okay?*

I'm great, he replied quickly. *That was crazy, hot, sexy. The client liked me. I was nervous, but it went okay.*

Just okay? I asked.

First time! he texted back. *It wasn't perfect, but he enjoyed himself. He said he was happy to "break me in."*

Did he hurt you??!!

He texted back a blushing emoji, and then a smiling one. *Not in any way I didn't like.*

You used protection?

Duh. Yes, mom.

I didn't realize until that moment how nervous I'd been for him. At least he didn't seem sad. *Always be careful,* I typed. Then I erased it. Then I typed it again and sent it. He sent back a heart emoji and three words.

I miss you.

A pause.

Are you still angry? he texted.

Yes.

There was no reply for a while. I chewed on my lip and tried to tune out the escalating groans of Cantor's partner, and the steady fall of his flogger.

Want to have breakfast tomorrow? I typed. *Big Apple Diner?*

He typed back a row of fifteen smiley faces, and the word *YESSSS!*

I could picture Andrew's smile in my head, and I knew I'd stay friends with him, even though it would hurt me to hear his stories about escorting. I knew I'd ask him for all tonight's details just so he could get it out, because the first time was always the hardest, and he'd need support for what he'd chosen to do.

I ended our conversation with a semi-lie. *Heading to bed.*

I was heading to bed very soon. I'd just have to leave the club to do it, and I wasn't ready to pull myself away from Cantor's performance quite yet. He'd put away the flogger and picked up a riding crop, and set about making his willing victim jump and squeak with pleasure. *You could have that*, my mind whispered.

And then I remembered *Good luck, starshine.*

Fuck.

I looked down at my phone. I could have amused Andrew by texting to him about my encounter with Cantor, but I didn't tell him, and I knew I wouldn't tell him, even at breakfast tomorrow. Somehow, it seemed better to keep it a secret. Maybe I didn't trust Andrew enough anymore.

Well.

The more likely scenario was that I didn't trust myself.

PRICE

I closed the drapes of my hotel window. I had no binoculars, because there was no Chere to look at. I was in Beijing, in a skyline hotel I'd designed three years ago, just before I met her. The grand opening had taken place today.

The ribbon-cutting ceremony had gone well. My speech on behalf of Eriksen Architectural Design was duly translated into Chinese by a doe-eyed young national, and seemed well received. That translator hovered near me all through the following banquet, the hunger in her eyes unsettling me. She was beautiful, gorgeous, but she was no Chere. She would have broken into pieces when I got her alone. She wouldn't have fought back, not like Chere. She wouldn't have had those moaning, struggling orgasms that looked more like pain than anything else.

I kicked off my shoes and stripped off my suit, and tossed my cufflinks on the desk. I got naked and sat at my laptop, and opened the most recent email from Beacon Investigative Services. I browsed through photos of Chere going to class, photos of Chere going food shopping, photos of Chere returning home. Andrew wasn't in any of them. They were apparently still on the outs.

There was another set of photos. Last weekend. Chere was dressed up, heading into the subway toward Meatpacking. Back to the BDSM clubs again. I didn't like that she went, because I worried for her safety. Sometimes I followed her, sometimes I let other people follow her so she wouldn't be alone, especially on the subway afterward in her tight dress and sexy black boots.

Jesus Christ, Chere. She looked gorgeous…and available. Her quest for closure weighed heavily on my mind. I massaged my hardening cock and clicked to another photo, this one of Chere inside Studio Valiant. She hid in the balconies there, as she hid in the corners and dark spaces everywhere else.

I jacked myself harder, gazing at her pretty face. She looked sad. Lost. My fault? It was horrible to stalk her like this, but I had to watch her and know about her, and it turned me on to look at photos of her going about her day. It was a little like having her, even though I couldn't have her.

I slouched back in the chair and closed my eyes. It was so quiet this high in the air. It was so cool, and I was so hot. Why hadn't I taken advantage of the corporate courtesan they offered me? She'd been even prettier than the interpreter, with a round face-fuck mouth and a long pretty neck.

Fuck, who cared about her? It was Chere I fantasized about as I came in a gasping mess. Cum oozed down over my fingers and dripped onto the designer wool carpet. Why wasn't she here? Why wasn't she with me?

Because you want what you shouldn't want.

When I jacked off, I usually thought about hurting Chere. I fantasized about binding her and torturing her, and fucking her ass without lube. I imagined raping her and making her cry. I never thought about why, or how, just the tears and her agony. If she were mine, in my apartment, in my dungeon, I'd find a way to make her cry every day. I'd make her come every day too, covered in my marks, covered in my cum, covered in my protection.

It was nice fap fodder, but it wasn't happening. I wouldn't let it happen, because you couldn't take a bright, ambitious person in the midst of a personal renaissance and make her your slave. You couldn't lock her in a dungeon and keep her there for your pleasure. Even if you wanted to do that very, very much.

I went to clean myself up, and returned to click through the last of the photos. They were grainy, covert, long-distance shots. I wished for the thousandth time that I was standing right in front of her, holding her in my arms. I'd stroke her velvet cheekbones, lick her freckles, kiss her pert nose. I'd hurt her and then I'd make everything better, and then I'd put her in a luxurious cage where she'd be safe until I wanted to hurt her again.

Holy fuck. What the fuck?

I stopped on the photo, enlarged it so I could see the man sitting beside her on Valiant's balcony. I clicked back to the email, scanned to the bottom. *Conversation with male, middle age, not identified. Subject went home alone.*

Fucking Jesus in hell, she better have gone home alone. As for the *male, middle age*, I didn't need any identification. I knew Martin Cantor, not just because he was one of Chere's professors, but because I'd attended Norton with him back in the day. I'd seen him at fetish clubs around the city, drawing in women with his sage, caring-Dom thing. I'd never liked him. He was a smarmy jackass with more ambition than talent, and the last thing in hell he needed to be doing was hitting on Chere in a club.

I clicked through the photos, seriously disturbed. She was his *student.* How dare he look at her that way? She didn't want his attention, that was clear from her hunched posture and the way she faced away from him. And Cantor, with his smiles and expressions. Smarmy fucking pervert.

She went home alone, I repeated to calm myself. *She went home alone.* In all this time, she hadn't hooked up with anyone, any other man, even casually in the BDSM clubs. She'd focused on school—and occasionally me—like a very good girl. Fucking Cantor. What the fuck was wrong with him? He was her teacher. Not only that, he was married with two kids.

I stood and started to pace. This wasn't her doing. It wasn't her fault. He'd gone up to the balcony and drawn her into conversation. The photos told the story...they just didn't reveal what words they'd exchanged. I wanted to trust that Chere wouldn't fall for his bullshit, but she'd fallen for bullshit before, like when that asshole picked her up after the Gansevoort debacle.

That man really hurt her. That's why I was so leery of leaving her without protection now. She was so easily hurt and so easily taken advantage of. She was honest with that jerk from the Gansevoort, and what did he do? Left her sitting at a table, alone, shunned, ashamed. When I heard that part of the story and saw the bitter look on her face, I wanted to put my fist through a wall. I mean, what the fuck?

Cantor wasn't going to get a shot at hurting Chere. If he was the reason she was looking for closure, then she wasn't fucking getting closure. I called downstairs for a limo to the airport, and started packing my shit. I was supposed to leave the day after tomorrow so I could spend a little more time in the city, but those plans were changing. Martin Cantor? Fuck no. I was leaving for New York tonight.

* * * * *

I figured I had two choices in this situation: confront Cantor, or confront Chere. The latter wasn't happening. I didn't trust myself to have anything to do with her, especially now that she was so close to graduating and moving on with her life.

So I looked up Cantor's office hours and paid him a visit. It felt strange to be back at Norton, in the administrative area where I'd come to arrange Chere's scholarship. When I knocked on Cantor's half-open door to get his attention, I realized there was a student in there. I saw long legs, delicate hands, the tight jeans co-eds wore. My heart turned over for one stricken, oh-shit moment, but it wasn't Chere. The universe wouldn't be so capricious, after all the effort and care I'd taken to avoid her the last two and a half years.

Cantor and the blonde co-ed turned to look at me. He regarded me with confusion, then recognition and surprise.

"Price? Price Eriksen?" He stood and came to the door. "It's good to see you. What brings you to Norton?"

"A private matter," I said, looking at the girl.

He turned back to her. She was already shouldering her backpack. "We were just finishing up. Academic counseling."

Academic counseling, my ass, I thought, as she moved past me with a blushing smile. Cantor took her arm as he said goodbye.

"Keep at the renderings, Simone. I'll see you next week." He turned his attention to me and shook my hand. "Come in. This is a surprise."

"How are you, Martin?" I couldn't quite keep the fuck-you from my voice. We'd never been friends. In fact, we'd been bitter rivals during our student days.

"I'm just...wow. Surprised." He spread his arms and shut his laptop. "Blast from the past."

I took the seat he offered and looked around. "Are you expecting anyone else? Any more appointments?" I asked.

He shook his head. "Most of my students are finishing end-of-semester projects. It's a little late now for them to be seeking my advice."

I looked around his neat, organized work space. He had a decent office for a has-been hack. Cantor studied me expectantly, leaning back in his chair.

"So, what brings you back to your old alma mater? What can I help you with? Are you here about internships?"

"What?"

"Internships. Want an intern?"

I shook my head. Norton begged me annually to take an intern, and I always said no. "I'm here for another reason," I said, allowing displeasure to creep into my voice. "I've come to discuss one of your students."

"I'm not allowed to discuss students. It's a matter of privacy, educational statutes, all of that."

"Her name is Chere Rouzier."

His lips tightened. "Oh. Yes. She's a third year design student, but I'm afraid I can't tell you any more than that."

"Can't you? Are you big on following the rules?"

He was starting to get the idea that this wasn't a friendly visit. He stood to shut the door, then sat at his desk and returned my hard gaze.

"How do you know Chere?" he asked.

"I know her…tangentially. I have an interest in her well-being."

Cantor shrugged, determined to play things off. "As far as I know, she's doing well. I've had no complaints."

"You're her teacher."

"Yes, I've worked with her in several classes, but I can't tell you anything more. Really, Price, I can't. It's against university policy."

"You know what else is against university policy?" I said with a scowl. "Hitting on students in lifestyle clubs."

He didn't ruffle easily. He never had. "Are you talking about last Saturday? We ran into each other at a club and said hello. That's the extent of it."

I couldn't call him a liar without admitting my investigator had timed a fifteen-minute conversation.

"What's your interest in Chere?" he asked, studying me. "What is your 'tangential' connection?"

"Friend of the family," I said. "We go way back. I look out for her."

"Is that so? Well, she's an admirable woman. A diligent designer, and enjoyable to teach." He lifted a finger on top of his laptop, wiggled it twice, and set it down again. Yeah, he found her enjoyable, all right.

"I won't tell anyone you're perving your students," I said, staring at that finger, "or that she's not the only one. But in return, you're going to do something for me. You're going to leave her the fuck alone."

He gave up any pretense of professional collegiality and smirked at me. "You're no friend of the family. Who is Chere to you? What's the story, Price?"

"The story is a married Norton professor hitting on a student at a BDSM club." I leaned closer to him. "I have proof it happened. Pictures. I'm sure the administration would love to look at them. Leave her alone."

"In a few days, she won't be my student anymore. How do you know she won't come after me? Chere seems very lonely." He paused, raised one black, arched brow. "Does she know you take pictures of her at clubs?"

"I didn't take them. A friend showed them to me." I stood and adjusted my tie, and walked to the door. "Leave her alone, Martin. You'll be sorry if you don't. Your wife puts up with a lot, but she might not put up with as much when you can't get a job."

"Are you threatening me?"

"Universities don't hire professors who prey on students. That was a really pretty girl in your office just now. Meet with her every week?"

"She's one of my students," he snapped.

"So is Chere."

I grabbed the door and wrenched it open. Fuckhead. I didn't know if my threats were getting through to him. I didn't know how much trouble I could make without Chere becoming involved.

"I'm glad you stopped by," he called after me as I left. "Glad we had this talk."

I didn't yell "Fuck you" back at him the way I wanted to. I was trying to keep it classy, which was more than I could say for him.

CHERE

Andrew came running up to me in Norton's cafeteria the last morning of fall semester, with fluttering hands and a magnificent smile. "Oh my God, oh my God, oh my *Gaaawd*! Chere! Guess what?"

"You finished that painting about the happy banana?" I murmured, shoveling sugar into my coffee.

"Better."

"What could possibly be better?"

His smile wilted a little. "Well, it's about...you know...the E thing."

Not E as in ecstasy. Andrew didn't use drugs. The E thing was escorting, and it was a lingering source of tension between us.

"Even if it's about the E thing," I said, "I guess you better tell me, or else you got me all worked up for nothing."

"Mr. Recaro is taking me to Vail!" The words burst out in jubilation. "Two whole weeks over the holiday break."

"And Mr. Recaro is...?"

"The gentleman I saw last week. The opera singer with all the muscles and hair."

"Hair?"

"I've never seen such a hairy taint, babes, I'm telling you."

"So, skiing in Vail for two weeks?" I asked, to get him off the taint talk. "Mr. Recaro must really like you."

His eyes lit up even brighter. "Do you think so?"

I put down my coffee and grabbed his face in a punishing grip. "No, I don't think so. That was a test and you failed it. You're not supposed to develop feelings for clients. It's the fastest way to go nuts in the escort biz."

"You developed feelings for one of your clients," he lisped through his crunched cheeks. "And you know he felt something for you."

"And where are we now?" I asked, releasing him. "I'm a lonely, neurotic mess of a woman, and he fucked off to God knows where."

"You're not a lonely, neurotic mess." He rubbed his skin where I'd gripped it. "Sort of cranky sometimes, when you haven't had enough coffee. You need to get laid."

I turned away from him, not willing to discuss that topic. The close encounter with Cantor was still on my mind. *I'm experienced and safe*, he'd said. And he was obviously willing to fuck me. I was one hundred percent sure of that, based on the way he'd looked at me in class ever since. Hot glances, small, speculative smiles, and far too many trips past my workstation for no reason. It amazed me that no one noticed.

"I don't need to get laid," I said, turning back to him. "And you don't need to be falling in love with your clients. It's wonderful that he's taking you to Vail. You'll get to ski and make bank, as long as you keep Hairy Taint happy. But it's work, not romance. Don't forget that, or you'll be heading into your last semester with a broken heart."

He promised me soberly that he would not fall in love with Mr. Recaro the opera singer, and I gave him one last menacing look. I hoped it was warning enough. I never, ever wanted Andrew to suffer the heartbreak I had.

I drifted through my last classes feeling morose. I wasn't exactly jealous of Andrew heading off on vacation for the holidays. Well, yes, maybe I was jealous. Andrew's family lived all the way over on the West Coast, and I didn't have any family, so I figured we'd hang out together, at least on Christmas Eve and Christmas Day. Instead, I'd be hanging out in my apartment alone, watching James Bond movies and eating takeout from the cheap Indian place on the corner.

No one else seemed very chipper today either. These were our last real classes at Norton, aside from senior seminar, which was basically just a time to get together and assure our teachers that our internships were going well. I wouldn't see a lot of these kids again, wouldn't sit in a classroom and talk about theory and marketing and technical design stuff. I wouldn't see Cantor every day anymore, wouldn't get to experience his predatory hovering and extra attention.

Maybe that's why I was so slow packing up my work space after he delivered our final critiques. Just about everyone was gone by the time I headed down the center aisle.

"Chere," he said as I passed his desk.

I turned to look at him. He gazed at me with that slow smile, the one halfway between seduction and mockery. "Were you going to leave without saying goodbye?"

His smile reminded me too much of Studio Valiant, and the way he'd spanked his sub's pussy. *No, don't think about that now.*

"Goodbye," I said. "Thanks for everything. Although I'm pretty sure I'll see you again."

I meant I'd see him here, at Norton, but I blushed, wondering if he'd misunderstood my meaning.

"That is... I still have one more semester to go," I clarified.

He nodded, and now I knew he was thinking about Studio Valiant, even if he hadn't been before.

"Do you have any plans for the break?" he asked.

"Not really."

"No family in the city?"

"No family anywhere," I said with a shrug.

"A holiday with friends, then?"

I was so, so tired of being dissected by him, scrutinized, questioned, stared at. I glared down at the floor and refused to answer.

"Well," he said, "we're officially not professor and student anymore. I've got your final grade here." He tapped the stack of printouts. "I'm sure you're aware you have an A. Well, an A minus. I docked you for all the dirty looks."

I gave him another dirty look. "Are you hitting on me?"

Everyone else had gone. There was only him and me, and his desk between us. He came from behind it and leaned against the edge.

"I'm not hitting on you," he said. "I'm stating a fact. I'm not your teacher anymore."

He was hitting on me. His eyes pinned me, dark and intense. The silence went from uncomfortable to stifling.

"Is there someone else?" he asked quietly. "If there is, he doesn't make you very happy."

"There's no one else. It's just…" I rubbed my forehead. "Why do you have this interest in me?"

"Because you're interesting."

"Why?"

He stood up. I took a step back, even though he hadn't moved toward me.

"Why me?" I asked again. "I don't understand."

He put his hands on his hips, then back at his sides, like he didn't know what to do with them. "You're unusual, Chere. I initially noticed you because you were older than the other students. There was more to see in your eyes. From the beginning, you've had this drive, this burning ambition. That hasn't changed, even though you've changed."

"Changed how?"

"You've become calmer, more dignified. In the beginning you were so anxious, not that I understood why. But you've subsumed all that, little by little. You've disciplined it down to the small, manageable things you make."

I let my bag slide off my shoulder. "You've thought a lot about this."

"Sometimes we get students who make us think, students who fascinate us in some way. Not very often, but we get them. You fascinate me, Chere. It's your detachment. Your control."

"My control?" I laughed bitterly. I had very bad control, otherwise I wouldn't still be standing here talking to him.

"When I hit on you at the club..." He grimaced. "When I invited you to scene with me, it was because you always seem so rigidly controlled. I want—" He paused and looked up to meet my gaze. "I wanted to see if I could break past that control to whatever's bubbling underneath. I wanted to get at all that pent-up emotion inside you."

"I don't want that," I said, horrified. "That's the last thing I want."

"It might be good for you."

"No."

He spread his arms. "Then I suppose you'll continue to be an enigma to me. Maybe it's for the best."

"I think it would be for the best, *Professor* Cantor," I said, to remind him that he was still a teacher in my eyes. We'd barely been out of class for half an hour. I picked up my bag. "I've got to go. I'll see you around."

"I hope so. Have a good break. Oh, and Chere," he said when I was almost to the door.

I turned back with a sense of dread, or maybe sadness. "What?"

"You're a great designer. A great artist. Forget everything else I said, because it doesn't matter. You do amazing work."

* * * * *

I tried to forget everything Cantor said, but it was difficult.

W was out of my life, gone, disappeared. He wasn't coming back, and I was lonely. The winter break stretched out before me, three weeks of drifting angst and inactivity. By the end of the second week, I was losing my mind.

I had to go to a club. I had to be around people. So what if it was the dead time just after New Years? Someone would be out and about. I thought about making the trek uptown to Evolution City, to the big, loud, busy place, but I ended up at Studio Valiant instead. For the balconies, I told myself. Because I liked the balconies.

Cantor wasn't there the first night I went, or the second night, but the third time I showed up, he was the first person I saw on the dungeon floor. He wore light colored jeans this time, jeans that revealed an alluring play of muscles. He oozed confidence as he flogged and teased another pretty blonde.

Him and his blondes. He would have loved me back in my Miss Kitty days. I didn't go up to the balcony right away, but stayed on the dungeon floor, twenty feet or so from where he was playing. Near the end of the scene, he turned to look around the room and caught me staring at him. I didn't try to duck and hide. I let him notice me, and that was when I realized I was ready to let myself be with him.

That sent me running for the balcony. Had I really come here to hook up with Cantor, the married dungeon playboy? The idea of it terrified me, because it meant I was giving up on my safety, my staunch independence from entanglement and heartbreak. I hunched behind the balcony curtains, rubbing my temples, slowly losing my nerve. I finally convinced myself to leave, but not quickly enough. I ran into him halfway down the stairs, in the dark, claustrophobic stairwell, to the strains of Mozart's Paris Symphony.

"I was just leaving," I said.

He slid an arm around my waist. He was shirtless, a little sweaty, but he smelled good anyway. "Why are you here?" he asked.

I shook my head. I was an idiot. "Professor Cantor—"

"I'm not your professor anymore. Call me Martin."

I clasped my hands in front of me like I was praying. It had been so long, *so long*, since anyone had held me like this.

"I don't know what I want," I said. "But I came here, and I think I did that to see you."

"I'm here. How can I help you? Do you want to play? We don't have to do anything complicated."

I shook my head. "I can't. I don't... I don't know..."

"You don't know what you want? It's okay not to know." He let go of my waist and took my hand. "Do you want to get out of here? Talk outside where it's not so noisy?"

I nodded. Yes. Getting out of here was a great idea.

We went out front, to a round concrete wall that banked the entrance. He sat down and gestured me to the space beside him. Aside from the tattooed bouncers, there were a few smokers standing around, and a Dom/sub couple engaged in a heated conversation. Groups of people flounced by on their way to other nighttime destinations.

We didn't say anything at first, just sat there next to each other. I didn't know what to say.

"Why do you like being lonely?" he asked after a while. "It seems like you try really hard to be lonely. I never see you with anyone. You don't hang out with the other students in class."

"I'm older than them."

"You never talk to anyone at the club. You hide in that balcony." He turned to me in the light from the street, propping an elbow on his knee. "Just so you know, anyone at Studio Valiant would play with you. Man, woman, Dom, sub, switch. You could take your pick."

"That's not true."

"It is true, Mistress Mysterious. I'm not the only one you've fascinated."

I looked at the nearby couple, whose discussion was devolving into a fight. "I'm not trying to be fascinating. Or lonely," I added. "I'm trying to protect myself."

"From what? From whom?"

"Everyone. Especially you."

He gave a small laugh and took my hand. I didn't hold his hand back, and he let go.

"What do you want?" he asked. "I mean, self-protection aside, what are you looking for? What would make you happy?"

I didn't even know how to answer that. I wanted something like what W had given me, but I didn't think there was anyone else who could provide that. What he did to me wasn't what the Doms at Valiant did to their subs. It wasn't negotiation and "play" scenes. It was roughness, grasping, breathlessness, peril. Craziness and emotional manipulation.

"I won't be able to find what I want," I said, because in my heart, I knew that I wouldn't.

"That sounds very negative," he said with a sigh.

"If you want—"

"It's not what *I* want," he interrupted. "It's clear to me that I'm not what you want. I'm trying to help you find what *you* want. I know a lot of people in the Manhattan scene."

"Did you ever know this guy...?" I paused, thinking how stupid it was to even ask. "Did you ever know this guy who was tall, blond, and kind of into rough stuff? I mean, really intense stuff, with no negotiation?"

"No negotiation? That's not safe."

"No, he wasn't safe. But did you ever know a guy like that around Manhattan, in the scene?"

He turned to me with a strange look. "Why? Do *you* know this guy? What's his name?"

"I don't know. I don't really know him."

"Is that what you want?" he asked. "Rough stuff? I know people who'll do that, but they'll want to negotiate first."

"Are any of them tall? Blond? Muscular? Around your age, with blue eyes? Maybe in a design career?"

A hint of anger crept into his expression, just for a moment. I understood I was describing someone who looked nothing like him. "No," he said, his voice still tight with an edge. "I don't know anyone like that. Sorry."

I crossed my arms in front of my chest. What was I doing here? The fighting couple was a noisy metaphor for the upheaval in my soul. Cantor was right, I didn't want him. I still wanted W, and hated myself for it. I uncrossed my arms and shoved myself up, thinking how to get out of here with the least amount of awkwardness.

"Chere."

"I'm sorry if I led you on," I said over my shoulder. "I shouldn't have. I was confused. I thought maybe I wanted to play with you back in the club, but now I'm sure I don't. Not that there's anything wrong with you. I don't mean to hurt your feelings."

"My feelings?" He snorted and came over to me. "Don't worry about my feelings. I'm a big boy. I would have liked to take a whack at that wall of yours, but it seems like you have someone else in mind."

"No, there's no one else. I don't want anyone else. I need to be alone. I've made so many bad choices. The fact that I don't want to get involved with you probably means that you're a good, healthy person, so you should feel flattered."

He rubbed his forehead. "You're hurting my brain."

"I know. I'd better go. You'll still have time to hook up with someone else if you go back in."

He glanced at his watch. "I think I'm going to go home."

He was going home to his *wife* and *kids*. His wedding ring shone in the neon glow of Studio Valiant's sign. I knew I was doing the right thing, even if it left me feeling lonelier than ever.

"Can I see you to your place first?" he asked.

"Sure. Thanks."

We walked together to my building, a long, quiet, awkward walk while I questioned my decision. What was better? Settling for a relationship I didn't really want, or living in loneliness? It seemed like the answer never changed. It was better to be alone, in control of my own miserable destiny.

I didn't ask him to walk me upstairs to my door, although I think he still held out a glimmer of hope. I just apologized again. When he asked if he could hug me, I said yes.

It was a respectful hug, a friendly hug. He held me against him longer than I was comfortable with, but he didn't do anything wrong. He just made me realize how dead I was inside, because I didn't feel anything. Loneliness, sadness, all of it bundled inside me like some insidious tumor, growing bigger each day.

I headed into the lobby and up to my apartment. Exhaustion washed over me as I turned the key in the lock. I was so tired, so wrung out from my fucked-up night. I threw my keys in the basket on my kitchen counter and went to the fridge for a water bottle. As I twisted off the cap, I heard a knock.

I froze. Cantor? No, he wouldn't have a key for the elevator. I took a sip of water, hoping whoever it was would go away. The person knocked again, louder this time. I put down the water bottle and moved toward the door. The lock turned before I got there, and the padlock too.

Shit, *shit*, someone was breaking into my apartment. I ran for the kitchen, gunning for my phone as the door opened and shut. The intruder grabbed me before I could reach it, and plastered a hand over my mouth.

"Don't scream," said a voice against my ear.

I knew that voice. I knew the body, the height, the strength, the scent of his cologne. I knew the scratch of his stubble against my jaw and the feel of his hand over my mouth. He'd stifled me that way so many times. I lifted my eyes and looked into the mirror across my apartment and saw him behind me, holding me.

I couldn't believe for a moment that it was him, but his body curved around mine the way it used to. He looked the same, like he'd left the note for me just last week. *Good luck, starshine.* His eyes were half closed in the dim light. He took a slow breath.

"Jesus," he said. "Chere."

He was here. He was in my apartment.

Two and a half years. It had been *two and a half years.*

Motherfucker.

I started to struggle, snarling and yanking at his hand. He moved his fingers up to cover my nose. Motherfucker. Not today. I drove my elbow into his ribs and was rewarded with a grunt. He released me and I spun on him. I didn't understand why he was here. I didn't understand his dark expression. All I understood was that W was in my apartment after *two and a half years.*

I flew at him, to hurt him, not embrace him. "Motherfucker," I cried, my voice breaking. "Tell me your fucking name."

PRICE

I'd followed her and Cantor in the heat of anger, after I saw them leave Valiant together. If she'd brought him up here, I would have kicked his ass and thrown him out. It was her apartment, but it was also my apartment and he wasn't allowed in it because he was a soul-dead, manipulative user.

I hadn't come here to bring her back into my life. That was what I told myself, that I was only here to warn her about Cantor, but as soon as I touched her, my will and anger disintegrated into need.

She was so beautiful, so much more beautiful than I remembered. As soon as my body aligned to hers, I lost it. I lost words, lost action, lost intention, everything. I couldn't move or loosen my grip on her, even when she started to shake.

I was surprised by her elbow to my ribs, or I wouldn't have let her go. She came at me, furious, which I totally understood.

Chere, sweet Chere. I love that you're a fighter.

I let her light into me before I lit into her, because she was going to get what was coming to her either way. She'd been a bad girl. She was supposed to be taking care of herself, protecting herself, and she'd left Studio Valiant with fucking *Cantor.*

"Tell me your name," she demanded as she punched me in the chest.

I grabbed her wrists after she landed a few blows. "Is he coming back?" I asked. "Is Cantor coming back here?"

"None of your fucking business." She pushed away from me, panting for air. She was flushed and beautiful and raging, her freckles standing out against her bronze skin. Her hair was a mess. She ran her fingers through it and glared at me.

"What are you doing here?" she shrieked. "Were you following us? Have you had a key all this time?"

"Of course I've had a key." I glared back at her. She was so close. Right there. I wanted to kiss her but she was too furious, and so was I. "Thank God I had a key, you little fuck up, because you're on the brink of making a terrible mistake."

"It's been two and a half years," she yelled. "You left. You went away. I don't understand why you're here!"

"I'm here because you need to stay the fuck away from Cantor. He's a bastard. You're too good for him."

She drew up taut, her hands in fists. "What business is it of yours, if I hang out with him or anyone else? You disappeared from my life *two and a half years ago*. You didn't even bother to say goodbye."

"What did the two of you talk about?" I pressed. "Are you fucking him?"

"Why do you care?"

"Are you fucking him?" I shouted over her.

"Yes," she screamed back. "We fuck like crazy every chance we get. He fucks me in every fucking hole. He makes me come harder than you ever did."

She was lying. She was upset. I grabbed her and shook her. "That's fucked up, Chere. He's your teacher."

"Not anymore. And how do you know he was my teacher?"

I swept away her stupid question with a wave of my arm. "Are you involved with Martin Cantor? Give me a fucking answer."

She pushed at me. "No! Is that why you've come back after all this time? Because you think I might start fucking someone else? I've fucked a thousand guys since you left me," she said, sticking out her chin.

"You haven't." Even knowing it was a lie, I couldn't bear to hear her say it. "You haven't been with anyone. I would have let you— If you'd found a good man—" I broke off, aware of everything I was revealing. "I would have left you alone," I shouted. "But Martin Cantor is a fucking piece of shit."

"What do you… How do you…?" Her voice wavered. "You've been *watching me*?"

She stared and tried to back away, but I wouldn't let her go. Her eyes. I'd forgotten the depth of her copper-brown eyes, and how easily she could use them to slay me.

"All this time, you've been watching me," she said. It wasn't a question anymore. "You've been *watching me*, you motherfucker. You've been keeping tabs on me?"

"I had to watch you to protect you," I said, the first thing I hadn't shouted at her. "I watched you to be sure you were safe."

I shouldn't have come here. I realized that now. I'd made a horrible, impulsive mistake. She wasn't for me, she could never be for me. I couldn't take her over and enslave her the way I'd fantasized. But now that I'd touched her again... *Fuck. Fuckity fuck.*

"I don't understand what the hell is going on here," she said, shaking off my tightening grip. "Let go of me. I hate you. I fucking despise you. Why are you here? Why are you back? How dare you put your fucking hands on me?"

"Chere."

"I hate you! Do you understand that? I'll never forgive you for what you did to me, for the shitty way you abandoned me."

"Abandoned you?"

"Yes, abandoned me! You abandoned me when I needed you most. You left me, and now you're standing here confronting me like you have any fucking right to do it." She pushed me back again, tears spilling from her eyes. "Fuck you. No. I hate you."

"Chere—"

"You *left me*!"

She lunged at me again but I was ready this time. I caught her in my arms and put my hand over her screaming mouth, not too hard, just hard enough to silence her. I pulled her closer with my other arm, squeezing her waist. Oh God, the solid feel of her against my body.

The more she struggled, the harder I held her. Just like old times. I dodged her kicks as I tugged up her skirt to get at her panties and rip them off.

"No," she groaned against my hand. "No."

"Yes." Now that we were this close, I couldn't resist. Her body went taut as I thrust two fingers into her pussy. She was hot. Wet. Aroused. I felt her teeth against my palm and repositioned my hand before she could bite me.

"No teeth," I hissed, and gave her a hard smack on the ass. This wasn't playtime. I was here, and she was in my arms. Never mind that she'd just finished screaming at me through tears. I had to have her, all of her. Now.

"I'll use a condom," I said. "I have condoms in my wallet."

"No," she cried against my palm, but her body was melting into mine. Her pussy was getting wetter by the second, and her hips arched toward me, trapped beneath my hand. She was my beautiful, lost, angry Chere, and I had to be inside her. I smacked her ass again, felt her gasp and press closer.

My cock was so hard, too hard. I might kill her if I took her now, but that wasn't going to stop me. She made a pleading sound in her throat and ran her hand over my fly, pulling at the button and pushing down the zipper. She should have been tied up, bound and hurt before I fucked her, but God, yes, *take me out, that's right, touch me...*

I let go of her mouth and grabbed her face. I kissed her hard, molding my lips to hers and then biting her until she whimpered. I walked her from the middle of her living room over to the wall. I could see this wall from my apartment. Now I was going to fuck her against it.

"You want it?" I growled. "You fucking want this?"

She grasped my cock, hungry, needy, unashamed. I pushed her hands away, *fuck, fuck, fuck...* I groped in my wallet for a rubber, ripped the package open. *I need to be inside you...*

I rolled it on with one hand and shoved her against the wall with the other. Through her dress, through her bra, I squeezed her breasts and pinched her nipples hard. "Say you want it," I barked. "Say you fucking want me."

"I want you."

"You better fucking mean it."

She groaned in answer, arching her hips even as I hurt her.

I knew she hadn't hooked up with Cantor. Their thing would never have worked, because what she needed was this, force and ownership and brutal hands making her hurt. I pinched her harder, as hard as I could through the goddamned material, and slapped one of her breasts. I mauled her everywhere, grasping, groping, scratching the skin I could get at while she humped mindlessly against my cock.

I wanted her naked, I *needed* her naked, but there was no time because if I didn't get inside her in the next three seconds, I was going to die. I yanked up one of her thighs, draped it over my arm and impaled her, everything, all of me balls deep inside her as I crushed her against the wall. The sensation, the explosion of bliss paralyzed me for a moment. I went rigid, feeling every inch of her hot pussy enveloping me.

She gasped and shoved at me, looking down between us. Poor thing, to find herself so suddenly filled up. I didn't move, just held her hips and waited, buried deep inside her where I'd longed to be for the last two and a half years. She squirmed, my tight, wet, tortured victim.

"Oh, please," she gasped. "Please."

I pressed her to the wall until she couldn't breathe, all the while jamming myself inside her. I wanted to rip off her clothes so there was nothing between us. My pants were around my ankles but I couldn't stop even to kick them off.

Later. I'd strip her later and stroke every part of her, from the top of her head to the tip of her toes. For now, it was about pushing inside her body and making her moan and pant, and remember. *Yes, remember me? Remember this?* Shuddering pleasure made my legs shake. The lust was so thick, so heavy between us. I could have come in a heartbeat but I wouldn't, not until she was coming with me.

"You want more?" I grunted, lifting her with the force of my thrusts.

"You're too big." Her voice whimpered against my ear, seductively alarmed. "I forgot. It hurts. You're so big."

"You like it big. You like a huge cock destroying your pussy." I twisted a hand in her hair, pulling hard. "You want my huge cock inside you, stretching you and hurting you."

"God, yes, yes, *yes*. Please, *oww*." She tried to stop me from pulling her hair and I slapped her face for it.

"You let me do what I want," I reminded her in a hard voice. "You let me do what I want to your fucking body. You're my slut, my cunt, my toy to play with." She made a little "uh" sound each time I surged into her. "And when I'm done getting off in your pussy, you're going to take this huge cock in your ass. Now put your hands over your head. Put them on the fucking wall and leave them there."

She obeyed as her body jerked in my arms. I was plowing her out, driving inside her with ramrod force. Her fists banged against the wall, a sound that resonated up my spine.

"I swear to fuck..." I wanted to yell at her to stop it, but most of the blood had left my brain. There was only the animal sense left, the need to overpower and subdue. She wrapped her legs around my waist and bucked against me. I shoved her dress up and over her head, and flung it away. Her raised arms jutted her chest forward in my face. I jerked down the cups of her bra so her tits were exposed, offered up to me like fucking candy, like brown sugar and cream.

I licked her bared nipples to sensitize them, then sucked each of them hard. She reached down to restrain me, trying to push my head away. *Ohhh, bad girl.* She didn't get to do that, as my angry growl attested. If she was my slave, I would have punished her with her hands cuffed behind her back, and painful clamps applied to her nipples over and over until she understood the consequences of resistance. Instead I spanked her bottom, five hard swats on each cheek, while she wailed and raised her hands back against the wall.

"It hurts," she cried. "Ow! Please."

"Yes, it hurts," I said, squeezing her breasts. "You deserve it." *Bad girl, for making me ache and starve, and want you.* "Are you going to be good?"

"Y-yes! Yes, Sir. Please. Oh God!"

That "Oh God" was shorthand for "I need to come." I could tell by the way she snapped her hips, and the way her muscles tensed as her thighs gripped me. I remembered how it felt when she was about to come, no matter how long it had been.

I ground against her clit, fucking her deep as she made gasping, begging sounds. Her whole body trembled, a delicate vase about to shatter, a firecracker about to explode. As for me, I'd long since lost my mind. *Animal.* I felt like an animal. I fucked her like an animal. She was riding me like an animal and banging her fists against the wall.

"Come on," I said. "You hungry little slut. I want to feel you come on my cock."

"I can't," she cried.

"You're going to." I took her down to the floor, or maybe my legs collapsed from the pressure building behind my balls. I shoved her thighs open, hard and wide, and stretched myself over her, pressing her wrists to the floor. I went even deeper in her now. She tossed her head back and forth, so beautiful in surrender. I felt the exact moment the struggle left her body. I saw the tension bleed away from her face and then I felt her pussy clamp around me. She sobbed, twisting her hips.

My balls contracted and my cock exploded, the built-up pressure shooting outward in waves that turned me inside out and left me enervated. "Jesus fucking Christ," I gasped. "Holy fuck."

The orgasm went on forever, pulse after pulse of rending bliss. She was still breathing hard, arching under me. I stayed buried in her pussy, riding the afterglow for all I was worth. At last I came back to earth, from animal to civilized man. Well, mostly civilized man.

"Good girl," I said when I could speak. "No. Don't move yet. I'm not done with you yet."

I eased off her a moment later. She reached for me, but I stretched her arms up again and held her wrists against the floor. "I said not to move. Stay there, or I'll blister your ass with my fucking belt. Do you understand?"

I wasn't sure she'd obey. Our hot, violent tryst had left her a little scattered. I knelt back, watching her with a warning look, and forced her legs open when she tried to close them.

"What are you going to do now?" she asked. I left her lying there, threw away the condom and started to undress. She sounded scared, petulant, horny, confused, all those wonderful emotions. She was the same old Chere. It was like I'd never left.

"I told you what I was going to do," I replied, throwing my shirt and pants over the edge of the couch.

She gave me a pleading look. "I haven't—I haven't done anal since you went away. I don't think I'm ready to take you in the ass."

"I don't care if you're ready. You'll manage. Don't you dare close those legs." They'd begun inching together again. Poor, scared Chere. Her pussy had gotten the quick, impulsive fuck. Her ass was going to get worked over for a whole lot longer. She remembered. She knew.

"Please," she said, but at my glare, she fell silent. She was under my control now, the way she ought to be. The way she *wanted* to be. I stroked myself for a few minutes, watching her, thinking how beautiful and open she was.

"Do you want to touch yourself?" I asked. Her pussy was so wet the moisture was running down into her ass crack.

Her thigh muscles tightened. "Yes, please."

"Well, you can't. Not yet. I'll let you rub your clit once I'm inside your asshole, if I think you deserve it."

Her quiet whimper of frustration brought me to full hardness again. I raised an eyebrow. "You're lucky I don't have any clamps."

I knelt between her legs and rolled on a condom, then jammed a few fingers into her pussy, collecting the copious wetness. "Look at me," I ordered as I smoothed my fingers down to her asshole. Her gaze met mine as her tiny ring tensed at my touch. I used her pussy juices to ease in a finger, then two. "You *are* tight," I said in a low voice. "This is going to hurt you."

"Please, don't. I haven't been fucked in the ass in so long. I wish you wouldn't."

"Girls like you need to be fucked in the ass all the time." I eased in another two fingers, stretching her open.

"Oww," she whined, arching her hips. I'd forgotten how much I loved her whining and complaining. So much drama, pretending she didn't like things. She was so worked up right now she was about to explode from it. If she was on her stomach, she'd be humping the floor, which was why I kept her on her back with her legs spread. No pleasure for her yet.

"Look at me," I said in a sharper voice, when her eyes started closing. She had four fingers inside her now, stretching, probing, making her squirm. It was so quiet, so still in her apartment. There was only her and me, and the halting sound of her breath.

"Tell me your name," she said between her teeth. "Tell me, or I won't let you do this."

"Oh, you're going to let me do it," I said with a chuckle. "And I'm not paying you for it either. You're not a whore anymore, except when I want you to be."

She was about to start whining again. I slapped her legs open when she attempted to close them. "Price," I said. "My name's Price, but when you're on the floor with my fingers in your asshole, you'll call me Sir."

"Price?" She looked dazed. Maybe the moment was anticlimactic? She'd waited all that time to know my name, and what had it really changed?

"Price," I snapped. "P-R-I-C-E. As in a sum or value, something to be paid." I spread her legs wider and gestured to my swollen cock. "You're about to pay with your fucking ass."

She tensed as I pressed the head of my cock against her hole. "Why did you disappear?" she asked. "Why did you leave? I would have been your 'whore' for as long as you wanted."

I wasn't ready to go there yet, to explain why I had to get the hell away from her, why I was anxious about being here even now. Instead I fisted my cock and tried to wedge the lubricated head past her clenching sphincter. "Let me in," I said, holding her troubled gaze. "I don't want to force things, but I will if I have to."

She bit her lip. I could see she was trying, but she was so small, and I was so large. Every time I pressed an inch inside, she pushed me out again.

"It's because I'm scared. You scare me."

I didn't reply to that. Yes, I scared her. I wanted to scare her and thrill her and turn her on. She was my perfect fit, even if she was having a little trouble accommodating my thick prick in her asshole.

"I have lube," she said in a small, guilty voice. "In my bedroom, in the bedside table, I have a bottle of lubricant."

I stared down at her with a stern look. "Why would you have lube? I thought you haven't had anal. You said that to me, not five minutes ago."

"Well, I haven't. But I..." Oh God, her shame was glorious. "I used the lube to..."

"To play with your ass?" The more she blushed, the more I would make her confess, in excruciatingly explicit detail. "Because I know you wouldn't need lube for your pussy. You drip like a faucet every time I so much as look at you. You must have been using that lubricant to play with your ass."

She couldn't hold my gaze anymore. "Chere," I said in a warning tone. "You fucking look at me when I talk to you. Did you masturbate your horny little asshole? Did you put things inside it?"

She brought one of her arms down to cover her eyes. I smacked it back up again. "Don't," she cried.

"What did you put in your asshole, girl? Dildos? Butt plugs? Any fucking thing that was hard and round and thick? Do you have butt plugs in your bedside table?"

"Yes," she admitted. "Only one."

"You lied to me then, when you said you weren't ready, that you didn't want to have anal."

"Can I go get the lube?" she begged, as I fisted my cock again.

"Hell no, you can't go get the lube. You lied to me, you little anal whore."

There was ample lube, between her pussy juices and what was on the condom. There was enough to get inside her, not that it would feel very good. But I didn't want this to feel too good.

"Bad girls who tell lies get punished." I pressed into her hole, and this time, I put the weight of my hips behind it. The head eased in as she wriggled in pain. Her body stretched for me, as it was made to do. "Pretend it's your butt plug," I taunted her.

"It hurts," she said, tensing, fighting. "It hurts, it hurts."

"That's because you're not surrendering. Let it happen. You deserve this. You *want* this, or you wouldn't have lube in your side table, would you?"

So delicious, to shame her and pry her ass open at the same time. The sensation, the pleasure, the intimate violence of the act nearly overpowered me. Her distress made my balls throb. I pushed deeper, four, five inches in, the lube on the condom making the invasion possible even without her cooperation.

"Don't," I said, when her hands came down to push me away. "Don't dare."

"It hurts. Can I touch my pussy now? Can I touch my clit?"

"No, bad girls don't get to touch their clits. You lied to me," I reminded her. "You were a bad girl."

"Please," she cried, but she could see from the look in my eyes that it wasn't happening. She tossed her head in a frantic way. Her spine arched as I drove in a few more inches. I was almost balls deep, buried inside her. Poor Chere. So horny, so needy, and all I gave her was pain. Her pelvis moved in tiny, gingerly increments. I took her hips in my hands and drove the rest of the way in.

"Oh, God," she gasped.

Yes, I felt like praying too. It was a moment for me, a scintillating moment of controlling her in this brutal way.

"Do you feel full?" I asked. "Does this feel good, baby?"

She shook her head, squeezing her eyes shut, but I just laughed.

"Admit it. It feels like heaven to you. You're the type of woman who needs more than a butt plug to feel satisfied. Were you thinking about my cock when you shoved things in your asshole? When you smeared them with lube and slid them deep inside you?" I started to move in her, all the way out, then all the way back in again with rough, dominating strokes. She shuddered, spreading her hands out over her head.

"Is this what you thought about?" I asked again. "Am I the one you fantasized about when you shoved toys in your asshole?"

She shook her head, hopeless, helpless denial, but then she admitted the truth. It spilled from her lips on a sob. "Yes. Yes!"

She trembled and bucked as I pumped her hole. I held her hips harder, so she couldn't evade me, couldn't move an inch to disrupt my steady pile-driving. "I'm back now," I said, facing the fact that this wouldn't be some one-off session. "You won't need that butt plug anymore. Or any extra lube, once I have you trained again."

Her breath came faster, disintegrating into gasps. I would have made her look at me but she was so gone, so wrecked. I didn't want to pull her from her world of dark, hurting submission. I wanted her to bask in all the surrender she felt.

"Oh, please." She sounded like some injured creature, emitting small whimpers and pants. "Please can I touch myself?"

"Yes, you can touch yourself. Squeeze your nipples. Hurt your nipples for me while I pound your ass."

"No. Please! My pussy!"

"Pinch your fucking nipples." I let go of her hips to guide her hands to her breasts. Her nipples were rock hard, standing up in rigid points. She started to tug at them with a beautiful, angry expression. "Pinch them hard," I said. "Harder! Twist them back and forth between your fingers."

I demonstrated briefly, wresting a cry of agony from her throat. She was happy to replace my fingers with hers. She didn't hurt herself as much as I could have, but she obeyed me, pinching and twisting her sensitive peaks.

"That's right," I said, enjoying the tortured expression on her face. "I would have let you jack yourself off, if you'd told the truth from the start. *I haven't done anal since you went away*," I sneered in a high, mocking voice. "*I'm not ready.*"

"I'm sorry I lied." She tossed her head back, jerking at the tips of her tits. "I'm sorry. I won't lie again. Please let me touch my pussy. Please let me come."

"How about if I touch your pussy for you, naughty girl? How about if I spank it, because you've been so bad?"

I slapped her between the legs, right over her clit. Her reaction was instantaneous, ball-busting, gorgeous. She arched and sobbed, clenching her sphincter around my dick.

"You want more?" I asked. I was barely holding back, and she was so wet, so messy and juicy. "You want me to spank your pussy some more?"

"Please. Yes. Please!"

"*Please, Sir.* Use your fucking manners."

"Please, Sir," she cried. "Please spank my pussy."

I spanked the shit out of her pussy. My fingers were coated in her juices, and she was coming apart at the seams.

"Don't you dare stop hurting your nipples." I pinched her clit between my nails to refocus her. She yelped and obeyed me, tugging at herself, giving her ass and pussy up for me to hurt to my heart's content. It was too much. It would never be enough. This visit would never be enough, and I wasn't sure what that meant for the both of us.

"Come, damn you," I growled. "Before I kill you."

Before she killed me. My mind, my body, every part of me was focused on one thing...living inside her. I wanted to devour her. I wanted to ravage her. I wanted to feel her come.

I wanted to lock her in my dungeon and never let her go.

She spread her legs wider for her pussy spanking, arched up and sucked in a breath. I drove deep just as she came. Her ass clamped around my length in pulsing contractions, wresting my orgasm from the pit of my balls.

Jesus. God. Holy Jesus Fuck Shit. I shouted expletives, half of them nonsense. Chere said nothing, only writhed and gritted her teeth. She let go of her nipples and pulled her arms up beside her, then covered her face.

Let her be ashamed. My little anal whore. I leaned over and stuck my tongue in her mouth, tasting her, licking the inside of her teeth. I kissed and savored her because I didn't dare bite her, not in my current mood. I would have drawn blood. I was still inside her ass, rigid and hard.

"Don't leave me," she said, and I didn't know if she meant her asshole or her life. She reached out to me. She was crying, not sexy crying, but the emotional kind.

I lowered myself over her, gathering her in an embrace. "Don't cry," I whispered, moving shallowly inside her. I brushed back her hair and kissed her forehead, and gazed into the confused, hazy depths of her eyes. "Don't cry, starshine. It's all right."

But it wasn't all right. I was bad for her, and now that she was back in my clutches, I wasn't sure I could summon the willpower to leave her again.

CHERE

My body woke before my brain started functioning. I turned and stretched, and winced. Why did I hurt? Why did I ache all over?

I stared out my window at the late-morning winter sun, and slowly things came back to me. A hand over my mouth. Shouting and fucking. More fucking, a shower. Kissing, more kissing, more fucking, a collapse on the bed. I felt a fingertip move along my thigh.

Oh God. W was back, and he was beside me.

No, not W.

Price.

I could feel his weight and sense his heat behind me. The fingertip crept up to my waist and then he pulled me back against him with a quiet groan. His stiff erection poked my ass.

"No," I protested weakly. "I can't."

"You can." His voice rumbled beside my ear, gravelly with morning roughness. "But we can't. I don't have any more condoms." He chuckled and tugged at a lock of my hair. "Unless you're hiding some of those in your nightstand too."

I put a hand over my face. I felt the strangest impulse to cry, to weep until my pillows were soaked. In the two months I'd worked as his escort, I'd never woken up with him, not once. This was new and unfamiliar ground. I'd never spent more than a couple of hours in his presence.

We'd shared finite scenes, sessions with clear beginnings and endings. It befuddled me to find him beside me, even though I'd cuddled up next to him just a few hours earlier, when we finally ran out of energy for fucking and decided to sleep.

Price. As in a sum or value, something to be paid.

"You won't look at me," he said in the quiet. "You don't want to look at me."

"I can't."

"Why?"

I didn't know why. I just knew that I didn't have the courage to turn to him, not now, not in the morning's bright light. My scrapbook of his poetry was hidden under my bed, the poetry I'd obsessed over and cried over and seethed over when I came to understand he was never coming back.

But he was back. He was beside me, but he wasn't W, he was Price, and he'd let himself into my apartment and fucked me all freaking night. He'd simply waltzed back into my life and taken me, no apologies, no explanation.

I let out a breath. I wasn't ready for this. Now that the sex was over and my body wasn't full of his dick, I didn't know how to feel. I was afraid to turn and see him there, *right there*, blond and strong and domineering and larger than life.

I pulled away from his embrace and sat on the edge of the bed, then catapulted up to run to the bathroom. I didn't have to pee. I just had to get away from him. As I scurried past his side of the bed, I could see him in my peripheral vision. A ghost, a blur. A specter. No, a real man. I still couldn't believe he was here, even after all the ways he'd defiled me the night before.

"I'll be right out," I muttered, shutting the door. My finger hovered over the lock. It was only a courtesy lock, so people didn't barge in while you were pissing, or undressing for the shower. It wasn't a lock for keeping out someone like W, not if he wanted to come in.

No, damn it. Not W. *Price.*

I left the door unlocked.

I went in the little partition that Andrew called the "shitter," closed that door too, and sat on the toilet with my head in my hands. I wanted to rage at him, to kick him out, but I'd already let him fuck me. I'd fallen to his daunting ability to control me. I'd forgotten how easily he could short circuit my brain. But before, when I was his escort and he was my client, I knew he would eventually leave.

Now, I wasn't sure he would leave. I was kind of terrified that he might stay and fuck me until I died.

Shut up, Chere. You're being ridiculous. He's just a man, like any other man.

When I opened the door, he was there in the bathroom, as I knew he would be. He leaned against the marble countertop, his arms crossed over his chest. His cock, even soft, looked too large and threatening. Too masculine. Too male. Too big. *Price.* Price who? I still didn't know anything about him. He studied me with a guarded expression, his lips turned slightly down, his ice blue eyes both alert and assessing.

"I feel better now," I lied. At least I'd finally managed to look at him, even if I was cowed by what I saw.

He brushed past me and pissed in my toilet with the door open. I suppose it was really his toilet since he'd bought this place for me. He had a key. All this time he'd had a key. He'd pretty much admitted that he'd been watching me, monitoring my activities. Perhaps he'd even snuck into my apartment while I was in class, or while I was sleeping.

I shivered and hurried into my fleece bathrobe and started brushing my teeth. I stared down at the counter, at the toothbrush I'd given him last night. He picked it up and brushed too, like a man, noisy and fast, spitting just after me.

"I want the key," I said. "The key you used last night. I want you to leave it with me."

He didn't answer, just grabbed me and drew me into a kiss.

It wasn't a tortured kiss like the one he'd given me while we were shouting at each other in my living room. It wasn't a rough kiss like he gave me after he fucked me. No. It was a soft, warm, gentle kiss that felt way too perfect and cozy there in my bathroom, with our toothbrushes lying next to each other.

I can't. I hate you.

I don't know you.

I'm not sure.

Maybe he wasn't sure either. Maybe he had no intention of spending time with me ever again once he walked out my door. He'd left me before, and he didn't impress me as someone eager to form enduring relationships. But this time now, and this kiss, felt different from our previous carnal sessions.

"I want the key," I whispered when he finished.

He pressed his cheek to mine, ran a hand up and down my back, and then yanked a handful of my hair. "Don't fucking boss me around."

* * * * *

He made toast and eggs for breakfast, while I washed fruit and piled it on a plate. I didn't have a coffee maker. He promised to punish me for it later, and I didn't think he was kidding. He stood at my stove cooking breakfast with no shirt, and his tailored pants riding just below the dimples of his ass. The eggs were scrambled, like my thoughts, but they were cooked just right, sprinkled lightly with cheese. He was so fucking competent at sex, and now this.

I wanted to be strong and independent. I wanted to be pissed that he'd come here and taken over me so easily, but when he put a plate down in front of me, I said thank you and started to eat. The eggs tasted wonderful. I hated that they tasted so wonderful.

"So, who's going to talk first?" he asked.

"What?"

"What do you want to say to me? You seem..." He waved a hand. "Angsty."

He'd disappeared for two and a half years, materialized out of nowhere, and now accused me of being "angsty"? I frowned and squished a piece of egg into a puddle.

"Am I supposed to be glad you're back?" I said. "Am I supposed to be happy?"

"You seemed happy last night when my cock was in your ass."

I couldn't deal with this. I wasn't prepared. "Do you know what this is like? Seeing you again? Having you come at me and…and…"

"And what?" He grabbed a handful of grapes and popped one in his mouth. "You're lucky I came back in time to warn you about Cantor after you were stupid enough to get drawn in."

"I wasn't drawn in by Cantor," I lied. "We just talked about some stuff."

"That's how he works. He talks. He flirts. He tells you you're interesting, at least until someone else interests him more. He uses women. I didn't want that for you."

"You want to fuck me instead."

"Chere."

"Why did you leave?" I asked, ripping the crusts off my toast. "You haven't answered me."

"I left because you decided to stop escorting. I wanted to support your decision."

"You disappeared because I decided to go to school? I told you I would have kept seeing you!"

"I know you would have kept seeing me."

He took a drink of water. I crossed my arms over my chest.

"Then why?"

"Why what?"

"Why to everything. Why wouldn't you tell me your name? Why did you give me this apartment, then take off? We could have had a relationship, even while I was in school."

"Not the kind of relationship I wanted."

"And what kind of relationship did you want?" I scoffed. "Considering how easily you left me?"

"You don't want to know."

His low, taut words were accompanied by a jeopardous stare. I'd forgotten what it was like to be at the mercy of his pale blue gaze.

"Stop," I said.

"Stop what?"

"Stop being that way. Stop trying to fuck with me and scare me. I'm never letting that happen again. I don't want this weirdo shit between us. I'm different now."

He laughed, and it wasn't a nice laugh. "You weren't different last night."

I stood, snatching up my plate and silverware with a clatter. "Last night is over. I regret it now. It was a mistake."

"Last night was fucking magical, and you know it." His sharp retort jolted me, made me pause on the way to the kitchen, then flee like a coward. He followed me, grabbed the plate out of my hand and tossed it on the counter with a bang. He stood against me. *Too close. You're too close.* He stood so I couldn't move, pinning me against the cabinets.

"Admit it," he said. "It was magical."

"It wasn't magical. It was the opposite of magical. It was desperate and impulsive and I regret it today."

His lips curled. His nostrils flared. "Get off me," I said through my teeth.

"You're not the one in charge here."

"This is my apartment!"

"This is my apartment." He pointed to the table. "Mine." He slapped a palm against the counter, rattling the dishes. "Mine." He swung an arm toward the living area. "This is my apartment, you ungrateful little bitch."

"You gave it to me. It's my apartment now. I signed the papers your lawyers sent."

"Did you read them first? Did you hire someone to look over them?" He smiled, a slow sadistic smile. "Do you really think I would have signed it over to you completely without some means of getting it back?"

I didn't know if he was fucking with me again. My body hurt and my brain hurt. I turned away and he put his hands on either side of me, daring me to move. I didn't.

"Look at me," he ordered.

After a moment of mulish resistance, I lifted my chin to meet his gaze. I heard his fingers tap on the counter beside me. *Tap, tap, tap.* "What do you think it would be like, Chere, to be in a relationship with me?"

I didn't answer. I couldn't answer. I didn't want to think about it.

"Consuming?" he suggested. "Difficult? Hurtful? Ultimately heart-breaking?"

"Yes," I said in a rasp. "All those things."

"And you wanted that? You wanted me to stay and give you that, when you were taking all those steps to make your life better?"

"I don't know."

I looked away from his intense line of questioning, only to have my chin dragged back.

"I left you as a kindness," he said, holding my face between his fingers. "I know you're ungrateful for everything I've ever done for you, but you should at least be grateful for that. I left you so you could go to school and get your degree and start your new life where you would be happy."

I wet my lips, which had gone as dry as my throat. "But now you're back."

"I came back to stop you from making a mistake," he said quietly. "But a relationship with me would also be a mistake."

"So go," I said, losing patience with his obscure threats. "Leave me alone. I don't want to make any more mistakes."

"I won't let you make mistakes. But I still think I'll need to fuck you every once in a while. I wish it wasn't that way. Jesus, I've tried to convince myself—" His features twisted and rearranged themselves, a fleeting show of emotion. "I've tried to stay away, but now that I've had you, I'm going to need more. I'm going to need to fuck you a few times a week at least."

His calm, entitled proclamation momentarily befuddled me. He'd just finished telling me that he wouldn't have a relationship with me, that I *shouldn't* want a relationship with him, but he'd help himself to my body whenever he pleased? It was fucking insulting. Fucking ridiculous.

"Fuck you," I said, pushing him away.

"You don't think it's a good idea?"

I stalked into the living room, trying to put distance between us. "I think it's a horrible idea. If we're not going to have a relationship, what's the fucking point?"

"The fucking point is the *fucking*," he said. "I like *fucking* you, and you like being *fucked* by me, as evidenced by your participation last night."

"The only reason I let you fuck me last night was because it'd been too long for me. I've been too busy at school to get laid. Too busy to hook up with anyone."

"Aside from your professor," he said in a snide tone.

"I want you to leave." I was tired of his mockery, his condescension. Yes, I'd fucked Price last night. Yes, I'd enjoyed myself, but it didn't mean anything, and it certainly wasn't a mistake I'd repeat again. "I want you to give me the key you used to get in here, and then I want you to leave."

He crossed his arms over his chest. "I'll leave when I fucking want to leave."

"I'm not sleeping with you again, ever, so you might as well fuck off."

"You're wrong about that, Chere." He started toward me, force and masculine beauty. "You're going to sleep with me whenever I fucking want you to."

I spit out more words, attempting to shield myself from his will. "You can't make me. You can't have me if I don't want to give myself to you. I won't let you back into my life after the way you left."

He took my arm and dragged me over to the living room window. He jabbed a finger, pointing across the street. "You see that building? Count up to the sixth floor, the corner window. That's where I live. That's where I watch you sometimes with a pair of hunting binoculars because you never shut your drapes. If I want to be in your life, I'll be in your life."

The word "hunting binoculars" chilled me. Not just binoculars. Not the ubiquitous telescopes that nosy New Yorkers used to "look at the stars." He'd used *hunting* binoculars.

"Are you serious?" I said, pulling my elbow from his grasp. "You've been watching me?"

"You didn't believe me when I told you last night?"

"You said you knew what I'd been doing. You didn't say you were staring at me through binoculars."

I took another step back from him, and looked out at his apartment. Sixth floor, corner. Holy shit, all that time I cried for him and missed him, and searched the Internet for blond, sadistic designers to try to find him, he was across the fucking street with his fucking hunting binoculars.

"This is fucked up," I said. "You can't—You shouldn't— People aren't supposed to act this way! I can't believe you spied on me."

"I was trying to protect you," he snapped. "I wanted to be sure you were okay."

"How does perving on me from across the street protect me? I think it invades my privacy. I think you're a psycho creeper."

He didn't like that I called him that. His eyes narrowed and his chin tipped up.

"You might show a little more respect," he said. "I was very generous with you over the course of our association. I gave you some of the best fucking sex of your life."

"Well, that's over. We're over."

"We're not over. I still want to see you sometimes. I won't make a lot of demands on your time."

He reached to touch my cheek. I pushed his hand away but he only grasped my wrists and overpowered me, trapping me against the couch. As he held me with his body, he ran his fingers down the line of my jaw.

"I'll make you feel good, Chere. I know how to make you crazy. I know what you need. What you want."

I shook my head. He was too close. He was too strong and hot and tempting. His eyes met mine as his hand moved down my neck, his thumb resting on my pulse. "I'll make you hurt and fight and come," he said in a soft, lurid tone. "I'll make you tremble and cry, and then I'll hold you afterward until you feel better." His other arm slipped around me, a firm band. A prison. "Then, when you're all better, all exhausted and fucked out, I'll leave. I won't interfere with your school, or your work once you graduate."

Once I graduate? That was months from now. Did he imagine I'd be his eternal fuck buddy, waiting at his beck and call? I started to twist in his embrace.

"Don't fight me, starshine," he said. "You know it'll be good."

Good luck, starshine…

"No. No, not again. I want you to go," I said, pushing at his chest.

"I will. Just tell me when I can see you again."

"Never! You can never see me again."

I struggled in earnest now, but his arms were longer and stronger. His body was a rock against mine.

"Let go," I snapped, pushing against him. "I'm not fucking you again."

His features twisted in irritation. "I thought you weren't in the escort business anymore, but if you need me to pay you, I'll pay you. Either way. Whatever will make it happen."

I lost what remained of my patience and slapped his face twice, way harder and more forcefully than he'd ever slapped mine. I raked his ear with my nails before he caught my hands and held them. I kicked him instead and he tackled me, upended me and covered me on the living room floor.

"I'm not your whore! I don't want your fucking money." I writhed under him, trying to free my arms from his grip. The bottom of my robe parted and I could feel his erect cock through the fabric of his pants.

"I can't fuck you right now," he said, and I could have sworn he was laughing. "Stop flirting."

"Get off me," I shrieked.

Within a second, he was gone. He stood and jumped back, out of kicking distance. I lurched to my feet and fixed my robe, and glared at him as I retreated behind the couch. I started to yell at him again, for him to leave, to get the fuck out, but he held up a hand.

"Don't scream at me."

I clasped my hands over my mouth, fighting tears I absolutely would not shed. I stared at the man who'd commandeered so much of my heart, against my will, against my better judgment. He'd consumed so much of my life. I couldn't let him have any more. Even if, deep down inside, I wanted more.

"I'm not going to scream at you," I said from between my fingers. "But I need you to go. I *really* need you to go."

"Okay," he said, very calmly and very coolly. "But I need you to comprehend something. You and I are not over." He walked closer to me. I shook my head and scrambled back until I was trapped against the window.

I stared at his intent expression, his broad shoulders, the ladder of muscles leading up to his chest. I thought of his poetry and the way he'd taken over my body in those hotel rooms. I thought of the pleasure, the longing he planted in me. I thought...maybe...

But no. No, no, no.

"You have to leave." Tears spilled over, panic in liquid form. What if he stood there forever, looking at me like that, making me want him when I didn't want to want him? "You left me!" I said. "I wish I'd never met you. I wish you'd leave me alone."

"Chere—"

"Go away! And if you spy on me, I swear to God, if you look at me through your binoculars or follow me around, I'll call the fucking police. I'll report you. I'll take out a restraining order."

He held up his hands, his strong, powerful fingers spread wide in protest. "Chere," he said. "Don't freak out." He reached to wipe away some of my tears. "Stop crying. Listen to me."

I shoved his hand away. "No."

"You're overreacting."

"I want you to go. You're crazy and scary and controlling."

"Yes." I heard his sharp agreement through the frantic whoosh of blood in my ears. "Yes, I'm controlling, but I would never, ever hurt you."

"Really?" I glared at him in disbelief. "You'd never hurt me? You're a fucking liar. You left me! After everything, after you took over my heart and my life, and twisted up all my feelings, you *left me*." I grasped at my chest. "That hurt me *so much*. It hurt me way more than you can ever understand. I loved you, but now I hate you. You've already hurt me as much as anyone could be hurt, and I survived it. Now I just want you to leave me the fuck alone."

I stood there clutching my heart, trying to collect myself. I hadn't meant to reveal so much. I hadn't meant to give him the pleasure of knowing how deeply he'd injured me. I hadn't meant to tell him that I loved him. He didn't deserve to know.

He watched me a moment, then pursed his lips and turned away. "I'll go get my shirt."

He put it on, buttoned it up and tucked it in like any normal man. He looked normal, but he wasn't normal. He wanted too much, demanded too much. Stalked me too much and scared me too much. He gave me orgasms that clouded my reason, but I wasn't going to let that happen again. He put on his socks and his shoes without a word, gave me another taut glance, and walked to the door.

"Thanks for the fuckfest anyway," he said. "It was epic."

The door shut behind him, and he was gone from my life, forever, for the second time.

Shit. *The key.*

Price

By the time I got home, her drapes were closed, every one of them. I put the binoculars in one of the guest room closets. I wasn't going to need them anymore.

So, Chere wasn't inclined to welcome me back with open arms? Okay. Understandable. Hell, I shouldn't have gone back in the first place, I *definitely* shouldn't have fucked her, but now that I had, I wasn't going to deprive myself. Those breathless hours we'd spent through the night, before her angsty emotions caught up with her…

Well, they were worth it, even if her defensive, distancing words had followed. *I wish I'd never met you. I wish you'd leave me alone. You're crazy and scary and controlling.* All the blather about police and restraining orders. I knew she didn't mean any of it, but she'd been pretty damn angry.

My little fighter. She'd always had a temper.

It pleased me that Chere hadn't lost any of her spirit, that none of her defining qualities had changed. Her hair color had changed, sure, and she'd pretty much lost that whore look she used to have. But God, the splendor in its place... Her curly, dark hair, her bold features, her eyes like liquid toffee. Her freckles. That pert, strong chin.

I lay back on my bed and undid my pants, took out my cock and stroked it to hardness. I had work to do, a meeting tomorrow, but I had a little sexual tension to take care of first.

Today sucked, but last night had been amazing, perhaps the most magnificent sexual marathon of my life. The way she resisted at first, the way she fought me and melted into me at the same time. Then...when I pushed inside her... My fucking God.

I worked my cock slowly, sensually, pulling hard with a firm grip. *This is for you, Chere.* I took my time, thinking back to the softness of her skin, the cinnamon scent of her hair. I didn't want to come too quickly. There was so much to remember. So much to look forward to when I won back her trust, which I fully intended to do. I wouldn't attempt to enslave her as I did in my darkest fantasies, or interfere with anything she was trying to accomplish. I'd just fuck her in that rough, intense way she liked, for our mutual satisfaction.

After I came like a storm, and cleaned myself up, I sat and scrawled some words on a stark white page. I placed it in an envelope, and wrote her name and address on the front.

You're so beautiful.

It wasn't enough, and someday I would do better, but for now it was the only poetry I had.

CHERE

Andrew looked down at the parts and pieces spread out in front of him.

"Chere, I swear to God we're doing this wrong."

"Read the directions again."

He held the flimsy paper up to his face and squinted at the tiny writing. "You read them. I can't make out a word."

"Your eyes are younger than mine."

He leaned back against the doorjamb and tossed down the paper with a sigh. "Why are we changing the lock again? If the building manager already changed it?"

"Because Price used to own this apartment. He might be tight with the manager. He might own this entire building. He might have been the one to send the locksmith."

"You sound kind of paranoid," Andrew said.

"Of course I'm paranoid. He was stalking me the entire time he was gone. I'm sure he'd love to have another key to my apartment, and if he knows the people who run this building..."

My friend looked skeptical. "He had a key for two and half years, though, and he never used it."

I glared at him. "Whose side are you on?"

"Your side, darling."

"And we can't really say if he used it or not. Maybe he came in here all the time while I was away."

At my quiet huff of outrage, he bent back over the directions. "Okay," he said with feigned confidence. "We'll figure this out."

I leaned over the directions too, trying to calm down. I shouldn't have been bitching at Andrew. He'd come over in a flash when I told him I needed him, even though he'd just returned last night from his rent-boy excursion in Vail. He was sun bronzed and wind burned and full of racy tidbits about his time with Mr. Recaro.

I hadn't told him as much about my reunion with Price. I left out the night-long carnival of perversity and stuck to the basics: that he'd shown up out of nowhere and let himself into my apartment, and freaked me the fuck out.

"We need more light to do this," Andrew said. "Can't you open the drapes?"

"No. Remember? Hunting binoculars."

"Oh, yeah." He grimaced and picked up one of the pieces.

After I'd sent Price away, he'd had a note delivered to my apartment. *You're so beautiful.* That's all it said, *You're so beautiful.* When I showed it to Andrew, he'd pointed out what I already knew, that it was an echo of something he'd written once on my arm. *Look at what you do for me. You're so beautiful.*

I had done way, way too much for him the other night, not that I admitted that to my friend.

We turned our attention back to the lock's pieces, and my metal design background eventually helped me figure out how it went together. My sweet but useless sidekick kept me company while I took out the old lock and installed the new one.

"Here's the thing," Andrew said, holding the lock while I went at the door with a screwdriver. "Mr. Recaro—"

"Why do you always call him Mr. Recaro? Two weeks in Vail, and you're not on a first name basis?"

"His first name is Maximo, but he only lets me call him Mr. Recaro, or Sir."

The "Sir" sounded familiar. I sucked in a breath. "How kinky."

"Girl, you don't even know. It's so sexy, how he knows what he wants, how he demands and takes and uses me for his own fulfillment.

It's the submissive thing. When I'm with him, I feel so grateful to be able to serve him."

"You're a natural submissive. I'm sure he realizes that, and values it."

A tinge of pink colored Andrew's cheeks. "It makes me feel special to serve him. He made me feel special, even though I was the one at his beck and call. Does that make any sense? Why do I enjoy giving myself up completely to someone else? What does that say about me?"

The lock was in. I clicked the bolt back and forth. "Maybe it's a thrill-seeking thing," I said. "Or a way of coping. Sometimes it's nice to not have to be in charge."

"I don't know." He watched as I tested the key. "I guess it's not crucial to understand the reasons. I just know it turns me on. God, it makes me feel high, to be under someone's control, and to please that person. Is that weird? It's weird, isn't it?"

"No, you're just kinky. It is what it is."

Andrew pushed his curls back, a smile playing at the corner of his lips. "The way he looked at me after our scenes... I can't even describe it. The way he kissed me… Pleasing him makes me feel like I'm high on drugs or something. I'm not falling in love," he said at my exasperated look. "I'm *not.* But I really respect him. He was good to me and I was good to him. I hope we'll keep seeing each other."

"I'm sure you will. I'm glad you had fun."

His smile turned wistful. "I know he's just a client, and that this is just for now, but I hope I meet someone like Maximo someday and have a real relationship. A real Dom/sub relationship that goes on all the time."

"You'll find your match," I said, trying to sound like I knew what the fuck I was talking about. "You're too kind and generous to spend your life alone. Someone is going to appreciate you one day, and give you everything you need, and you'll live happily ever after."

"You think so?"

"I hope so," I said, even though I didn't believe in happily ever after. Now that the lock was in, I took the spare key and handed it to Andrew. "I want you to have this. You're my best friend in New York. Maybe my best friend anywhere. I've always wanted someone to give a spare key to."

"Oh gawd." His smile widened as he took it. "I'll treasure it forever."

I rolled my eyes. "You want something to drink?"

We sprawled on my couch with a couple of sloppy cocktails. Andrew launched into more Vail stories, apologizing for all the details. I didn't mind as much as he thought I did. The escorting was obviously working for him right now, and if he was going to be a good friend to me, I had to be a good friend in return. I had to support him to the best of my ability, and keep an eye on him in case things started to go wrong.

Keep an eye on him, like Price kept an eye on you?

I frowned and shook my head. *Not the same.* Andrew's voice drifted off mid-story as he realized I wasn't listening. He was so sensitive to my mood swings. If he wasn't gay, he'd be the perfect boyfriend.

"Still thinking about him?" he asked in a hopelessly gentle voice. "You were right to tell him to fuck off. But it must have been hard."

"Honestly, it wasn't that hard. He acted like an overbearing, obnoxious prick. I don't know what I ever saw in him, how I got so emotionally attached. I feel so stupid now." I leaned back against the cushions and put up my feet. "I romanticized him. It was the poetry, maybe. It made everything seem more romantic and beautiful than it was."

"You were a different person back then, weathering a difficult time in your life. Don't beat yourself up. Hey, at least you know his name now."

"I know his first name. That's all I got."

He sat up straighter. "I feel a search engine session coming on. I mean, you've looked, right? You've searched for designers in Manhattan named Price?"

"I searched every combination of 'designer' and 'New York' and 'Price.' But when you search 'designer' and 'Price' you get a bunch of links to online clothing stores."

"Why didn't you just ask his last name?"

I scowled at Andrew. "I kind of forgot to do that in the middle of all the fighting and stalking revelations and sex."

He held up a hand. "Hold. Up. You did not tell me you had sex."

I covered my face. Holy shit. I hadn't just had sex with him. I'd submitted to all his crazy, rough, perverted demands like we'd never been apart, like I was still his prostitute, meeting him for sessions at a luxury hotel.

"I don't know how it happened," I said, looking up again. "We were fighting, and then he was grabbing me and kissing me, and then..." I pointed across the room, at the wall. "We did it there." I pointed to the floor. "And there. And in the bedroom."

"You did it three times?" Andrew gawked at me.

"After that, he ran out of condoms."

"Well." He looked like a shocked old church lady. "I'm glad to hear you're having safe sex, but why didn't you tell me you slept with him? I told you everything about Maximo."

"You certainly did."

"So why—"

"Because it's stupid," I said, cutting him off. "It was stupid and weak of me to sleep with him and I didn't want to admit I did it."

"No wonder he wants to start things up again. Was the sex hot?"

"It was so fucking hot, Andrew. I can't even describe it."

"And that's why you keep zoning out with that tortured look on your face," said Andrew, shaking his head. "That sucks. It sucks that we always want the things we shouldn't have. That we want the things we shouldn't want."

Bless him. He always understood. "Why can't you be straight?" I groused. "You're fun and sexy, and you get me. Why don't you straighten the fuck up and be my boyfriend?"

"Cougar," he muttered.

I climbed in his lap and started riding him, which led to uncontrollable laughter and a pillow attack.

"Stop," he shrieked, whapping me upside the head. "Consent violation."

He tackled me to the couch and pinned me under his body. He wasn't as big as Price by a long shot, but he was still a man, and bigger than me. We gazed at each other, laughing, and then he leaned down and pasted a messy kiss on my lips.

"Gross," I said, sticking out my tongue. "I don't want your gay cooties."

"I don't want your cougar cooties." He sat up and helped me right myself. "Forget it, babes. Stop flirting. I'll never live up to Price's mystique."

"I wouldn't want you to." I moved into his arms when he opened them, and rested my head against his chest. "You're my safe place. He's my scary place."

"Ah, but Chere..." He stroked my hair and wrapped one of my curls around his fingertip. "I think you like to be scared." He was silent a moment, while I mulled that over. "I'm not saying he's a good person," Andrew went on, "or that you belong together, but, honey, let's be honest about something. You pined over him for *two and a half years.*"

"I didn't 'pine over him.'"

"You pined over him," Andrew repeated. "You gave up on relationships because of him. I think that's why you're so upset now, so conflicted and messed up."

Ugh, I was definitely conflicted and messed up.

"It doesn't matter," I said. "He's not relationship material."

"Are you sure? Girl, think about it. Think of his actions, his machinations with the apartment, just to be able to look at you after he left. The poetry was only part of it. Think about the planning. The ongoing surveillance."

"I have," I said, burrowing my face into his neck. "That's why I'm so scared."

"He's scary," Andrew agreed. "But I'm a little jealous. He watched you for two and a half years." He made a low sound in his throat. "That's kind of insane."

* * * * *

Andrew got busy after that, with Mr. Recaro and a couple other clients. I didn't see him again until the first morning of our internships, when we met for an early breakfast. My normally unkempt friend looked strange in his white starched shirt and tie, with his curls tamed back in a ponytail. He was going to spend half his internship as assistant to a curator at the Metropolitan Museum of Art, and the other half working at an up-and-coming gallery in Soho. Norton contacts were a powerful thing, and an aspiring painter needed all the connections he could get.

My design assignment was more practical: an architectural firm on Park Avenue. Their website was glossy and high tech, and maddeningly devoid of information, aside from a striking portfolio of their projects.

"Eriksen Architectural Design," said Andrew, studying the site on my phone. "Hey! They designed that crazy building on Driggs Avenue, and that new skyscraper on Wall Street." He scrolled a little more. "And the

Anand Valley Bridge in Mumbai." He looked back up at me in puzzlement. "I thought you asked for a jewelry placement."

I took back my phone and stuck it in my recently purchased leather briefcase. "I did ask for a jewelry placement. I didn't get it."

"Why would they match a small-metals designer with a bridge-building firm?"

"I don't know. Because they're Norton and they think it's cool and artistic to be disproportional." I shrugged. "I don't care. I'm just ready to finish the program. I like Norton, but I'm ready to get on with my career."

"I doubt Eriksen and friends will have a lot of connections in the jewelry world."

I'd pointed that out to my academic advisor, but my complaints had fallen on deaf ears. "I guess design is design, whether you're designing bridges or earrings. I don't know. They didn't offer me a second choice."

"I love that suit," said Andrew, gazing jealously at my outfit. "You look amazing. You're gonna impress them for sure."

I felt slightly guilty about using sex appeal on the first day of my internship, in some bid to impress my new boss. I'd chosen to wear one of the designer numbers I wore when I was escorting. Exquisitely tailored and wonderfully expensive, the Burberry suit looked right at home in the lobby of a luxury hotel, and, hopefully, in the conference rooms of Eriksen Architectural Design.

We finished our coffee and stood to give each other hugs. "Enjoy the museum," I said, squeezing him tight. "And tell them to make some room on a wall somewhere. Your work's going to hang there one day."

"I love you, babes. Knock 'em dead at Eriksen. Maybe they'll let you build a bridge or two before your time's up."

We shrugged into our coats and headed out into the January cold. The office wasn't far up Park Avenue, so I walked, dispelling nervous energy and swinging my briefcase at my side like I was as confident as all the bustling New Yorkers around me.

I arrived at the office building a few minutes early and gazed up at the structure of metal and glass. I went through revolving doors to the lobby and was directed to the eleventh floor. That was when my butterflies started. I kept my head down on the elevator, murmuring "Eleven, please" to a wall of pinstriped suits.

Get your shit together, Chere. This is what you wanted, what you've been working for all this time. I wasn't an escort anymore, and the chapter with Price was closed. I had nothing on my plate but building a kickass career, and I intended to make the most of it. On the eleventh floor, I headed for the frosted double doors emblazoned with an etched bridge and the initials "EAD" in a stylized script. A perky receptionist greeted me the moment I slipped inside.

"Welcome to Eriksen Architectural Design. May I help you?"

"I'm the new intern from Norton. I start today."

"Of course. Mr. Eriksen is expecting you. He's meeting with the staff in the conference room this morning. If you'll follow me?"

She led me down a carpeted hallway, past more office doors. She pushed one open, revealing a spacious room with a large table, and a meeting in progress.

"Ms. Rouzier has arrived," she announced.

"Ah, there she is."

My gaze shot to the man who'd spoken. Price stood from his place at the head of the table and strode to me with a hand outstretched in greeting.

You can't. My God. What the fuck?

"Welcome to Eriksen Architectural Design," he said, squeezing my fingers with a firm grip. "I'm P.T. Eriksen, and this is the rest of the team." He introduced me to each of the six people in turn, professional men and women of varying ages. They smiled and said hello, forcing me to compose my scattered emotions. Price was P.T. Eriksen of Eriksen Architectural Design? At last the ridiculous internship placement made sense. I felt manipulated, humiliated, and furious that I had to stand like an idiot in front of his smiling staff.

He was dressed in his armor: a dark suit and tie, and a pair of silver cufflinks. As he walked back to the head of the table, I realized they were my design, a pair I'd submitted to the Norton student shop a few months earlier. He turned to me with a taunt of a smile.

"Won't you join us, Ms. Rouzier? We'll be wrapping up our meeting in a moment, and then you and I can speak in more detail about your internship."

Oh, I couldn't *wait* to speak about my internship. I sat at the end of his high-end conference table and stared at the polished tabletop. I'd bought a briefcase for this ridiculousness. I'd dressed up for this. This was my senior internship, my life, my career, not some fucking game.

"Don't worry," he said to the men and women at the table. "She's not here to replace anyone. I just thought I'd give back to my old alma mater by taking on an intern."

"Norton has a great design program," said one of the women, an older Latina with salt and pepper hair.

"Are you thinking about moving into architecture after graduation?" asked the guy beside her.

"No." I allowed some vitriol in my voice. "In fact, I'm afraid there may have been an error in my placement."

The staff members seemed troubled by this possibility. Price smiled and leaned back in his chair.

"Design and architecture are two sides of the same coin," he said. "We'll find ways to engage you. This will be a highly productive internship for you, Ms. Rouzier, if I get my way."

* * * * *

"This isn't going to stand," I said as soon as we were alone in his office. "I'm going to get my internship changed."

"Are you?"

He moved to a side table and poured a glass of ice water from a frosted carafe. I stood in the middle of his elegantly furnished workspace with my briefcase clasped in front of me. I refused to be impressed with his world-famous architectural firm, and his breathtaking office with its massive iron-and-glass desk and drafting table.

"Sit," he said over his shoulder.

"No," I retorted. "I would rather stand. I'm not going to stay."

When he brought me the water, I ignored him, staring out his picture window at Manhattan's Lego-like cityscape. After a moment, he set the glass on his desk and leaned on the edge next to it. I turned and moved toward the door.

"Don't leave," he said.

"I'm not staying."

"You're not leaving either, not until we talk. You can stand if you like, but put down your briefcase."

My fingers tightened on the handle. He was so good at giving orders. I hated him for it.

Still, I put down my briefcase.

"Is this your idea of a joke?" I said. "Because I don't find it funny."

"No joke. You're required to complete an internship if you want to graduate." He shrugged. "We can keep it professional, if you'd like."

"I would like to keep it professional," I said, shaking with anger at the situation. "Not that it's very professional to force someone who hates you to continue interacting with you."

He gazed at me, piercing blue eyes beneath blond lashes. "You *hate* me, Chere?"

Just like that, I knew he had my number. He saw through my false bravado to the needy confusion underneath.

"I don't want this," I insisted, but some part of me couldn't stop looking at his hands, his broad shoulders, the way he filled out his suit.

"I think we'd enjoy working together," he said. "And doing other things together."

I backed away when he reached to touch my arm. "I'm not doing anything with you. You're an asshole. I can't believe you arranged this." I scowled at him. "You're playing with my life."

"I've been playing with your life for a while now. Have I done you any harm?"

"Yes!" But when I tried to think of some instance of real harm, real danger or malice, I came up short. "You harm me by...by freaking me out. By trying to control me. You arranged this so I'd be forced to hang out with you."

"Not just hang out with me. Fuck me, Chere." He cast a glance around the office. "Imagine it: over the desk, over my drafting table, in the conference room, in hotel rooms when we travel."

"Fuck you. I don't want you. I don't want this."

He strode toward me, and caught me when I tried to evade him. "Don't be a fucking liar. And don't use bad fucking language in my office, you unprofessional piece of shit." He jerked my face toward his and kissed me. I resisted for all of five seconds. His lips coaxed mine open, his passion mixing with my anger. My hands opened against his suit, texture and fabric and the muscles underneath. The scent of his cologne went right from my nose to my pussy. Everything clenched.

He ended the kiss and leaned back to gaze at me. "Now that we have that out of the way," he said.

"Nothing's out of the way." I wiped my lips like I could wipe away my unwanted attraction to him. "I'm leaving now to return to Norton. I'm going to explain everything, and make them change my assignment. It's completely inappropriate for us to...to do this, considering our past."

The corner of his mouth turned up in bemusement. "Going to tell them everything, are you? All about our sessions?"

"No. I'm just going to tell them that we have a history, and that we don't get along."

"But we do get along." His fingers stroked my waist, making small, caressing circles. "And they won't let you change this internship, not when I requested it. They know we have a history, Chere. They've known it since you applied."

I stared at him. "How do they know?"

"Did you ever wonder how you got that new, highly specific and exclusive Elberta Stephensen scholarship? Elberta Stephensen was my grandmother, and I've paid every dime of your tuition at Norton, not to mention yearly stipends for your metals and materials."

I gawked at him. "*You* paid for my scholarship?"

"Yes. Although it did, admittedly, come out of my grandmother's trust fund. She would have liked you. That's what I told them at Norton, that she would have liked to see you succeed. I've paid them enough that I've pretty much earned a say in whatever decisions they make about you. And I don't think I want you to have a different mentor. I think I'm best for the job."

"Is that what you think?" I asked, covering my shock in sarcasm. "I'm sure I'll learn a lot as you're fucking me over various pieces of office furniture."

His cool gaze betrayed a flash of heat. "So ungrateful. Do you know how much Norton costs?"

"I never asked you to pay for it." I tried to push his hands away. "I never asked you for anything."

My bid at escape was quickly arrested. He pulled me back against him, then turned me around so my back was pressed to his front. His hand went to my neck.

"Don't," I whispered.

"Ungrateful interns are bad interns," he said, tightening his fingers around my windpipe.

I arched my neck, pushing back against him. "Let go," I begged. "I don't want this." But my body was growing aroused by his force.

"A good intern is grateful. Obedient. Attentive to her boss's needs," he said into the curve of my ear.

I could feel his cock hardening against my ass. "No. No!"

"Interns don't say no. They say '*What would you like me to do?*'"

"Had a lot of interns, have you?" I asked, clinging to my last shards of control.

"No, you're the first one." His hand tightened on my neck until I had to struggle for breath. When I flailed and tried to dislodge his grip, his other arm wrapped around my body.

"I've always dreamed of having an intern," he went on in a casual, bemused tone, like he wasn't a squeeze away from strangling me. "A cooperative, sexy, eager-to-please young professional. Good interns say things like '*What would you like me to do?*'"

I knew I'd have to say it if I didn't want him to choke me to unconsciousness. I didn't want to wake up from a faint on his office floor with him on top of me.

"What..." I tried to speak through the pressure at my throat. "What would you like me to do?"

His grip loosened a little, a reward for obedience.

"Lift up your skirt," he said.

My fingers moved to the hem of my skirt, traced over the material. My nice skirt, my professional, expensive skirt I'd put on to impress my new boss. This wasn't how things were supposed to go. I thought I was starting my career today, and instead, I was back in Price's grasp.

"No," I whispered for the third time.

"What?"

I fought his grip and gave voice to the agony roiling inside me. "No," I repeated, and this time it sounded awful, like a cut-off screech. I jerked away from him, and he let me go. I turned away, rubbing my neck and staring down at the muted diamond pattern of his office carpet.

I had too many feelings, and none of them were sane. Some part of me wanted him. Some part of me wanted to lift up my skirt and see what he'd do to me, but a greater part of me was viscerally opposed to becoming his intern-whore.

"I can't do this," I said. "I'll be your intern, but I won't... I can't..." My voice shook. "I've worked so hard for this."

He was silent a moment. Maybe he was going to kick me out of his office. Maybe he was going to force me anyway, against my will. It wouldn't be the first time.

"Please," I said. The carpet pattern blurred. So many hopes, so many feelings, and all he had for me was "*Lift up your skirt.*"

"Chere."

I tensed and turned my head to the side. "What?"

"Look at me."

"No."

I didn't want him to see my tears, because I knew him. They'd only turn him on. I spun the other way and hurried for the door. I didn't make it. He caught me and wrapped his arms around me, not a chokehold this time. Just a hold. A rough sob shook me as I tried to break away.

"Don't." His voice sounded as ragged as my voice sounded when I had said no. "Don't cry, Chere."

"I can't do this."

"You don't have to. I thought..." I heard him sigh beside my ear. "Fuck."

I pulled from his arms and turned to him, wiping away my tears. "You know where I came from. You know how much this means to me, how hard I worked to get to this place."

He moved back to his desk, reached into a drawer and produced a tissue. He shoved it at me. "Stop crying."

That was easy for him to say. I swabbed at my cheeks and tried to pull my shit together. He leaned and picked up my briefcase, and handed it to me.

I took it with a sense of relief, but also a sense of devastation. This thing between us was so ugly and so raw, and so unfathomable. I wanted to be over him, but I clearly wasn't.

"Thanks," I said, taking the polished handle.

"You should go," was his only reply.

He went back behind his desk, avoiding my gaze. I wondered what he'd tell everyone when I was gone. *Not a good match. She wants to make jewelry.* My cufflinks shone at his wrists, elegant squares of polished silver. Someone as wealthy as him should have been wearing gold.

I turned and headed for the door. I heard him sit, then stand up again.

"What if we were professional?" he said.

My hand froze on the doorknob. I tilted my head so I could see him in my peripheral vision. "I don't… I don't think we can be professional."

"I can be a fucking professional. I built this business. I can be professional when I need to be. I can help you. I would like to help you, Ms. Rouzier."

The lazy mockery was gone from his voice. I turned and braced my back against the door, and stared at him standing behind his desk. He was a beautiful man, a tempting, powerful man. A man I wasn't sure I could trust. "I don't know," I said.

"One hundred percent professional, I promise. I'll give you the best internship any Norton student ever had. I know hundreds of designers in Manhattan. Big designers, small designers. I'll help you meet them all." He held up his arms in a helpless gesture. "What do you want out of this? Tell me and I'll try to make it happen."

"I just want to work and learn," I said. "I want to focus on my career. I don't want to be fucked with, especially after what happened with Simon, and then you."

I could see by his expression that he couldn't stand being lumped together with Simon as one of the men who'd fucked me over. Too bad. I didn't want him to think this would turn out the way he wanted, that he could chip away at me until I fell back into his arms. It wasn't happening.

Even if I desperately wanted to fall back into his arms.

"I'll give this one week," I said. My eyes were dry now. I recklessly tried to be the one in charge. "I'll be your intern for one week, but if it's not working out, if you're not being professional the way you promised, I'll go back to Norton and have my placement changed. And if they won't change it, then I'll drop out. I won't graduate."

I knew he'd never let that happen. I couldn't understand a lot of things about Price, especially as they related to me, but one thing I understood very clearly was that, somewhere along the line, he'd become invested in my decision to change my life and go back to school. He'd given me a place to live, and apparently paid my way through Norton with his made-up scholarship. If I didn't graduate, all of it was for nothing.

He gave a low, regretful laugh. "You and your threats."

We glared at each other across the resonating space between us. There was so much emotion in that space, so much history and frustration, and unspoken desires. There was need and sadness and complication that seemed insurmountably fucked.

"Okay. One week," he finally agreed. "One hundred percent professional, I swear."

PRICE

I always intended to give Chere a legitimate internship, and her refusal to play games with me—really fun games—didn't change that. Instead of fucking, I decided I'd use the time to get to know her better, to analyze her skills and talents and refine them to a razor point. If she wanted a design internship, I would give her a design internship. I was P.T. Eriksen, for fuck's sake. They'd begged me to mentor Norton students for years, and now that I had one I was interested in, I planned to mentor the fuck out of her on a daily basis.

As for physically fucking her, there was time to work on that. I had all the time in the world now, an entire semester, if I could convince her to stay beyond the first week. The second day, I took her to lunch with a friend who worked at Chopard. The fourth day, I set up a meeting with a friend at Bulgari. By the end of the first week, she didn't talk anymore about having her placement changed.

The following week, I set up a powwow with the upper brass at Schumacher, who'd heard about my new condo contract and were interested in collaborating on some of the finishes. I had no say in the unit finishes, but they didn't have to know that.

The third week, I took her to Queens to see the Neustadt Collection of Tiffany Glass. While she drank up the designs, I used my credentials to talk us into the back, where we met the museum's curator as well as a Tiffany & Co. designer. With the woman's assistance, Chere made an appointment to visit Tiffany's design labs the following week.

At each of these meetings, I was careful to explain that I'd brought my intern along because she was such a prodigy, a real up-and-comer. I hinted that she'd be the *next big thing*, because everyone was looking to recruit the next big thing into their design house. I could do these favors for Chere forever. She made it easy, because she played the role of the hungry prodigy so well. The ambition was there in her voice and in her questions, and in her direct gazes.

I understood the pressure she put on herself to succeed, the drive to make something of herself as some penance for her secret, squalid beginnings. I wanted to tell her to relax. She wasn't going to fail, because she was fucking incredible. She was going to bring beautiful things to the world, things as beautiful as her smile. I tried to make her smile sometimes to balance out the tension between us. Provocative power flowed back and forth, even without sex. Especially without sex.

She probably realized by the end of the first week that denying the pull between us made it twenty times stronger. We could not be purely sexless together. Not "one hundred percent" sexless, as she would want me to agree. We had moments of focus and concentration when thoughts of sex were pushed out by pure inspiration, but that's all they were. Isolated moments. The rest of the time we simmered in a morass of unsated, roiling lust. I would have done anything to have her, but her walls were up hardcore.

Denial. She was subjecting me to a course of sexual denial. Someday I'd punish her for this, and she wouldn't fucking like it.

But that day wasn't now. It wasn't even soon. There were weeks left in her internship, and I'd promised "one hundred percent professional," so I watched her, day after day, without touching her. Without lingering close to her. Without pressing my face against hers and breathing in the scent of her hair. Maybe it was good for me to practice this restraint.

Ha. Restraint. There was no restraint in me. I didn't watch her through her windows anymore, but I put her desk inside my office so I could look at her all the time. If my colleagues thought that was weird or predatory, they didn't say anything. I told them I wanted her to be intimately involved in all my projects, to be a party to all my phone conversations, meetings, and drafting sessions, and she was. She saw everything and heard everything, and observed how I worked from brainstorming session to plans to revision.

Whenever I went to lunch, I took her with me, pointing out buildings as we walked, grilling her on aesthetics and techniques. I asked her to show me the small things, not that I didn't notice the small things. But there was large design and small design, and Chere was a zealot for small design. She dissected bevel degrees and chisel depths for meaning. We spent an hour once going over a statue in Gramercy Park, no element unturned. I wanted to shove her up against that statue and fuck the everloving hell out of her, but I didn't. I didn't even take her hand.

And that was really fucking difficult for me, because the more she denied me, the more my mind fixated on making her mine, getting her to a place where she couldn't deny me. I wanted her naked, aching, crying, orgasming, begging for more pleasure or pain. Every time I looked at her I thought of it.

But I couldn't tell her that. I couldn't tell her how much this denial between us made me burn. She'd leave if I did. She'd quit, disappear, even with all the help and contacts I afforded her. She needed space for now. She needed distance and time to forgive me, just as I'd needed distance and time when I left her before. For her, I could have patience. The hottest fires burned the longest, and were the most difficult to put out.

I could wait until she felt brave enough again, and I knew she would. Chere was a fighter. She'd stuck with me this long, through all her fears and misgivings. She still wanted me. I think she probably cried sometimes that she couldn't have me.

Your choice, starshine. Not mine.

* * * * *

Her trip to Tiffany's design lab took place exactly one month after her internship started. She went on her own, leaving my office quiet and empty of her presence, her little shifts and sighs. After the first day she was invited back, and then invited back again, until her one-day visit stretched to a week. She called me every evening, breathless, inspired, telling me everything she'd seen and asking for more time. What was I supposed to do? I gave it to her.

She returned to the office the following Monday with stars in her eyes, and a thousand ideas to put on paper. I told her to go where her inspiration took her. She was full of excitement about diamonds and fittings, and the shape of the body.

Oh, the shape of her body...

I had plans to work on, a bridge to envision. We sat across from each other, designing our wildly disparate products. She'd been gone for a week. Now that she was back, her nearness taunted me almost more than I could bear.

"Chere," I said abruptly, in the midst of our industrious silence. "I missed you."

Those three words, *I missed you*, sounded so much more weighted than I meant them to. She looked up at me, alarmed.

Shit. *One hundred percent professional.* I thought I should add more words, words to take the edge off the ones I'd just spoken, but I didn't.

"I..." She swallowed, thinking what to say. "I appreciate you giving me the time to spend at Tiffany's. I know I'm supposed to be helping you here in the office."

I gave a short, bitter laugh. "Helping me what? Lose my mind?"

A blush rose on her cheeks. She was wearing a necklace she'd made, so delicate, so intricate, gold and silver against her chest. She tugged at it, perhaps regretting that she'd worn such a low-cut blouse. "Don't do this," she said. "Don't wreck everything."

I wouldn't have said anything if I hadn't missed her so badly, if I wasn't straining so hard to subdue the fantasies that preoccupied my mind. I turned back to my blueprints, trying to concentrate on lines and equations. Instead I imagined tying her up and fucking her, and hurting her. The memories were always there between us, palpable in the room. I glanced back at her, gave her one of the old stares.

"Please don't," she said.

"Don't what?" I pretended innocence, while I gazed at her with all the fire of my lust.

"Internships aren't supposed to be like this," she said, putting her face down against her desk.

"Your internship is like this because that's what you chose," I replied. "One hundred percent professional." I brushed a hand over the front of my pants. She couldn't see my raging erection from where she sat, but I wanted her to understand it was there. "I'm one hundred percent ready to fuck you right now. My cock is one hundred percent at full boil."

She put her hands over her ears. "You promised."

"I know I promised. I just think it's stupid. There's no reason we can't work together and still assuage our hunger for each other."

"Our *hunger for each other*?" She glared up at me, frowning. "Speak for yourself."

I held her gaze with a warning look. *Don't make me show you.* Because I'd do it. I'd strip off her clothes and show her how hungry she was, show her just how much she'd give up to me if I demanded it. After a moment of quivering mutiny, she looked away.

If I could have, I would have spanked the shit out of her for lying, for pretending. For denying. I would have bent her over her desk and punished her for putting both of us through this hell. I wished I had a strap, a paddle, a leather-wrapped cane, but even if I did, the blows and her cries would have been too loud in the office. Frosted glass walls only muffled so much.

Later. I'd punish my little mutineer later, at some future time when things weren't so fucked up between us. For now, I could only punish her with her own ridiculous, blushing shame.

"Stand up," I said. "Come here."

"No."

"Come the fuck over here. I'm your boss, you fucking listen to me."

She finally stood and obeyed, cringing like she'd already been punished. Maybe I sounded uncontrolled. Frightening. I was only so tired of the divide between us, the artificial chasm of her making. *Chere, you're my fighter. Why won't you be brave?*

"Look at me, damn you," I insisted, taking her by the arms.

She raised her eyes to mine with a look of such conflicted desire and loathing that I almost went off in my fucking pants.

"I want you to admit it. You want me. You want this." I took her hand and made her trace the length of my cock. I was rock hard beneath the gabardine twill. She curled her fingers around the shape of me, then tried to pull away.

"I don't want it," she said.

"You're not getting wet right now? Your heart isn't beating faster?"

I let go of her hand and grabbed her neck. She reached to balance herself against my chest, gasping, but making no other complaint.

"I can feel it," I whispered. "I can feel your pulse racing. I can feel your breath hitch."

"Because you're choking me," she rasped.

"Are you wet for me? Tell the truth."

"No."

I reached under her skirt. When she tried to pull away I tightened my grasp on her neck. She made a rough noise. Her hands were free. She could have fought me. She didn't.

I ran a palm up her thigh, over silky skin to the gusset of her panties. She stared at me, swallowing against my grip. She didn't want me to touch her horny, wet pussy, because then she'd reveal the depth of her need.

But another part of her ached for my touch. I could see it in her eyes, feel it in her body's tension. The stubborn, hiding part of her wanted me to force her and humiliate her by driving my fingers inside her. I stopped my slow explorations just above her panty's smooth gusset. I wanted to ravage her with my fingers, to shame her and fuck her, but I wouldn't.

"Let's have a little honesty," I said instead. "You want me every day. You want me every hour, just as I want you. You fantasize about my control, my commands, my gaze on your naked skin. You want me to hurt you. You want my cock inside you, fucking you until everything else falls away."

With every word, her gaze flickered a little. The front of prim professionalism would never hide the need inside her.

"Just admit it," I said quietly. "To me and to yourself."

I waited with one hand grasping her throat, and the other between her legs, not quite touching the heat of her arousal. I'd wait an hour, if she needed that much time to come clean about her feelings. In the end, it only took a minute.

"I admit it," she said in a pained voice. "I want you. But I don't want to want you. The thing is... We can't. I don't want anyone in my life right now, especially you. You have too much power to hurt me."

Jesus Christ. My cock was so hard. She was too near. I had to let her go. My fingers opened, releasing her.

"Go to your desk then," I said. "Go do your important work, and pretend you don't want me every day for the rest of this internship, but know that I miss you. That I want you. That will never change."

She flinched like I'd just slapped her. *Yes, starshine, remember when I used to slap your face? How horny you would get? How you'd bare your teeth at me and beg for more?* She scurried back to her desk, like it was some fortress that would protect her. My desk, in my office.

This isn't your safe place, Chere. It's only safe because I'm hanging on to my last fucking shred of control.

"I just can't right now," she said, staring down at her design book. "Price, I can't. I'm sorry." She bit her lip and went silent.

I looked back at my blueprints. Someday I'd punish her for this. Someday I'd exact revenge for all my suffering and make her beg for my touch and my cock.

She thought I had too much power to hurt her? She hadn't seen anything yet.

CHERE

My internship continued, real work and real education stirred together with constant temptation and Price's unsettling stares. He was teaching me useful things, but the real reason I sprang out of bed every morning was to spend time in his presence. I admitted this to myself, after fruitless efforts at denying it. But I would never admit it to him.

P.T. Eriksen was a monarch in the design arena, a brilliant, admired star-chitect to whom everyone deferred. He held multiple advanced degrees, spoke multiple languages, and possessed more money and influence than I'd ever imagined. He'd hidden it from me on purpose when he was my client, and now, every day, I struggled to reconcile this capable, famous person with the man who'd shoved his cock down my throat and slapped my face.

Don't misunderstand me. He was absolutely the commanding man I knew from those sessions, but he was also so much *more*, and I didn't know how to deal with that. Every day, I caught myself remembering touches and grasps, low, hissed words, and the feeling of him inside me. I feared I was falling for him all over again, which scared me to death.

On the weekends, I tried to refocus, to move past my misguided obsession with my lover-turned-boss, but I only found myself eager for Monday again. I didn't know how to explain all this conflict to Andrew. I tried. I babbled to him about the way Price looked at me, and the crazy shit he said to me. Did I think it would make more sense in the telling?

It didn't.

"Jesus, Chere." Andrew sprawled on my couch, a pizza box balanced on his chest. "He's not giving up, huh? He wants to get inside you."

I reached for another piece of pizza. "He wants this extreme sexual relationship," I said. "Even when we're talking about stuff like metal composition and architectural casting, the sex vibe is pouring off him. It oozes out of him. When I come home, I feel like I have to shower it off me."

"You're supposed to be having your final internship, not showering off mental jizz."

"Psychological bukkake," I murmured. "It's starting to get to me."

That was a lie. Price had gotten to me long, long ago, but I kept going back for more, skirting the line of my own destruction.

"He messed me up so bad before," I said to my friend. "I can't start up with him again, right?"

"No. You definitely can't." Andrew shoved another piece of pizza in his mouth. "I love you, babes. I don't want you to get hurt again. You don't need him, and no matter how much he pushes the sex thing, he doesn't need you."

Shit. No. He didn't need me. He had money and success and everything going for him, and if I didn't eventually sleep with him, he'd move on to someone else. The thought of that made a sick feeling tremble in my stomach. I put down my pizza and pushed away my plate.

"Tell me about your gallery," I said, to get my mind off my mentor. "Tell me—"

"Don't change the subject yet. Are you going to be able to resist Price?"

"I kind of have to."

"You have to, or you're going to? What happens if he disappears again?" he lectured. "What happens when your internship is over?"

"I'm trying to keep a distance between us. A space. That's what I asked for, pure professionalism."

"If he was giving you pure professionalism, you wouldn't be showering off mental jizz. I've met lots of hot guys during my internship, and there's been absolutely no jizz involved."

"I'm sorry to hear that."

Andrew shrugged, looking out my living room window at the rain. It was a cold, drizzly Saturday, one of the rare Saturdays when Andrew didn't have a date and I wasn't haunting the metals lab. Cantor had caught me there last weekend and grilled me about my internship. It was the most uncomfortable conversation of my life. I could have sworn he was trying to warn me about Price—like I didn't know the danger.

"Tell me about your gallery internship," I said, trying again to turn the conversation from my object of obsession. "Tell me about this guy you met."

Andrew went from looking stressed to totally blissed out. "Craig."

"Craig. Ooh. What a strong name. Is he strong like an animal?"

Andrew hardly needed egging on. "Yes. Kind of," he said, sitting up straighter. "I see hints of animal in him. He's just a gallery manager now, but he's ambitious, and he's a talker, and Jesus, he's so Dom."

"Yum."

"He's very calm and very kind. Authoritative, but in a good way."

"How old is he?"

"Ten years older than me. And so much wiser." He gave a wistful sigh. "He's flirted with me, more than once, but I don't know if it's real interest or just some game to him, you know, mindfucking the new intern."

"I didn't know mindfucking interns was such a thing."

"You should know, sister. *Anywaaaay.*"

I leaned my head back against the cushions. I liked Craig already, because he wasn't an escort client. "My advice is to keep it professional with this Craig dude until the internship is over, and then see where it leads. Even if things don't work out, he'll be a contact, maybe with enough influence to get you a show someday."

"He's talked to me about my work." He got all fluttery again. "I showed him a few paintings on my phone. He says he'd like to see them in person."

"Take him to the paint lab at night, put on the music, the whole deal."

"I know. It'll happen." He clutched at his chest. "I'm just kind of freaked out. I really like him. It's scary, how much I like him." He let go of his chest and carried the pizza box into the kitchen, and tossed it on the counter with a pensive look. "Craig doesn't know anything about the escorting. I mean, of course he doesn't know. If he knew... I don't know. I don't want to keep secrets, but I don't want to tell him either."

I watched the conflict play across my friend's angelic face.

"You can stop the escorting anytime," I said. "And you don't have to tell anyone. You're the only one of my friends right now who knows I used to do it."

He sighed and hunched up his shoulders. "But I know I would end up telling him. If I fell in love with him, I'd spill everything. Especially if we were Dom/sub."

"Which you would be." I shook my finger at him. "I told you the escorting was a big decision, not to be taken lightly. Once you do it, you can't erase it from your past."

"I enjoyed it for a while. I'm still enjoying it. The money's great. It's just..."

"I know." I walked over and embraced him. "I remember. If you want to stop, just tell Henry. He won't be angry. He won't pimp-slap you or anything."

Andrew pressed his curls against my cheek. "That's too bad. I probably would have liked it."

I was glad Andrew and I were friends, even if he bitched at me sometimes about Price. We understood each other because we were equally fucked up in the head.

"Price wants me to travel to Oslo with him," I said. I'd been saving that little nugget until Andrew calmed down. "He's been offered a commission there, to design a historical museum. We'll be there a couple weeks, for meetings and financial stuff."

"Let me guess, it's just an internship thing?" Andrew pulled away from me. "I guess you've already told him yes?"

"I won't have sex with him. We won't be alone there. Three of his associates are coming too."

"Great, an orgy then. How exciting!"

"No sex. No orgies. No choking and fucking and mayhem," I emphasized. "One hundred percent professional."

Dear religious, all-powerful entity, please help me be professional. Please help me resist sleeping with my sexual titan of a boss on this business trip.

In the name of God or Krishna or Moses, or whoever can freaking help me. Amen.

PRICE

We weren't alone on this flight to Oslo. It wasn't a lovers' getaway, unfortunately. In my fantasies, yes. In reality? No.

Three of my firm's associates were with us, and one of them, Raneesh, had taken the seat beside me on the plane. Hannah and Jennifer sat in the adjacent row, and Chere was one row back, in the seat I'd intended for one of them.

Fuck. I couldn't oust Raneesh so Chere could sit beside me, because I had business to talk with Raneesh, and Chere was just along to "learn." Still, I wanted to do it.

I didn't.

In all this time, not one of my associates had come to suspect that Chere and I had a history together. They treated Chere the way you'd expect them to treat an intern, with polite and stand-offish condescension. If they thought it strange that I paid for an intern to accompany us to Oslo for two weeks, they didn't comment on my decision.

Chere wasn't even in front of me, damn it. If she was in front of me, I could have at least stared at the back of her head. Instead, I had to control the number of times I zoned out on Raneesh to glance back at her. I cursed myself for not hiring a private plane, large enough for two passengers and a bed. I could have been inside her all the way across the ocean. Oh, but I couldn't. Professionalism and all that.

When we arrived in Oslo, it was evening, local time, and Jennifer suggested dinner before we headed to the hotel.

Fuck me. Of course we would go to dinner. That's what associates did on a business trip, and I was the only one fluent in Norwegian. At least I could look at Chere during dinner, if I couldn't touch her and lick her all over the way I wanted to. Travel made me horny. No, not exactly. Traveling *with Chere* made me horny.

I stared at her as we waited for a car to take us to the restaurant. She was in full intern mode, silent, sober, listening to Hannah and Jennifer go on as if their idle conversation about Oslo's skyline was of utmost importance.

"Hey, boss. You all right?"

Raneesh's question stopped the ladies' conversation and brought all eyes to me.

"I'm fine," I said.

"You look tense."

I raised my shoulders. "I might be a little tense. I worked late last night, getting some final idea sheets together." Actually, I'd worked late last night masturbating to the fantasy of fucking Chere over my drafting table. "I'll order a massage at the hotel," I said, as they continued to regard me with concern.

Hannah was the first to drop her gaze, but not before I saw the invitation there. She'd give me a massage if I asked her to. She'd even let me fuck her over my drafting table, but she was the ball-busting, corporate-climber type, and I was pretty sure if I ever let her touch my dick, she'd break it off.

At dinner, I played a game called *How long can I go without looking at Chere?* Some of the glances were gimmes. It was natural to look at someone while they were talking, or while they were ordering. It was less natural to look at someone as she chewed bites of lemon-sauced salmon, and took sips of wine that seemed increasingly seductive. I wondered what the others would have thought if I ordered her under the table to suck me off. If they weren't here, I might have tried it just to see what would happen. I was that wrought up.

As dinner dragged on, Chere made it more difficult to look at her by growing increasingly silent. Raneesh didn't bother to ask her if *she* was all right, the asshole. In fact, they pretty much ignored her until the end of the meal. Our waiter brought coffee and cream, and Jennifer finally turned to Chere.

"You graduate soon, don't you?"

"Yes." Chere glanced at me briefly. "Next month. The end of April."

"That's exciting," said Raneesh, who got excited about everything. "What are your plans?"

"Well, I've been putting together a portfolio. Some projects I've worked on, accessories and metalware, silverware, rings and earrings, cufflinks." Her eyes darted toward my wrists. I sported another pair of her creation, small, spare polished-silver ovals in her signature style. "I hope I can interest some of the bigger jewelry houses in my work."

"Or you could start your own company," I said. "With your own vision. Your own designs."

I'd been considering how to give Chere a leg up in a highly competitive business. I thought I might give her some seed money to start her own jewelry line. She could make exclusive pieces for the rich and famous, glittering works notable for their delicacy. She could design under her own name, instead of disappearing into the back rooms of some big conglomerate.

Hannah raised a glass to me. "That's what you did, isn't it, Price? Started your own business right out of school?"

"But he went to school for ten years," laughed Raneesh.

"Yes, and I got four degrees in those ten years. Mainly because I didn't know what I wanted to do." I clinked Hannah's glass, ignoring the way her eyes raked me in the ambient light. I looked across the table at Chere. "Do you know what you want to do, Ms. Rouzier?"

I knew what *I* wanted to do. I wanted to take her back to the hotel and fuck her, and she knew it.

"I'm not completely sure yet," she said after a moment.

"I was younger than you when I started my firm." I stirred my coffee to watch the cream swirl on top. "I made a ton of mistakes, but I had an end goal. I still have an end goal. Do you have an end goal?"

My associates watched me, admiring and silent. I was the boss teaching the intern, passing along my experience and power. They thought I was mentoring. No, I was badgering. *Do you have an end goal, Chere? Does it involve surrendering to my sexual needs?*

"I haven't made any decisions. My world is kind of..." She spread her hands. "Kind of wide open right now."

I wanted to spread her legs wide open. I wanted to be inside her. It was so hard to sit across from her and pretend I was just her boss. Why had I brought her here? So I could suffer from 24-7 temptation, instead of the usual 9-5 agony? *Great job, Price, you stupid prick.*

It would be better at the hotel. Out of sight, out of mind. To reduce temptation, I'd had her room booked onto a separate floor. I hoped she appreciated my efforts.

I raised a hand and signaled the waiter for the check.

* * * * *

The first few days were busy. We were overscheduled and jetlagged, and Chere bore the brunt of everyone's irritation. We sent her for coffee and food and electrical adapters, and medicine when Jennifer developed a recurring headache. She was the intern, so she did what we asked.

Then Saturday arrived, and I told everyone to head out and explore the city. I knew they wouldn't. I knew all of them would work so they'd be ahead on Monday. That was why I'd hired them.

But I didn't want to work. I went to Chere's floor and walked by her room, as I'd done a dozen times by now. This time I allowed myself to knock.

No answer. I knew she was there, that she could see me through the goddamned peephole. I knocked again. "Open the door."

She did, looking irritable and rumpled in her robe. I looked past her into her room.

"Were you sleeping?"

"Resting."

"You've been a sport," I said, acknowledging her thankless grunt-duty over the past few days. "I'd like to show you Oslo, if you're interested. If you'd like to go for a walk."

"A walk?"

"A walk," I repeated acerbically. "It's this thing where you advance your feet in a forward motion, perambulating by your legs—"

"Okay. All right. Give me a minute to get dressed."

She made me wait in the hall, which was wise. I'm not sure I could have restrained myself in a hotel room with her, even a small, rather ascetic hotel room in downtown Oslo. Once she was ready we set off, bundled in warm, high-collared coats. I was relieved we didn't run into the others on the way out of the hotel. I wanted Chere and only Chere, because I wanted to see the city through her detail-oriented eyes. If I couldn't have her body, I could at least wallow in her mind.

I took her to the Parliament Building and the National Theater. We spent a couple hours talking, pointing, discussing, taking things in. We posed with the statues in Vigeland Park, the naked men and women carved in stone. We grabbed food from a takeout place and headed to the City Centre to look at the ships. She was cold. I knew she was cold but I didn't want to go back to the hotel where we'd retreat to our separate rooms, leading our separate lives. I tried to sit where I shielded her from the wind. My leg pressed against hers as we hunched forward, scarfing sandwiches and cake.

"Thank you for bringing me here," she said when we finished eating. "And for showing me around Oslo. It's a beautiful city, and I know this trip is costing you a lot."

"It's nothing."

She gave a little laugh and looked out at the harbor. The cold pinked her cheeks, or maybe she was blushing. "It's nothing to you, with your big, fancy architectural business, but it's a lot to me. I never imagined..." She pursed her lips and blinked. "I've never really thanked you for everything you've done. Not just this trip, but everything. I'm sure these words are way too late in coming, but your generosity changed my life. So…thanks."

Her shy, clumsy gratitude made me feel ridiculously pleased. She was so close I could have kissed her. I didn't.

"If I had to pick a life to change," I said instead, "I'm glad it was yours. You've capitalized on everything I've done for you. You impress me every day."

"I impress *you*?" She shook her head. "That's difficult to believe. You're the most impressive person I know."

"You don't know enough people."

"Seriously..." She put a hand on my coat and my whole body tensed. "You do these amazingly difficult things, and you make it look easy. You design buildings, you create bridges out of thin air, out of your mind and your imagination. You make all this money and you use it to help people, not just Norton, not just me. You give money to dozens of charities in dozens of countries."

"I'm not perfect." She ought to know that better than anyone else. "Don't make me into a saint."

"Not only that, but you speak Norwegian like a native. You just..." She moved her hand, waved it in the chilly air. "You just speak it, and everyone understands you."

"My grandmother made me learn it. It wasn't that hard."

"What other languages do you speak?"

"French. Spanish. German. A little Mandarin."

She put her head in her hands. "I don't know," she said between her fingers. "I don't know how you do all this stuff, how you're so good at everything. I guess you're a genius."

"I'm not a genius. I got lucky. I was born to rich parents and I've always had everything I wanted." *Except for you. I don't have you.*

She shook her head, just sitting there bent over with her forehead on her knees. A whole minute went by. I wondered if she was crying. I took off one of my gloves and touched her nape. I don't know why I did it. Because I'm not a genius.

She sat up and looked at me, but she didn't say anything like "Stop" or "One hundred percent professional." I curled my fingers around my glove to keep from touching her again, touching her cheek, her hair, her knee that was so close to mine, encased only in department store jeans.

"Are you cold?" I asked.

"Sort of."

"Do you want to go back to the hotel?"

Her lips parted like she was going to speak, but then the lower one trembled. I couldn't hold her gaze. I could only watch that trembling lip and think about kissing it.

"I don't want to go back to the hotel," she said.

She blinked, the winter sun shining through her lashes. And I know, *I know*, she was the first one to lean toward me. She was the one who opened her hands on my coat and slid them up to my collar, and shook back her hair and looked at me, but I was the one who kissed her, nipping that trembling lower lip between my teeth. Thoughts rampaged through my brain. *She's kissing me. Pull her closer. Her hair, her warmth, her scent. She's skittish. She tastes like berries and marzipan.*

People walked by us, right by our bench, but she seemed oblivious, and I didn't care. I scooped her into my lap and held her cold cheeks between my palms, and simply existed in the reality of her embrace. Her hands slid inside my coat and around my waist. I kissed her harder, clasping her to my front. My cock went rigid, trying to fight out of my pants even in near-freezing weather.

So that was all I'd needed to do to melt her reserve. Bring her to Norway, feed her cake by the harbor. Ask if she was cold. I wasn't cold at all. I burned. I was on fire after all my waiting and lust. *Kiss me. Touch me. Berries and sugar. Starshine, with sun through her lashes.*

She pressed closer to me, moving her thigh against my cock. I wanted her thighs around me. I wanted to be inside her pussy, making her arch and cry with lust. *This isn't professional*, I thought as her fingers traced my spine. But we were never meant to be professional together. We were meant to connect on a much more animalistic plane.

"I know you said you don't want to go back to the hotel," I managed to say between kissing her. "But I think we ought to go back. I think we need some privacy."

"Privacy," she breathed. "Yes."

"Naughty girl," I said in a low voice. "Naughty intern, throwing herself at the boss." I grabbed her hair and pulled hard. "Do you know what happens to sexy, naughty interns like you?"

She gazed at me. "Something bad? Something awful?"

"Absolutely." I squeezed one of her breasts until she gasped, hurt her right through her coat and bra and sweater in front of everyone. "Bad, awful things that you absolutely deserve."

CHERE

I barely remembered the cab ride back to the hotel, barely remembered the route we took or the few words we exchanged. Price gave orders to the driver in Norwegian, but all I recognized was the name of the hotel. Maybe he told him to hurry. I wanted the driver to hurry before I regained my sanity.

Not that I thought Price would allow me to backtrack at this point. He held my hand until the cab pulled up at the hotel doors, and only let go to pay the driver. He hurried me through the lobby to the elevators and took my hand once again as soon as the doors closed. His fingers felt warm, firm, encompassing. Demanding. If I tried to back out now, he'd insist upon my attendance. I was already under his power.

Our scene had already begun.

He took me down a silent hallway to his door and keyed it open, then tugged me inside and led me to the center of the room, over by the window. His room looked very much like mine, only neater. The bed was made, the sheets turned down. Everything was white in this hotel. The pillows were white, the counterpane was white, the sheets were white, the padded headboard was white, upholstered in tufted linen. I felt conspicuously dark as he moved about the room, setting down his room key, kicking off his shoes and shrugging out of his coat.

He hung our coats up in his closet, and then he turned to me with such purposeful resolve that I shied away.

"Don't shrink from me," he said. "You fucking face me."

But his rough voice and force made me shy away more. I snatched at my sweater as he drew it off, taking it over my head and flinging it sideways. My jeans were next. He pulled the button hard and parted the zipper by ripping it open. He yanked them roughly over my hips. They were slim, tight-fitting jeans but he got them off by pure intent, tossing them away with a grunt.

He stopped then, and raked a glance over my body, my silk panties and bra. I knew he wanted to touch me. It frightened me that he declined to do so. Was he afraid he'd hurt me? I was afraid he'd hurt me. Why had I decided to do this after protecting myself all this time?

I could still run away. He'd never let me out the door, but I could lock myself in the bathroom, or barricade myself in the closet and scream until someone came to help me.

I didn't scream. I didn't run, but my body moved away from him on instinct. I saw his hands come up, to hit me or grab me. He didn't do either, just caught me from behind, wrapping one arm around my waist. The other caught my chin, pressing my head back into the curve of his neck.

"Going somewhere?" he asked.

I shook my head. "No. Don't. Don't hurt me."

I meant that I wasn't ready yet, that this was happening too quickly, or that maybe I hadn't thought things through. I wanted him to do bad, awful things to me, but with Price, I never knew how bad and awful they'd be. I clutched at his arm where he held me pinned against his front. My shoulder blades slid against his sweater as I squirmed to get away.

"Listen to me, starshine," he said in his patient and terrifying voice. "I've waited weeks now to touch you. You made me wait, you made me suffer, never letting me have you. Now I'm going to have you. I'm going to take you until I'm done with you, and until I'm done, you're going to do whatever the fuck I say."

My breath came in pants. "I... I'm..." *I'm afraid.* That's what I was trying to say.

His fingers tightened around my jaw and slid down the front of my neck. "*Yes, Sir,*" he said. "That's your line. Say it." He gave me a shake.

"Yes, Sir." I sounded weak, whimpery. I sounded every bit as scared as I felt. I still clutched at him, like he might relent.

"Put your arms down, Chere. Stop trying to get away from me. You heard what I said."

Oh, yes, I'd heard. *Until I'm done, you're going to do whatever the fuck I say.* Later, I'd masturbate to those words. I'd picture his face as he said them, although he wasn't letting me see him now. That was always part of his control, to make me feel blind and helpless. I put my hands down at my sides, releasing some of the tension in my body.

I could feel his muscles respond behind me. His arm left my waist and moved up to my bra. He pulled the cups down so my breasts were exposed, lying on the shelf of the folded-over satin. He slapped each breast and pinched my nipples. I rose on my toes and reached again for his arm.

"Put your arms down," he repeated, in a voice that dared me to disobey.

I held my hands stiff at my sides as he pinched my nipples hard as any nipple clamp ever did. His fingers tightened around my neck as I moaned and wrenched my head from side to side. I bowed out my middle, trying to get away from the pain.

"Ow. Please," I begged. His sweater was soft against my back, but his muscles were hard and his hands were hurting me.

"Push your panties down."

The agony of his touch compelled me to obey. I slid my fingers under the waistband and jerked them down over my hips with frantic tugs.

"More," he said impatiently. "Push them down to the middle of your thighs."

The fingers at my neck went tight again, and I scrabbled to comply, shoving them down with my fingertips. I could feel the unyielding girth of his cock through his jeans, pressed against my bare skin. I imagined him unzipping his fly with that intent, angry look of his, pulling out his monster cock, and then...what?

"Please," I whispered, not even sure what I was asking for.

"Shut the fuck up. I tell you what to do and you listen. That's how our thing has always worked. Now, part your pussy lips."

"What?"

"Did I stutter?" His fingers tortured my nipples, first one and then the other. "Part your pussy lips with your fingers."

I reached down and delved between the hot folds, ashamed by my crazy wetness. His rough orders, the nipple torture, his hand threatening to choke me, all of it had me creaming myself. My fingers went immediately to my clit.

"No." He let go of my nipples to give me a short, sharp crack on the ass. "Did I say to touch yourself? I said to part your pussy lips, not to rub one out. Have you forgotten how to follow directions?"

I gave a soft sob and nudged my labia apart to hold myself open. It was so humiliating, so cruel to make me do this. It was also so fucking hot. I was suddenly twice as wet as before.

He made me stand like that, tits out, panties down, exposing my wet, needy clit, burning all over my body in a blush while he massaged my neck and kissed me, and nibbled at my ear. "This is how you should be all the time," he said, sliding his arm around my waist again. "In my control, with your sex open to me, and your body open to me, all wet and ready for me. Doesn't this feel good? Doesn't it feel right?"

I shook my head, blinking back tears. "No."

"Sometimes it's hard to admit what you really want. That's why you need me. I take away the choice, and make you accept all the filthy, dirty cravings inside you."

The grip around my middle loosened. His hand slid down. I could have pulled away then. I could have escaped, but I didn't move. I felt paralyzed with need, with lust. With shame.

He touched me one place, one single, specific, slick and swollen place. He laid a fingertip atop my clit and my knees almost buckled. One touch, one second of pleasure, and his finger was gone.

"Oh God." The words burst out of me with angry frustration.

He released my neck to cover my mouth. "Quiet," he snapped. "Not one word. Keep holding yourself open. I didn't tell you to stop."

I complied, knowing I'd die if he didn't touch me again just that way. He did, several times, but never long enough to satisfy me more than a second or so. I moaned behind his hand.

"This is what happens to girls who tease, and say no," he said. "They get taught lessons. Look how wet you are." He left my clit to slosh his fingers through my drenched pussy. "You told me you didn't want this.

You told me you didn't want sex, that you wanted us to be one hundred percent professional, but feel how wet you are. If you don't want sex, why are you humping my hand?"

I whipped my head back and forth, voiceless, breathless, humiliated by his demonstration of my hypocrisy, but too worked up to care. He returned to torturing me, delivering fleeting, electrifying caresses and pinches to my swollen clit, chuckling when I bucked helplessly against his hand. I knew he'd only give me what he was willing to give me, and he was punishing me at the moment, so it wasn't very much.

Why had I chosen this? Why was I subjecting myself to his whimsical sadism, his torturous scenes? Just to feel his power and have his cock, and earn those magical orgasms if he deemed me worthy?

Yes. Good God above, yes, that was why. I held my pussy lips open for him like an obedient masochistic slut, dreaming of sex and kisses and poetry. I forgave him for everything that came before: the secrecy, the desertion, the binoculars, the machinations with my internship. I forgave him and cursed myself for denying our bodies the pleasure they could have enjoyed for weeks now. I deserved the torment he was heaping on my poor, exposed sex.

"Please, no more," I begged from behind his hand. "Please, just let me come."

"I don't think so," he said with a chuckle. "Not this time. Not after all the time you denied me. Maybe later, if you're good." He rubbed my clit a little longer, a little harder, just to drive me those last few inches to insanity. As I strained back against him, he whispered in my ear. "Don't you wish you could come? Don't you wish I'd fuck you hard and fast, until your walls clenched around my cock? Don't you want to feel that release? That bliss?" His fingers traced around the petals of my clit. "I wanted it. But you wouldn't give it to me. Bad girl."

His fingers ceased their wandering and clapped over my held-open pussy with a squeeze and a firm slap. A tear escaped the corner of one eye and slipped down my cheek. I wanted to come so badly, but he wasn't going to let me, and I didn't dare do it on my own. I was so weak. He was so much stronger. I was in so much trouble, and now I was getting what was coming to me.

He let me go, waiting a moment to be sure I didn't collapse. I almost did. He straightened me and gave me a look. Now that I could see his face, the gleeful sadism in his eyes, my humiliation was complete.

"Stay right there, naughty slut. No, keep holding yourself open. Don't dare rub your clit."

It took all my brazen determination not to scream at him to go fuck himself while I wildly masturbated myself to orgasm. It would have taken about six seconds from the place I was now. But I didn't scream at him or masturbate, for two reasons. First of all, I was scared of what he'd do to me in reprisal. Second of all, I knew any orgasm I gave myself would be a mere shadow of the orgasm he would give me. *Please, God.* He was going to give me an orgasm, wasn't he?

He went into the bathroom. I heard running water, the sound of him washing all my messiness off his fingers. I could have masturbated now without him seeing me. I knew it. He knew it.

Still, we both knew I wouldn't do it. That wasn't the way we played our game. He came out of the bathroom with his sweater off and his pants undone. His cock jutted from the front of his fly, thick, straight, hard. He worked his palm up and down the length of it, and leaned over his phone.

I salivated, watching. *Put it in me. Please. I'll never, ever deny you sex again.*

"The others want to go to dinner," he said in amusement. "I *am* kind of hungry."

Oh God. He wouldn't. He couldn't.

"Meet you in the lobby in fifteen minutes," he said, reading me his response as he typed it. "I'll tell Chere." He turned back to me. "Can you be ready in fifteen minutes?"

I shook my head in agonized dread. His laughing gaze raked over me. How did I look, close to tears, on sexual display for his amusement and pleasure?

"Can't...go to dinner...now," I managed to say.

"You can and you will, my horny little penitent. But first..."

He pushed me down on my knees. When I tried to reach for him under my own power, he made a noise that stopped me.

"Keep your hands behind your back." He showed me what he wanted, making me grip my forearms with my pussy-slickened fingers.

Then he tipped my face up and looked at me as if searching for some answer.

I had no answers, only questions. *Why are you doing this to me? Why do you love hurting me, and why do I love being hurt by you?*

I didn't have to ask the questions. He already knew my conflict, had understood my conflict from the start and knew exactly how to exploit it for his benefit. He shoved his cock in my face and I opened my mouth, feeling naked and vulnerable and so, so submissive. How had Andrew described it? Like being high on drugs, but to me it was much more grounded than that. I felt secure when Price was controlling me. I felt emptied out, carried away. I felt surrendered to a power greater than myself.

He wasn't gentle. His cock choked me, shoving deep in my throat. His hands twisted in my hair to keep me from doing anything so self-protective as pulling away. I was his mouth, his hole, his wet, shameless thing who was willing to hold her pussy open and be tortured only because he demanded it. I had his cock now, at least, which was what I'd wanted.

The only thing I wasn't getting was an orgasm. When he finished shooting his cum down my throat, I swallowed and contemplated the consequences I'd receive if I dared hump my aching pussy against his muscled calf. In the end, I wasn't brave enough to do it.

He released my hair and patted my head, and let out a long, contented sigh. He dressed for dinner while I knelt with my head bowed and my arms still clasped behind my back, then he told me to dress. I pulled my panties on over my wetness, and my tight jeans. It made it feel so much worse. My sore, tender nipples were once again protected by my bra, but they were sensitive now to every movement.

He went with me downstairs to change, to be sure I wouldn't be "naughty." I would have been. At this point, I would have masturbated if he'd given me even three seconds of privacy. He made me put on a dress with no panties underneath. It would be cold, but maybe that was a good thing.

To keep up the facade of a professional relationship, he made me walk down to the lobby first to meet the others. They couldn't know I'd just come from his embrace. They couldn't see the nakedness he insisted upon beneath my sweater dress and my coat. They'd never understand the nakedness I felt, even if they could see it. It was like he was still grasping me between my legs, even though he wasn't there. When he stepped off the elevators and walked toward our waiting group, he barely glanced at me, and greeted me like the fifth-wheel intern I was.

But I felt so owned, so completely owned by him in that moment, that I had to press my thighs tighter together, or die from my vulnerability. I was so owned by him, it was a miracle none of the others knew.

PRICE

Chere squirmed through the ritzy fixed-price menu dinner, looking beautifully distracted. She understood now what happened to naughty interns who drove their bosses out of their minds with denial and teasing. I hoped she was learning her lesson, now that the shoe was on the other foot.

Oh, the glances she sent me. The injured looks. She delighted me so much with her secret, frantic agony that I took pity on her after the second course. I got out my phone while Raneesh and Hannah were jabbering about what to order for dessert, and sent her a text.

Go to a stall in the ladies room. Spread your legs, pull your dress up to your waist, and masturbate to orgasm. In all caps, I emphasized: *ONLY ONCE.*

I didn't have to add the "or else." She knew the "or else," had gotten a good taste of it about an hour ago, when I'd made her a miserable little slut for her crimes against me. I must have been going soft, to let her orgasm now, but when she came back, she at least seemed a bit more composed. She met my eyes, smiled faintly, and put the tip of a finger to her lips. I knew it was the one she'd rubbed herself off with. I would have licked it myself, but the others would have questioned. I contented myself with a glance that said, "Later."

And there would be a later. She'd need more orgasms, and I'd need more orgasms, and we'd have orgasm after orgasm from this point forward, because I wouldn't let her retreat from me again. We'd tried that experiment and it had failed.

When Jennifer, Hannah, and Raneesh decided to go bar hopping, I developed a sudden headache and Chere pretended to be exhausted. We said goodbye to the others and got our own cab to return to the hotel. I held Chere's hand during the ride back, not feeling any particular need to talk. We were still in the giddy stage, the reuniting stage, and I didn't want words to ruin things. I didn't want to ask her *Is this okay?* or *Want some more sex?*

It was okay. We were going to have more sex.

Once I got her inside my hotel room, I pushed her against the door and gave her all the groping, sloppy kisses I couldn't give her at dinner. I yanked off her coat while she pulled off mine. We dropped them to the floor. She tasted like wine and her hair still held the currant-floral scent of the restaurant. When we returned to New York, I was going to buy her flowers. I was going to send dozens of them to her apartment to recreate that smell.

By the time I broke the kiss, she was gasping, gazing up at me with eager appeal.

Yes, I know you want to fuck. Yes, I'm going to torture you for a while first, because that's what I do.

I brushed back a lock of her dark, curly hair. It was so much lovelier than her bleach-dyed, straightened, Miss Kitty hair. She was so much lovelier in every way, now that I wasn't paying for her, now that she was herself: complicated, conflicted, rueful, charming. Smiling. She was smiling at me with a sex-drunk look on her face. She was opening up to me. I cupped her cheek and brushed a thumb across her lips.

"You little slut," I said. "Were you grateful I allowed you to orgasm at the restaurant?"

"Yes, Sir. Very grateful."

"I'm sorry I missed it. I bet you put on quite a show. Did you stand or sit?"

"I stood. Germs, you know, on public toilet seats."

I found that hilarious, that she worried about germs and not the fact that I'd sent her to masturbate in a restroom stall. I pulled up her dress and slapped her naked ass, and gave her another rough kiss. "I'm going to put my fucking germs all over you tonight. But I like this vision of you standing up. It seems so desperate."

"Oh, I was desperate. You should have seen me." Her smile broke into a grin. "It's really hard for me to orgasm while I'm standing up, but I managed."

"And you only did it once?" I watched her face closely. I'd know if she lied to me, but she shook her head with a perfect lack of guile.

"I only did it once."

"Was anyone else in the restroom?"

"Yes."

She blushed. Naughty slut. I decided she was going to get another orgasm right now, because the image of her standing in a bathroom in a ritzy Oslo eatery, jilling herself to oblivion, was too enticing to resist. I grabbed the hem of her dress and pulled it up and over her head.

"I want you to do it again," I said.

"What?"

She watched as I folded down her bra, exposing her nipples. I loved her sexy, structured bras, and the way the doubled-over cups made a perfect shelf for her flawless tits.

"I want you to do it again," I repeated. "I want you to sit on the edge of my bed and spread your legs and make yourself come. I'd like to see it."

She hesitated. I waited, my expression darkening. "Or perhaps I should make you stand up, if it's more difficult for you."

"Please, no. It's just..." She bit her lip. "The whole time...at dinner... I thought when we came back..."

I waited patiently for her to make her point, because I figured it would be entertaining.

"I mean, it's been so long since you…"

"Put my cock in you?"

"Yes."

"And whose fault is that?" I turned her toward the bed. "Go spread 'em, starshine. I want to see a show."

She gave me a long-suffering look. Silly girl. I was going to fuck her to pieces before tonight was through, but I wanted to play with her a while before she got the cock she hungered for.

"Get to it," I said in my most threatening voice. "And spread your legs wide enough for me to see everything, or I'll use my belt on your pussy and make you come that way instead."

She probably would have loved to get whipped on her pussy, but she wasn't in charge here. I was, and I wanted to see her jack herself off. She went to the edge of the bed as I'd instructed, sat down and spread her thighs. Oh God, her legs, her tits, her shining, swollen pussy. I sat in a chair by the desk and leaned back, and unzipped myself.

"Spread them a little more," I said. "Arch your hips. I want to see every fucking thing you're doing."

"I don't know if I can come with my hips arched."

Her and her sassy mouth. I glared at her. "You'd better try."

With one more sigh of protest, she started to stroke her clit. She was a little slow to warm up—it was hard to get off when you were angry—but soon she was going at herself with rough, jerky movements. Well, I knew she liked it rough. Why wouldn't she masturbate rough?

I stroked my cock as I watched her abuse herself. She was gorgeous, thrusting her breasts out and rocking her hips. Why had I never made her masturbate like this before, for my enjoyment? I never saw her masturbate when I was watching from across the street. She must have done it shamefully, under the covers. I thought of the ass plug and lube in her bedside table and smothered a smile.

When it looked like she was getting close, I went to stand in front of her. She'd been in her own little world, but when she felt my presence, she opened her eyes and sat up a little straighter.

"Keep going," I said, flicking one of her taut nipples. "Never stop until I tell you to stop." I played with her breasts, pinching, teasing, caressing. Mostly pinching, because I loved to hear her gasps.

She whimpered and bucked her hips forward. I could have put on a condom and stuck my dick inside her. She would have come in an instant, but this was about making her perform for my amusement. It was about watching her writhe and whimper, and wish I was inside her.

"It's so hard to come when you're hurting me," she said. "It's hard to come sitting up like this. It's so hard."

"I don't care if it's hard. You do what I want, and I want you to come."

"Will you fuck me? Please?"

I let go of her nipples and popped her on the cheek. "What did I tell you?"

"Please!"

"Maybe later."

She groaned. "I'm sorry. I'm sorry I wouldn't sleep with you for so long. But I've changed my mind now. Please, I want you to fuck me! Please forgive me. Please fuck me!"

Her babbling beg-session was gorgeous. Her frantic masturbation was gorgeous.

"You need to come in the next sixty seconds," I said, starting to strip, "or you're getting it in the ass."

I threw my clothes over a chair and grabbed some condoms from my luggage. Of course I'd brought condoms. Never, ever went anywhere near Chere without condoms. I dug out the travel-sized bottle of lube, too, just to scare her, but I wasn't in the mood for anal. I didn't want to force myself into her asshole tonight. Tomorrow, maybe, when I wasn't so wrought up from our re-connection.

She watched me as I rolled on a condom. "You're running out of time," I said, flicking at the lube's cap with a blasé expression.

The threat of forced anal turned her on enough to make her come. I could tell because she gave that little hitch of breath that always signaled her climax. She jammed her fingers into her pussy and rode it out, bouncing on the edge of the bed.

"That was beautiful," I murmured, fisting my shaft. "That was a very entertaining show."

She stared at my cock in that hungry, desperate way she had.

"You want this now, don't you?" I said, brandishing it at her. "You want me inside you?"

She nodded, still pawing at her pussy. I took her chin and gave her a few choice slaps.

"Say it. Use your words. You want my cock?"

"Y-yes, Sir. Please. Please, Sir, I want your cock."

"Louder."

"Please, Sir, I want your cock!"

I let go of her chin and shoved her back on the bed, and yanked her hands over her head. I slapped her breasts a few times, her reddened nipples still offered up by her helpful bra. She wanted to shield herself but she couldn't. Her struggle was gorgeous. The small pleas in her throat had me driving for her entrance. When I pushed inside her, she groaned and opened her thighs wider to accommodate me.

Oh God. Oh fucking God in fucking heaven. I gritted my teeth against the sensation of her body opening, stretching, clenching around me. Her pussy was so tight, so fucking tight and responsive. She squeezed around my dick and I almost went off.

"Wait," I growled. "Don't move."

I blew air through my teeth. I didn't want to come too fast. I didn't want to fuck her too hard and possibly injure her. *Get your shit together, Price. Take a fucking breath and man up your shit.*

When I had control again, I started to move, sinking deeper. I'd forgotten how soul-searing it felt to be inside her, how everything in the world came down to my shaft and balls, and the electrified jolts of pleasure every time she moved her hips to take me deeper. Electrocution. Destruction. Violence. I needed to give her violence to find peace, so I gave her violence, driving into her, using my knees for leverage to fuck her across the bed. She ended up at the headboard, braced back against it.

I gazed at my wanton slut, my whore, my Chere, her dark hair and caramel skin a delicious contrast to the pristine white upholstery. I lifted her up, held her hard and fucked her from my knees. To a voyeur, it might have looked like I was worshiping her, because I was kneeling before her, and her head was thrown back like some priestess in ecstasy. Maybe we had a spiritual moment. I don't know. I was too busy fucking her to figure that out. She clung to my shoulders while I fucked her and fucked her and fucked her, and grabbed her by the neck, and kissed her through her moans.

I know, starshine. I know you like it. That's why we belong together.

She snapped her hips against me, close to another climax. No more denial tonight. I let her have her squeezing, shuddering orgasm with my cock wedged up inside her like a club. As her walls contracted, she started crying, perhaps from the intensity of it all.

I yanked her under me, planted my hands on either side of her, and pummeled her with driving thrusts. I'd burned so long, waiting for her, aching for her. Chere was still sobbing, and I realized she was coming again. Her pulsing walls milked me to orgasm, and massaged me all the way through a series of magnificent aftershocks. I shuddered and collapsed on top of her, holding her head between my palms. Tears flooded her cheeks. I brushed them away with my thumbs, searching her gaze.

"What?" I asked. My voice sounded raspy. My cock was still inside her. I was afraid I'd been too violent. "Did I hurt you?" I pressed when she didn't respond.

"No. I'm not hurt." She sniffled and wiped at her eyes. "It's just... I missed this. I'm sorry I didn't let you have me for so long. I'm sorry. I was scared."

I pressed my lips to her forehead. "You were worth waiting for," I said. "You're always worth waiting for. Now stop fucking crying."

She squeezed on my cock. I gritted my teeth and withdrew from her. It was too much sensation now, too much everything. "I'll be right back."

I went into the bathroom and threw away the condom, and started running a hot bath. The two of us might have sore muscles after all. I wondered how my associates' club hopping was going, and then I quickly shoved them from my mind. I only wanted Chere and me in this moment, no one else. I went back in by the bed. She was lying where I left her, sprawled in a heap. I took her ankle and dragged her over to me, and lifted her in my arms.

Mine also, little painted poem of God. I kissed her, licking the corners of her lips, her nose, her dark eyebrows. She laughed and pushed at me, and let me carry her in to the tub. We lay together in the hot, relaxing water, barely talking. Mostly touching.

"I'm glad you agreed to come with me to Oslo," I said, stroking her hair. "It wouldn't have been the same without you here."

I didn't only mean the sex, although that was great. No, it was her secret glances, and our walk around the city. It was lying in this tub with her head against my shoulder, and our legs intertwined. If the damned museum ever got built, I'd find some way to put a memory of Chere inside it, in some lovely angle, or a bank of windows.

"I never would have imagined we'd be here like this," she replied softly. "I mean, years ago, when I first met you, I never would have imagined this."

I didn't answer, because I wasn't sure what she meant by "this." I had to think long and hard about how to proceed from "this." I had to be careful not to lead her on again, and make her want more than I could give her. I had to be careful not to destroy everything she was working for. I had to figure out how to get enough of her to satisfy my needs, and still allow her to be free. Well, free enough.

It was hard being an ultra-possessive, ultra-protective sadist and pervert. It made my life complicated as shit.

For now, there were more immediate tasks to work on, like moving her to a closer hotel room, and making sure she was sitting beside me next week when we flew back to New York. We'd stay a secret for now, for professionalism's sake, but she'd be a secret beside me.

I'd gotten drunk on her tonight, but there was so much more of her I planned to drink.

CHERE

Our time in Oslo passed like a dream. It was so beautiful and cold and white, with Price's hands hot on my skin. Then we returned to New York and nothing seemed as clear anymore. I questioned the wisdom of my choices. I'd avoided entanglements for two and a half years because of what he'd done to me, and now, for some reason, I was allowing him right back into my life.

I sat in his office during the day, trying not to think about the things he might do to me later in my apartment. His apartment. Our apartment, now. He was there at least two or three evenings a week, fucking me, terrorizing me, renewing my acquaintance with nipple clamps and zip ties. Sometimes he stayed over, but more often he left, stealing away in the wee hours while I slept off the sexual high.

We still hadn't gone to his apartment, and I didn't ask to go. I sensed a continuing preference to hold me at arm's length. It wasn't about privacy now, as it had been in the escort days, but about personal space. He insisted that we shouldn't get too close, that a relationship with him would be *bad for me.* I remembered how he'd turned me inside out last time I'd fallen under his spell, and agreed that a relationship was off the table for now.

Still, I asked him for poetry, and he humored my requests. He left verses on my bedside table, whispered poems to me, and sometimes scrawled them on my body where they wouldn't show. Andrew said I should demand more, but he was young and naïve, and trying to be a caring friend. He didn't understand our history, and how anxious I was to avoid heartache. In the end, I understood that our thing was just about sex and release.

And design.

Price had a fertile mind for design, just as he had a fertile mind for perversity. I'd learned a lot from him over the course of my internship. I'd learned that the same principles for beauty and utility applied whether you were designing an eighty-story building or a bracelet. I'd learned about tempering vision with collaboration, creating with serenity, and keeping your cool when nothing was working. *There's always a way*, he told me over and over. *Don't let people tell you no.* His words inspired me to try designs that people like Cantor used to discourage, designs that were avant-garde, asymmetrical, or excessively delicate.

"Chere?"

I looked up from my most recent sketches. Price was at his desk, leaning back in his chair. He crooked a finger at me. "Come hither."

I went to stand beside him, and followed his pointing finger to an open email from Norton.

"I have to submit a formal evaluation of your work during this internship," he said.

"Oh. Yes. I need that to graduate." I frowned at the questionnaire, thinking how supremely silly it was for him to have to do this, and how supremely hard he was going to make me suffer for it.

"Why don't you have a seat?" he said. "We'll work on it together."

His idea of having a seat was for me to sit on his lap. He hooked an arm around my waist and he pulled me against him as I glanced at the door. We were supposed to keep things professional at the office. That was what we'd agreed upon after we'd returned from Oslo, that we'd keep a dividing line between business and sex. When I tried to stand up, he pulled me down again.

"Sit."

"What if someone—"

His fingers untucked my blouse and tightened against my skin. I squirmed in self-protection.

"Don't pinch me. Ouch!"

"Hush and be still."

He read the first question, running his fingers over the bit of skin he'd just tortured. I had no doubt he'd do it again if I tried to get up.

"Let's see. *Did you find the candidate cooperative and well-mannered?* Not always," he said, giving me a look.

"What? I'm cooperative and well-mannered."

"Yes, when it fucking suits you."

I glared at him. He stifled a smile and typed *Yes*.

He went on to award me high marks for punctuality, appearance, and professionalism, while he muttered under his breath that professionalism could be overrated. I laughed at his snarky commentary, and his arm tightened around me until it almost felt like a hug. *Don't fall for him. Don't.* Sometimes he made it really hard not to fall for him. Sometimes he was sweet and playful, like this. It never lasted. Nothing between us would ever be lasting and *I had to remember that.*

I sobered as he answered questions about my level of design capability and my willingness to learn. He wrote that I was detail oriented and ambitious, and a pleasure to have in the office.

A pleasure to have in the office. I knew that wording was intentional, just as I knew his thigh working itself between my legs was intentional.

"*What strengths did this candidate display in the course of the internship?*" he read next. He thought a moment. "Flexibility, for sure. Patience. Horniness," he said, running a hand over my breasts.

I waited. He didn't type any of those things. He typed this:

Ms. Rouzier exhibited an immense number of talents under my purview.

I expected him to start listing sex acts. He didn't.

From the first day, he typed, *the candidate exuded an unwavering focus and willingness to learn. I found her to be an articulate and thoughtful designer, and I was constantly surprised by her attention to detail. Her creativity will serve her well in future endeavors, but her determination is her greatest asset.* He paused a moment, typed a few letters, backspaced, and typed again. *Ms. Rouzier is ready for whatever her future holds.*

"Do you think that's good?" he asked.

I couldn't say anything. I had all the feelings. *Her determination is her greatest asset.* He was the one who'd sparked that determination, who'd made my vague aspirations seem possible when I was working as an escort.

"Too gushy?" he asked when I remained silent.

"No, it's good. It's nice."

"It's true," he said gruffly, like he was angry that I'd accused him of being nice. He moved the cursor down to the final question.

Is there any task you wish the candidate had completed during the internship, which was not completed?

I watched as he typed *Blowjob under my desk* in the space allotted.

"You can't write that," I said, turning to him in exasperation.

"Why not? You never did it."

"You can't write that on my actual evaluation. They'll never let you mentor anyone again."

"I don't want to mentor anyone else. I made an exception for you."

I glared at him. He frowned back at me and shrugged. "If you don't want me to put that on your evaluation, then I suppose you'd better get busy. Your internship ends in a week."

His fingers spread under my blouse, tracing along the line of my waistband. I could feel his cock solidifying against my ass.

"You said no sex in the office," I reminded him.

"Uh, no. *You* said no sex in the office."

"But you agreed. You promised."

His hand moved higher, to caress the underside of my breast. His voice rumbled against my ear. "You know I'm not to be trusted. My promises are shit." His thumb grazed my nipple, a flash of sensation over the silk cup of my bra.

I wanted to argue with him, but that brush of his thumb resonated in my pussy. It resonated everywhere as he gazed at me with his intent blue stare.

"I know you'll find this hard to believe," he said, "but I've never had a blowjob under my desk."

"Poor, deprived man," I replied with as much sarcasm as I dared.

My gaze dropped to his lips. Any moment now, I knew he would make me. I saw it in his face, felt it in his body's tension. I could have saved both of us the trouble and slid down under his desk where he wanted me, but no, that was no fun. I looked at the door.

"What if someone comes in?"

"No one will come in," he said.

That was true. When people knocked, they waited outside until he barked "Enter" like a commanding sovereign. "But what if they do?" I asked.

"Then I guess they'll discover what a whore you are."

His gaze dropped to the front of my blouse. He unbuttoned a couple of the buttons, just enough to expose my bra and the tops of my breasts. He smoothed back the fabric, and raised me to stand in front of him, between his legs.

"Lift up your skirt," he said.

"I thought you wanted a blowj—"

He slapped me before I even got the words out. "Do what I fucking tell you."

I bit my lip and yanked my fitted skirt up to my waist, feeling cool air against my skin. My cheek stung where he'd slapped me, flaring with heat as I held his gaze.

"Now push down your panties," he said. "Leave them around your ankles. If anyone comes in, I want them to see just how slutty you are."

His desk faced the door, so once I was kneeling under it, giving him a blowjob, everything between my legs would be on display. It was so scary and hot, and twisted. I pushed down my panties, half ashamed and half turned on.

"Take out my cock," he said in a low voice. "Touch me."

Five minutes ago we'd been working on my evaluation. Now we were working on something very, very different. I reached for his fly and released him. He offered brusque assistance, rearranging himself in the chair and pushing back the sides of his pants so only his cock was exposed.

"Get on your fucking knees," he said. "If I have to fill out this evaluation for you, you're going to blow me while I'm doing it. You'd better make it good."

"Yes, Sir."

"And don't be sloppy." He grabbed my hands and shoved them behind my back. "Just your mouth. Just your tongue. No drooling and acting stupid. If there's one fucking drop of spit on my pants when you're finished, you won't be able to sit down for a week."

"Yes, Sir."

I was so turned on by his rough handling and his coarse words that I could hardly speak. When he shoved his cock in my mouth I took it as deep as I could, but not so deep that I'd start drooling. I held my hands behind my back in obedient fists and sucked him with warm, steady pressure.

After a moment or two he let go of my head. I heard him start typing again on his laptop. Work and blowjobs. Why wouldn't they go together in Price's perverse world? I thought about what I must look like, kneeling under the desk with my ass stuck out and my panties around my ankles. It just went to show how much I would do for him, how much I was coming to accept, even enjoy, the depraved humiliations he bestowed on me.

As for Price, he stayed rock hard between my lips. Sometimes he touched my hair, a silent signal that I was doing it right. If I wasn't, he would have let me know that too. I wanted to do it right, if this was really his first under-the-desk blowjob. I wanted it to be memorable, so any that came after me would pale in comparison. I used all the tricks and titillations I'd developed in my escort days, all the techniques he didn't allow me to use when he was in control. Eventually the typing ceased. His legs trembled where I leaned on them.

"You fucking slut," I heard him whisper. A moment later he spurted into my mouth. I swallowed the cum as fast as I could, fearful of getting anything on his pants. Since we'd returned from Oslo, I'd become reacquainted with the sting of his whips and belts. He kept an entire selection of them at my apartment, and I knew he'd punish me later even if he couldn't do it now. I sucked until he was dry, until he pushed me away with a groan.

"Enough," he said. "Overachiever. I need to put that on your evaluation somewhere."

I lay my head against his lap as his breathing returned to normal. I was horny now, my pussy hot and untouched. I wanted to touch it.

"Please, may I...?"

"No. No sex in the office, remember?"

He made me scoot back so he could tuck his cock away and refasten his pants. I watched in disappointment.

"That's not fair," I said. "You got sex. Why can't I have sex?"

He looked down at me as I trembled on my knees. He'd been attempting to teach me about submission, about giving myself over to his will, but the lessons were hard.

"We have sex when I want, not when you want," he said. "Remember? I'm the Dominant in this relationship, you're the slut toy. Now go back to your desk and do some work."

I frowned. I may have actually pouted as I pulled up my panties and rearranged my skirt. When I reached to button my blouse, he stopped me with a sound.

I took a deep breath and returned to my seat, aware that anyone who came into the office would have an unobstructed view of my exposed bra. Having him as a client had been difficult. Having him as a boss and Dominant truly and magnificently sucked.

"Sometimes I hate our relationship," I said. "I thought Dominants were supposed to be caring."

"I care about you."

"You care about making me miserable."

He pointed to his laptop. "I haven't sent your evaluation yet. You might want to watch what you say to me."

"I can't wait until this internship is over," I muttered just loud enough for him to hear. It was a reckless lie that directly related to the frustrated horniness of my pussy.

"If you don't stop sulking, I'll give you something to sulk about, starshine."

"Like what?" I sassed.

"Like a long and difficult lesson in surrender." He held up a finger when I opened my mouth to protest. "My control and your submission is the whole basis of our dynamic. If you're going to poke me and act like a fucking brat—"

"Maybe I'm acting like a fucking brat because I don't enjoy our dynamic."

He dismissed my angry words with a flick of his wrist. "Tell me something, Chere. How do you feel after our scenes? At the end, when I'm holding you and soothing you, and telling you it's over? How do you feel?"

I gritted my teeth, refusing to answer.

"Do you feel calm? Do you feel serene, like everything's perfect in the world?"

That was exactly how I felt, although I wasn't in the mood to admit it. I pulled my open blouse together and leaned over my laptop.

"No answer," he said with a sniff. "It figures. Open your fucking blouse. Let me see your tits."

I looked up at him, holding the sides more tightly together. He was across the office in an instant, stalking toward me with all his force and heat. He reached down and yanked the two sides of my blouse apart, so all the buttons came open. One of them popped off and rolled across the carpet.

"Stop," I said, pushing his hands away.

"Show them to me!"

I swallowed and looked up into his ice blue gaze. I hated him. No, I *wanted* him. Why did this aggressive, obnoxious behavior turn me on? I leaned back and let him look at my breasts.

"Take them out. Show them to me."

I started to fold down the cups of my bra.

"No, wait." He grabbed a pair of scissors off my desk.

"What are you doing?"

"Sit still, or I'll cut something that shouldn't be cut."

I watched with a mixture of horror and fascination as he cut two nipple-sized circles from my lacy bra cups. He pinched each nipple, tugging at them through the holes in my bra. "What I wouldn't give for a pair of clamps, bad girl." He thought a moment, then snapped his fingers and went to his desk. He returned with a pair of small silver paper clips. I shook my head, tried to close my blouse again.

"Don't dare," he said, tugging it open. He bent one edge of each clip until there was enough space to slide it onto my nipple. It pinched the tender flesh into a flat, painful shape.

"It hurts," I said. "Please! Why are you so mean? I gave you a blowjob."

"And then you bitched and whined because you didn't get what you wanted in return." He tweaked each of the paper clips. "Now you get punished."

There was a tap at the door. I reached up to cover my breasts. He took my hands hard and lowered them again. "Yes?" he asked.

"Your three-thirty appointment is expected in fifteen minutes."

"Thank you," he called out. "We'll be in the conference room a few minutes ahead of time."

The receptionist went away. I let out the panicked breath I'd been holding. "It hurts," I said again.

"As much as nipple clamps?"

Not really as much as nipple clamps. I just felt exposed and ashamed.

"Ten minutes," he said. "I'll take them off before we head to the meeting."

Thank you, God. I wouldn't have put it past him to make me wear them the whole time he met with his clients. I cringed, looking down at my reddened nipples and my ruined bra. I'd have to wear my jacket the rest of the day. This was why I'd insisted on the no-sex rule in the office, because he took shit too far. "I don't know why you do things like this to me," I whispered.

"I do them because you need me to do them. How does your pussy feel right now, with those clips on your nipples?"

I shook my head. I couldn't even describe how wrought up I was, how tormented and fucked up and horny. I placed my palms flat on the desk to keep from stroking myself through my skirt. "Please let me come."

He leaned closer, and forced me to meet his gaze. "Tell me you belong to me, bad girl. Say it. *I'm yours.*"

"Will you let me come if I say it?"

"Don't make me smack your fucking face. Say it."

My nipples throbbed from the clips. My pussy was about to explode. "I'm yours," I said, my voice trembling with the hell of denial.

"That's why I don't let you come every time," he said, tracing a manicured fingertip over the paper clips. "Because you're mine, and I get to decide. Because you're my beautiful, horny fuck slut, and I have the control, and right now I'm not going to let you come."

"Will you let me come later?" I asked. "Please?"

"I'm going to punish you later, Chere, for being a mouthy, horny brat. I think we ought to start having regular lessons in surrender. You need them."

I squirmed in my chair. Regular lessons in surrender sounded like hell. "Please. I'll be good."

"I think I'll take you to my apartment after dinner. There's more equipment there."

In all this time he'd never taken me to his apartment, but now that he was inviting me to visit for this 'lesson in surrender,' I didn't want to go.

"I have plans with Andrew," I lied. "I'm not sure I can make it tonight."

"You're going to make it tonight." He flicked my aching nipples one last time and walked to his drafting table, and leaned over the set of plans for his three-thirty meeting.

"You've got five more minutes to go," he said when I heaved a melodramatic sigh. "You fucking brat."

CHERE

He ordered me to sit on a couch in his silent, darkened living room until he was ready for me, then he disappeared down a hallway. No tour of the apartment, no after-dinner cocktails, no clicking on the TV. Maybe this was part of learning to surrender, having to sit here and worry with my heart pounding in my chest.

I looked around, trying to calm myself. Finally, I was able to see his world, his lair, the apartment he retreated to after he finished tormenting me. The soaring space was a showcase of design and understated elegance; I would have expected nothing less. The furniture was old-world, heavy and varnished. The leather couch I sat on probably went for twenty thousand bucks, if not more.

The end tables were thick, polished wood. A similarly furnished dining area opened up on the left, and beyond that, I suspected, a jaw-dropping kitchen. Bookshelves lined the opposite wall, perhaps laden with all his poetry anthologies? I didn't dare leave the couch to investigate. It was a beautifully welcoming residence, I just didn't know why I'd agreed to come here. Had I temporarily gone insane?

Not temporarily, Chere. You've been insane for almost three years.

I heard him in the hall. He returned and beckoned me. "I'm ready for you now."

Oh, fuck. *I'm ready for you now.* Price didn't do the fun, playful power exchange people engaged in at the BDSM clubs. This was twenty levels higher, and I knew his lesson on "surrender" would be twenty levels higher as well.

He led me to a room that had to be his bedroom, with more heavy, classically designed furniture, chests and an armoire, and an iron poster bed covered in smooth gray-blue sheets. As soon as I saw what he'd lined up on that bed—mask, ball gag, cane, Lucite paddle, a tangle of black rope, condoms, lube—I deeply regretted my decision to come here, and turned immediately to leave. "I'm not ready for surren—"

He silenced me with a hand over my mouth and used the other hand to shut the door behind us. I shook my head, meeting his intent gaze, pleading in the only way I could, with my eyes.

"You earned this," he said. "You need this."

"I don't. I can't." I babbled behind his hand, anything I could think of as he dragged me to the bed. He took his hand off my mouth. "Please, no," I cried. "Please."

He held my chin hard. "You don't just need a lesson in surrender. You also need to be punished for running your mouth at me. Say it. *I need you to punish me.*"

"I can't say that!"

"Say it."

He waited. I balked.

"I need you to punish me," I finally admitted. Tears rose, along with my anxiety level. "But I'm afraid."

His fingers brushed across my cheek. "Do you deserve this?"

One of my tears fell, coursing down the same cheek he stroked. "Yes. Probably. But—"

"Say it, then. Admit it. *I deserve to be punished.* Ask for it."

"I—" I knew the words he wanted, but it was so hard to say them. "P-please punish me, Sir. I deserve it."

A spark of satisfied mayhem glinted in his eyes. "That was very nicely done. Maybe I'll go softer on you because of it. But probably not."

He put the mask on me first, so I wouldn't keep panicking over the things he'd spread out on the bed. The gag came next. I tried to close my lips against it and got a slap for my efforts.

"Open your fucking hole," he said. "You're supposed to be learning a lesson."

All I was learning was how terrifying he could be and how stupid I was to repeatedly place myself at his mercy. *It's okay, it's okay.* I tried to think of Andrew, tried to think about submission as a high. I usually felt pretty high by the time Price was done with me, but tonight...with the mask and gag, and the scary black rope…

"Take off your clothes," he said.

I kicked off my shoes, then scrabbled for my skirt's zipper by feel. I took off my blouse and panties next, and then my adulterated bra, fumbling with the clasp. I couldn't see where to put them, so I just dropped everything on the floor. I hated being blindfolded. I hated that I couldn't see, but I didn't dare reach up and take the mask off. During our first date, yes, I would have done it if my hands weren't zip-tied behind me. But now, I knew better.

He put me on the bed, face down, and pulled my arms over my head. I felt the scratch of rope around each wrist, and pictured the jet black color against my skin. He worked in silence to secure me hand and foot, and then shoved pillows under my hips to raise my ass. He drew the ropes tight so I was spread eagle with hardly any slack.

I wish I could say I endured all this in stoic submission to his will. I didn't. I whined behind the ball gag each time he encircled one of my limbs with the rope, and full-on panicked when he tried to secure my left ankle. I kicked him hard enough—once—to hear a grunt. A moment later I felt a searing explosion of pain across my ass. It had to have been the clear Lucite paddle with the holes. To get whacked full blast, without a warm up, almost made me piss myself.

"Surrender," he reminded me sternly. "You'd better start trying to figure it out."

After that, I cried softly into the gag, but refrained from any more kicking. Jesus, he hadn't even started on me yet and I was terrified to endure any more of that paddle.

You allowed him to bring you here, Chere. You knew it would be bad.

I squirmed my pelvis against the pillows as he moved around the room doing God knew what. I heard only rustles and his faint breath. I pulled at the rope but he was a Boy Scout with the knots. I turned my head with a jerky movement when he finally spoke.

"Relax," he said in an even, soothing voice. "You can't get away. You can only surrender to me. You *want* to surrender to me, and we both know it. It's time to stop fucking around."

I heard a whoosh, a whisper through the air, and then the slicing heat of a cane stroke before I had time to brace. I meant to say *no*, to say *stop*, but all that came out was a long, ragged shriek.

"Yes, I know it hurts like hell," he said as I stiffened in agony, "but I think that's for the best."

The cane fell again, and I screamed again as I fought to escape. We were half a minute into this punishment and I was dying. *Oh my God, oh my God.* I would never, ever survive this. It killed so bad.

"You're getting ten of these" *Whack.* "and then I'll work you over" *Whack.* "with the paddle" *Whack.* "and we'll see where we are."

Each time he hit me, the pain felt hotter and more impossible. The mask forced me into darkness, into my own agonized mind.

"I can't, I can't, I can't," I babbled, although the ball gag just turned my words into muffled nonsense. "Please, please, no, stop, please."

Whack. I tried to turn away from each successive stroke, pressing down into the pillows, but I couldn't do anything to get away.

Whack.

Oh God, I'm dying!

I cried louder through the gag, harder, as if that might move him. He only whacked me again. "Hush. I have neighbors."

I needed his neighbors to bust through the wall and rescue me. He landed the last two strokes on the backs of my thighs. I squealed at the fresh slices of pain and wished I could go back in time and categorically refuse this lesson in surrender, our dynamic, everything. No more canes. Never. I tried to sob quietly but it was hard with the burning heat radiating from each throbbing stripe.

"Had enough of the cane?" he asked.

I nodded in the direction of his voice, trying to look apologetic. *I've learned my lesson. Surrender only from now on. No more rebellion. No.*

I felt the bed dip. He traced each of the ten cane tracks while I tried to collect myself. "Are you ready for the paddle now?" he asked when he finished. "It's going to feel pretty torturous on top of those welts you already have."

No. I didn't want torturous. I wanted more stroking, and his reassuring weight beside me. He rose from the bed and I braced, squirming, whining, tensing my ass cheeks like that might protect me.

It didn't.

I screamed through the gag as he gave me five hard paddle cracks in a row. The sting erupted in the shape of a big painful rectangle, rather than the razor fine line of the cane. Either way, it was unbearable. I needed to be untied. I wanted to be left alone to nurse my aching ass and my aching psyche.

"Are you letting go?" he asked. "From here on out, are you going to accept the fact that you like to surrender? That you live to surrender?"

It wasn't surrender I lived for. It was his voice and his force and his capability. Even now, the more he hurt me, the more I wanted him. I was tired of trying to understand. I supposed that was surrender enough. I moaned behind the gag and nodded.

"Are you going to show me your fucking tits when I want to see your tits?" he asked. "No more sulking and whining and behaving like a brat?"

I nodded as hard as I could, making urgent sounds behind the gag.

Another spank, another shriek. "I'm happy to hear that."

He might have been happy to hear it, but he paddled me some more anyway, at least a dozen hard, steady strokes on my one-thousand-degree butt cheeks. They felt like they were on fire, like flames must be licking up into the air and setting off his building's fire alarm. I pictured the sprinklers dousing us, although I doubted even a deluge of sprinkler water could put out this fire. *Ow, ow, ow...* I understood now why he'd shoved so many pillows under me. I probably would have injured myself otherwise.

I'll do better. I'll try harder to surrender. Please...

My muscles strained within the bondage. I couldn't turn my body, but I bounced up and down with every stinging blow. My face was damp, my eyes streaming with tears behind the mask. When he stopped, I kept crying, because I was afraid he'd start up again.

"I'll take the gag off if you promise to be quiet," he said.

I didn't answer right away. I didn't know if I could be quiet if he paddled me some more, or God, started in with the cane again. I felt his hands in my hair, pulling it tight between his fingers. "Are you listening? Will you be quiet?"

I just moaned, a plaintive, animal sound begging him to stop.

He left, walked across the room. I heard water running, probably in an adjoining bathroom. I wondered if I was bleeding, if he would have to patch me up. My ass felt swollen and numb and throbby, like he'd opened some spurting artery. He came back and unbuckled the gag, and wiped the drool from my mouth and chin with a damp cloth.

"Am I bleeding?" I asked in a broken voice.

He chuckled next to my ear. "You're not bleeding, my little drama queen. You're just a hot, deep shade of red." He rubbed my ass. The abrasive contact made me cringe.

"Ow," I whined. He rubbed harder. "Ow. *Owww.*"

"Hush, or we'll start all over."

I pressed as close to him as I could, still blind and caught in my bonds. *Surrender, Chere. Surrender.* A shivering sob shook me every few seconds. He'd gotten me so worked up, I couldn't calm down.

"Pain and sex," he murmured, stroking a finger up my spine. "Such a potent combination. Do you like when I hurt you, baby?"

My shiver turned to a shudder. I answered truthfully, trying not to feel ashamed. "Yes."

"Yes, what?"

"Yes, Sir, I like when you hurt me."

He stroked my shoulder blades, my hair, my nape, his firm, possessive touch making me fall deeper in love or lust or whatever the hell it was I felt for him.

"It's okay to like it," he said. "Say it: *It's okay to like it.*"

"It's o-okay to like it," I stammered.

"You're going to get fucked now. You're going to take it in your sore, red-hot ass to learn a little more about surrender, and I'm not going to use very much lube. I think it should hurt you a little. Don't you?"

"Yes, Sir," I whimpered, even though I wasn't sure how much more hurting I could take.

He parted my cheeks, depositing a scant amount of lubricant around my clenching hole. His body covered mine, a warm, masculine weight that would be pleasant if he wasn't positioning himself to drive into my ass. I wanted to beg him to be gentle, to be careful and go slow, but I was afraid he'd be rougher on purpose, so I kept my mouth shut. Soft, strained panic noises escaped my throat.

One of the hardest parts of being the submissive member of our twisted relationship was that he kept me so helpless. I wanted to be fucked, yes, my pussy was dying, aching with lust, but it was so hard to be trapped at someone's mercy. I had no recourse, no choice. I was tied hand and foot, with my ass propped in the air by a pile of pillows. He was going to fuck me and I was going to deal with it. I loved being overpowered by him, and *it was okay to like it*, but oh my God...fuck...

The head of his cock slipped against the lube at my entrance, pushing, poking, not quite making it in. He pushed harder, stretching me open by pure physics. Hard cock, steady pressure.

"Ow, ow, ow," I chanted as the pain intensified. "Ow, ow, *ow, ow, please...*"

"Let me in." He sounded so much calmer than I did. "I'm getting in either way."

I panted as he stopped just inside me. I felt so full, just from the tip. My "ows" had become low, pleading groans.

"Does it hurt that much?" he asked.

"Yes!"

His thighs were warm against the insides of my tied-open legs. He grabbed a handful of my hair along with the mask's strap, and yanked my head back.

"Ask for the rest of me."

Holy shit. The harder he pulled, the louder I whined. My ass clenched around him, trying to push him back out.

"You're hurting me," I cried.

"Ask for the rest of me."

"Please..."

"Please what?"

Surrender, Chere.

"Please give me the rest of your c-cock," I said, my voice faltering over the words. "Please push it deep inside me. I want it. I *like it.*"

He made a satisfied noise and proceeded to jam his length into me, inch by excruciating inch, until I felt his nut sack brush against my sodden slit. By then, the acute pain of entry had passed. Now there was only the feeling of being split in two, of being filled with something way too large in a space that was way too small. I pursed my lips and lay absolutely still.

"Is that better?" he asked. "Is it deep enough inside you to hurt?"

I whimpered. "No, Sir."

He let go of my hair and parted my ass cheeks, holding each in a firm, painful grip. He thrust the last inch or two into me, hard enough to push me down against the bed. My clit slid across the pillows as I clenched around him. My dark, surrendered world was filled with his dominance, and a fine edge of pain.

"Are you rubbing your pussy on my pillows?" he asked.

"Yes. I can't help it."

"You filthy fucking whore."

He may have called me a filthy fucking whore in that growly voice of his, but the only thing that registered was that he hadn't told me to stop. I gasped in time to his thrusts, like he was fucking the life out of me, and rubbed my clit against his soft designer pillows for all I was worth. The pleasure was so hot, so exquisite, because Price was being so mean to me and *it was okay to like it.* Sometimes I thought I was a shitty submissive compared to Andrew, that my heart wasn't really in it.

But now, tied down with Price's cock plowing my paddled ass, my heart was in it. I was surrendered, one hundred percent. The more I ground against the pillows, the harder he fucked me. Each time he pressed deep, I felt so, so close to coming. He let go of my ass cheeks and held my hips, drilling me. I lost myself in the steady fuck, and the feel of his hands grasping my skin, forcing me to take him, and my God, the pounding felt so...good...on...my...clit.

"Please, please, please," I murmured over and over. I meant *Please don't stop*, and *Please keep hurting me*, and *Please let me survive this. Please never untie me. Please fuck me like this every hour of every day.*

When I could hardly bear it anymore, my orgasm exploded, unraveling in an agonizing series of pulses, hot pleasure constricting my pussy and ass. I wished he had been embracing me. I needed someone to cling to, someone to shudder against. His cock felt wonderful deep inside me, but he wasn't holding me, and it didn't feel like enough.

I guess that was the punishment part of it. *Good girl. Bad girl. Play these games with me and I'll make you orgasm, but only on my terms.*

Now he was coming too, nice and deep and firm. Since I'd already come, I let myself lie there and experience his power and his own harsh gasps.

"Fuck. Fuck. Fuck," he said. "Holy fuck."

He collapsed on top of me, twitching through a few last shallow thrusts. My body still clenched around him in intermittent pulses, unwilling to let the last throes of ecstasy fade.

"Are you alive?" he asked, when I didn't move for long moments.

I pressed my face against the bed. "My ass hurts."

"An occasional side effect of surrender. You did great though. You were very…determined," he said, borrowing a word from my evaluation.

I could hear true pleasure in his voice, and it gave me a warm, trembly feeling. He kissed my shoulder as I blinked behind the mask.

"*Star-shadows shine*," he said beside my ear. "*How many stars in your bowl? How many shadows in your soul?*"

"I don't know." My voice sounded quavery compared to his. "Whose poem is that?"

"D.H. Lawrence." I felt him stretch, felt his ab muscles slide against my back. His wet, warm tongue traced my skin from earlobe to jaw. "He was a pervert. Most poets are perverts," he said when he finished with the tongue bath.

I shivered as he pulled back and left me. I always felt so empty after I'd been assfucked. Not empty enough to beg him to do it again, but still.

"Are you going to untie me?" I asked when I heard him return from the bathroom.

"When you answer my poetic questions." I felt the bed dip between my legs, and then his palms running up my thighs. "How many stars in your bowl, Chere?"

"I don't even know what that means."

He traced his fingers back and forth over my ass cheeks, over the lines he'd put there earlier. They still ached, a sharp reminder of his power, and my hunger for it. He asked me again, in an insistent tone that demanded an answer. "How many stars in your bowl?"

"Let me think about it."

I closed my eyes behind the mask, and thought about all the things I had to be happy for, and all the things that challenged me, and my intimate circle of trusted friends. "Eighty to ninety stars. Maybe."

He laughed at that. "Am I one of them?"

I wiggled my ass. *You're my sun*, I thought. *My main star. No matter how I wish it otherwise, everything in my life revolves around you.*

That was a scary thought, because, surrender aside, I still didn't know if he could be trusted. I didn't know if the violence or the tenderness was his true face. He was being so tender now, stroking me, soothing all the places he'd hurt.

"How many shadows in your soul?" he asked.

"Shadows?" I thought a bit longer about that one. Simon, for sure. Cantor? Kind of. My parents, definitely. My old clients? How many of them had there been? Hundreds over the course of a decade? "I have a lot of shadows," I said. "Maybe four or five thousand, if you're talking about my entire life."

The bed creaked. He shifted, then pressed his lips to the base of my spine. He kissed me there, a soft, tentative kiss that was over too soon.

"I'm sorry I have to hurt you to get off," he said. "Thank you for being brave enough to surrender to me. It means more than you know."

This sudden, and no doubt fleeting, show of sincerity made me feel shy. He was like a star and a shadow, light on one side and dark on the other.

"I want to see you," I said. "I answered your questions. Now you have to take off the mask."

"Oh, do I *have* to?"

But I felt his fingers at the back of my head, undoing the buckle. He took it off and I blinked. Every light was on in his room. I strained to watch him as he disappeared to the foot of the bed to untie my ankles. A moment later, he sat beside me to untie my wrists. He was quiet, his expression somber as he manipulated the black rope. Was he disappointed in my answers to his questions? Was I not poetic enough?

When my arms were free, I sat back from the pillows and watched him. My ass still hurt, and I wasn't sure of his mood. I couldn't tell if there was going to be more sex, or an argument, or kissing and whispering and making out.

"Shower?" he asked, raising an eyebrow.

"Yes. Please."

His bathroom was as beautiful and luxurious as the rest of his place. We stood in his huge glass enclosure, a marble and glass structure that raised hygiene to a fine art. There were two shower heads, but he kept me under his, half washing me, half groping me. I closed my eyes when he started to kiss me.

All the time I'd spent tied to his bed, I'd been blind and wanted to see, but now that I could open my eyes and look at him, I wanted to retreat into touch. He held me close, stroking up my back, and then trailing down to squeeze my sore ass. He massaged my nape, a caress and then a grasp to draw me against his muscled front. The kiss deepened, went on for so long I lost myself.

I was drowning in him. It wasn't only the kisses—although he was great at the kisses. It was the way he held me and stroked me, like he could never have enough of me. It was scary and thrilling, and dangerous to my psyche. *Don't fall in love again.*

I pulled away and looked at him, brushing back a wet strand of his hair. "Why does my surrender mean so much to you?"

"Because you're a fighter," he said, without thinking about it at all. He tried to kiss me again, but I held him off.

"I answered your questions. Now I want answers," I said. "Why do you prefer pain instead of love? What happened to you to make you this way?"

"Jesus, Chere," he said, turning away. "Shut the fuck up."

"No, answer me." I nudged him until he turned back to me. "Why do you say you can't be with me? I know why I don't trust love, but what happened to you?"

I couldn't make anything of his expression. It looked like too many emotions at once, shuttered into a concealing mask. "Love lies," he said.

"Someone lied to you?"

"Everyone lies." He forced a laugh. "You and your questions, your stupid girly shit."

"How many stars in your bowl, then? How many shadows in your soul?"

He shut off the water and got out. The question-and-answer session was apparently over. He'd withdrawn from me in that whiplash manner. One minute he was there, engaged, smiling and caressing me, and the next he was a ghost, impossible to touch. While I sat in his room and brushed my hair, he lay back on the bed with his arms crossed behind his head. He didn't say anything to me, or glance my way.

How many shadows in your soul? He had to have a lot, none of which he seemed willing to discuss. I stood to get dressed, but before I could grab my clothes, he held out his hand.

"Where are you going? Come here."

"It's late," I said.

"Come here."

Our eyes locked. His gaze drew me to the bed and into his arms. He enveloped me in a hug, this confusing man who'd just finished pushing me away. His hands moved over me, drawing me right against his body. Did I love him or did I fear him? Did I want to get closer to him, or should I be running away?

"I don't understand you," I whispered.

His lashes flickered, darker golden-blond than his hair. "Is it so important to understand?"

"Yes. For me it is. After everything with Simon, it's important."

His languid look wavered into irritation, as it always did when I mentioned my ex's name. He lifted my arm, stroked his palm up the underside, across paler, sensitive skin. He brought it to his lips and bit the inside of my forearm. I watched his mouth open, watched his teeth close and bite down.

It hurt. I whined and he let me go, and bit my wrist instead. He licked over the place he hurt, and sighed.

"I want you to sleep here with me," he said.

"Are you going to keep biting me?"

"Biting is the least of my crimes against you. Will you stay?"

I wanted to stay. He was warm and comfortable, and the surrender part was over. For now.

"I used to hate leaving," he blurted out, before I could answer. "I used to hate the time thing. The sessions. It was so fake."

"You could have paid to stay with me all night."

"It still would have been a session. It would have ended. We would get so heightened, you know, physically, psychologically, and then our time would be up. I hated it."

"You don't have to leave, not anymore. And I'll stay."

He touched my fingers, tracing them one by one. "Remember that time you left? The time you just fucking took off and left me?"

"The Standard Hotel. Yeah, I remember. I don't think I'll ever forget that session. That was the first time I realized you were a stalker."

"I didn't stalk you. I just dug up a little information on your boyfriend."

"That's called stalking."

He took my chin and gave it a little shake. "No. Stalking is giving someone an apartment so you can watch them with binoculars from across the street."

He was joking, but it wasn't funny. "Why did you watch me like that?" I felt like we could hash over this forever, and I'd never come to a place where I was okay with it. "Was it a voyeuristic thing? A sex thing? A control thing?"

He rolled away from me and ran his fingers through his hair. "I don't know. It was a Chere thing. I told you, it was hard to leave. Every session, it was so hard to leave you. If I couldn't leave you for a week, how do you think it felt to take an extended vacation from your life?"

"A 'vacation'? So you always meant to come back?"

"I don't know what I meant. I wanted you to graduate and start your life, and then, I thought, maybe..." He covered his eyes and made a frustrated sound. "I don't know. I want too much of you. I still want too much."

"What does that mean?" I wasn't in the mood for his vague, distancing conversation. "I don't understand why you keep saying that. How can you want too much from someone who's already giving y—?"

"I have a dungeon," he said, cutting me off. He took his hands away from his face and glared at me. "I have a dungeon, Chere, right here in this apartment, on the other side of this room. It's got everything, all the furniture and equipment. But I brought you here to the bedroom instead, because..." His voice trailed off.

"Because you thought your dungeon might scare me?"

He gave a mirthless laugh. "I know it would scare you. I would have liked that part. No, it's... I can't..." He let out a harsh breath. "Look, I've always been straight with you. And here's the truth: since you came back into my life, I've been getting it ready for you. I've been buying things with you in mind. I fantasize about taking you in there and..."

"And what?" I asked, even though I was kind of scared to hear the answer.

"Enslaving you. Training you and hurting you and fucking you up until all you know is *Yes, Sir* and *No, Sir*, and *What can I do for you, Sir?*" He frowned. "You're going to graduate in a month. You're going to go out into the world and start a career. You're going to be happy. You and I..."

He made a rough sound. "I'm bad for your happiness. I'm not safe. You know I'm not safe."

"You're safe," I argued, like he hadn't just revealed that he'd been outfitting a dungeon for me. I felt annoyed, because I wanted him to be safe. I wanted us to be two normal people without a bunch of fucked up issues. "You try hard not to hurt me," I pointed out. "You exercise control. You're not a vampire, or a lion, or some feral coyote."

"I might be a feral coyote. That would actually explain a lot."

He started kissing me again, hard, soft, licks and nips all over my face and shoulders. He cupped my breasts and then reached down to rake his nails across my tender ass. When I complained, he muffled my whimpers with more kisses, violent ones. I lost track of what happened after that. More sex, more pain, more tender caresses. More sex.

I was dying to see this dungeon now. *Yes, Sir. No, Sir. What can I do for you, Sir?* I begged him for details as I drifted to sleep but he wouldn't answer me. He just left the specter of a Price-designed dungeon hanging over my head. I pictured something awful, cold, and elegantly sadistic. I fell asleep dreaming of a dark, dank cement room with chains looping down from the ceiling, and whips lined up along the wall.

When I woke the next morning, Price was gone. I vaguely remembered him kissing me around seven, and pulling closed the curtains against the morning light. I stretched my limbs, thrilled by the ache and burn. I felt weak and emptied out, and confused as ever about what had happened between us last night.

The dungeon.

I sat up and listened. I didn't hear him, didn't hear any sound in the apartment. I grabbed my towel from the night before, wrapped up, and tiptoed out into the hall to look for the dungeon door. He'd said it was right next to his room, but there was no entrance on either side. Damn. The doors on the other side of the hall stood open, revealing tasteful guest rooms and a home office. I sighed and retreated back to his bed.

"You're fucking me up," I said to no one, in the luxuriant silence of the room. I curled up in the smooth sheets, then leaned down to smell his pillow. It held his scent, just like my aching body held his marks and bruises. I rolled back to my own pillow and noticed a note from him on the side table.

Went for a run. Back soon.

Help yourself to whatever's in the kitchen.

I picked up the note and found another one underneath, also in his handwriting.

Number of stars in my bowl: 1

Number of shadows in my soul: 1

Holy fucking shit.

PRICE

First mistake: taking her to my place.

Second mistake: admitting I had a dungeon with her name on it.

I only left her alone in the apartment because I knew she wouldn't find it. It was hidden, sort of like our feelings toward each other.

Third mistake: quoting D.H. Lawrence right after mind-blowing sex.

I'd named her the star in my bowl, the shadow in my soul. What was that shit? Most of the time I had my emo side under control, but her fucking questions in the shower had tapped a bunch of unwanted memories. My relationship history was a morass of rejection, castigation, and deceit. I didn't trust love. I didn't trust any woman on earth, but I was starting to trust her. That morning, looking down at her snuggled in my bed, I'd confessed too much. My bad.

Now she'd take that paper home and put it with the rest of them, and fantasize that I loved her when my love was a toxic, hurtful thing.

I couldn't really say where I expected us to end up. I just knew my love wasn't good for her.

I also knew I was getting worse, not better. I wanted all of her, every day.

PRICE

On a drizzly April afternoon in Lower Manhattan, Chere graduated from the Norton School of Art and Design. She graduated panty-less, for the record. I thought that was important, and no one could tell thanks to the long, black robe she wore over her dress. My grandmother would have been proud to see the first Stephensen scholarship recipient graduate with high honors. To my chagrin, Martin Cantor handed her the diploma. Fucking Martin.

I took her to dinner afterward, to a glitzy, ritzy showplace with no prices on the menu. She always said these kinds of restaurants made her uncomfortable, but I loved making her uncomfortable, so it all worked out. I enjoyed her anxiety almost as much as I enjoyed the gourmet dishes set before us.

"So what happens now?" I asked as our waiter whisked away the final course.

"Dessert?" she said.

"No, I mean, what are you going to do now that you've graduated? What's next for you? Where are you planning to look for a job?"

"Oh." She rubbed her forehead for a moment. "Tiffany, maybe. Or one of the smaller jewelry firms that recruited at Norton."

"In other words, you haven't thought about it."

She gave me a withering look. "My internship was at an architectural firm, so I'm kind of behind the curve on my job search."

"What about my investment idea? Using some of my cash to start your own company?"

She looked sideways at me and tugged her hair. "I don't know."

"What do you mean, you don't know? What don't you like about the idea?"

"I feel like you've already given me too much."

That response sounded distancing. Protective. Maybe she questioned my motives. Hell, *I* questioned my motives. I didn't want to help her start a business, so much as I wanted to prevent her from working for someone else. That someone might overwork her or exploit her, or ask her to relocate to a branch in Hong Kong. We'd have to go back to arranged visits, to occasional, fleeting sessions in hotel rooms.

No.

"You should do what you want to do," I said brusquely. "Like I said on your evaluation, you're ready for whatever your future holds. Just don't..."

"Don't what?" she asked, when I didn't finish.

"Don't let some asshole take advantage of you."

I said this with a straight face, like I wasn't a huge asshole who took advantage of her at every turn. But she'd had worse assholes in her life, like her ex-boyfriend, Simon, or her ex-pimp, Henry, both of whom had exploited her for their own gain.

"I won't let anyone take advantage," she said, rearranging her napkin in her lap. "I know better now."

"If you're not sure you're getting into a good situation, ask for my opinion. Tell me what's going on and I'll tell you if it's legit. I've been involved in design for a while. I've worked with a lot of great people, but I've worked with a lot of fuckheads too."

I shut my mouth because I sounded like a know-it-all idiot. The waiter brought dessert, some chocolate goo with smears of raspberry garnish that looked like blood.

"Mahogany sacrifice," I murmured. "Next season's colors."

Chere burst out in laughter that was too loud for the opulent surroundings. The couple next to us looked over in disapproval and I glared at them until they looked away. Chere covered her mouth with her napkin.

"Sorry," she said, catching her breath. "Am I making a scene?"

"Yes, you fucking are."

That sent her off into more peals of laughter.

"Eat your fucking dessert," I scolded. "The chef worked very hard to make it look as if the cake was slaughtered. It's all the rage. Primal *patisserie*."

"Stop," she begged. She had tears in her eyes. Not angsty tears for once, but laughter tears. She finally managed to compose herself. "I'm sorry."

"I'll make you sorry, you fucking slut."

She grinned at me over a bite of cake. "I love when you're in a flirty mood."

I stared into her dark eyes, into lust and humor and miraculous acceptance. No other woman would consider those words flirting. I'd never let her go to Hong Kong. If she tried it, I would stop her. I'd fucking tell her no, that it wasn't allowed.

"I don't want you to leave the city," I said.

"What?"

"When you look for jobs, look for something in New York. In Manhattan, if possible. I don't want you to leave the city."

I'd told her so many times that I wouldn't interfere in her life, or do anything to affect her career. I saw the confusion in her silent regard.

"I can't fuck you if you're not here," I explained, which was the basic point of this conversation.

"You work outside New York all the time."

"But I come back. I'm here. I want you to be here too."

She was suddenly very interested in the tablecloth.

"What?" I said impatiently. "Am I being unreasonable?"

"Well, I mean..." She looked up at me. "Do you get to choose where I work? Which job I accept?"

"I'm only explaining that you need to work in the city or there's no fucking point."

"No point to what?" She hunched up her shoulders and glanced around the glittering room. "What are we doing, Price? Where is our thing going?"

Fuck. I hoped she wouldn't ask that, because I didn't fucking know.

"Are you going to start up with the girly shit again?" I snapped, because the best defense was a good offense.

"It's not girly shit. It's a legitimate question. I have to make some decisions about where my life's going."

"And?"

"And," she said, with a barely restrained eye roll, "are we headed anywhere, like, commitment-wise?"

Neither one of us touched our plates of chocolate cake. They sat between us, berry stained monstrosities.

"I mean, I just want to know," she said.

I sighed and pushed the cake to the side. "I thought you were done with relationships. I thought you wanted us to stay detached. You know about our 'thing,' Chere. I want to fuck you. I want you available for fucking. Are you going to start whining about your feelings now, and my lack of commitment? Because I'm not going to put up with it."

"Oh, are you going to leave?"

Fuck!

It was a perfectly timed and scathingly executed reminder that I didn't hold all the power in our anti-relationship. It put me off my game for a moment. The waiter brought the check, providing me some time to gather my shit.

Why was she pressing me for these kinds of answers? We'd both agreed we didn't want to get embroiled in some complicated relationship. I took out my card and studied her stiff posture, her guarded expression. I wished I had the laughter back.

"This is stupid," I said. "You just graduated. Why are we discussing this tonight?"

"Because I just graduated."

"So what? Nothing has to change. All I said was that I wanted you to get a job in the city. That's all."

"You can't make those decisions. Unless..."

"Unless what?" I asked, even though I knew the answer.

"Unless we're a couple," she said. "A committed couple."

I snorted. "Is that what you want, Chere? That hot fucking mess?"

"It doesn't have to be a mess."

"Any relationship with me would be a mess. Trust me. You'd end up a miserable wreck, and you've been there, done that, right? You said you didn't want that again."

"A miserable wreck? Really? You keep saying how bad you'd be for me, all dungeons and torture all the time, but I don't believe you." Her steady gaze skewered me. "You give me poetry. You have feelings. I know you have feelings," she repeated when I looked away.

"Keep your fucking voice down."

"You care about me. You wouldn't have done all the things you've done if you didn't have a heart. Why can't we try a relationship and see where it goes?"

It'll go to hell, starshine. It'll go to sadness and destruction. Out loud I said, "I don't want a fucking relationship with you. Get over it. There's no fucking way."

She kept at me like a fucking badger. "All through the internship you told me *there's always a way. Don't let anyone tell you no.* I know we're both fucked up. I know we both have issues—"

"I meant that there was always a way in *design.*"

We fell silent, scowling from opposite sides of the table. The waiter slunk back to get my card. Once he left, she frowned at me and sat up very straight.

"There's a way for us, Price," she said.

"Oh yeah?" I sneered. "Love? Marriage? Children?"

"If you want it. You said to never accept the answer no."

"Too bad. I'm telling you no. That's not what I want."

"The dungeon then. A slave and a lover."

A slave and a lover. Would that be so bad?

Yes. For her, it would be the worst fucking thing of all.

"You just graduated," I said again, and now I sounded like I was pleading.

"What are you afraid of?"

I'm afraid of your unhappiness. I'm afraid you'll want to go, and I won't want to let you go.

"Can't we wait?" I asked. "Can't we wait a fucking month or two, until you're settled in a job? I like things the way they are. Why do we have to force ourselves into some kind of serious relationship just because you're out of school?"

She looked away from me, hunching her shoulders even higher. She didn't understand. *There's always a way*, she insisted. Why had I told her that? Every relationship I'd ever entered had ended in drama or litigation.

There was no happily ever after with a guy like me, which I'd repeatedly tried to explain to her.

But maybe…this time…

She's not like the other ones.

That was the danger. She wasn't like the other ones. She didn't just want my cock or my money. She was after my fucking soul.

CHERE

"So, can you come?" Andrew asked, bouncing up and down on my couch. "You have to come. It's going to be a huge party. Craig's invited tons of his art friends, and three or four of the curators from the Met."

"I'm definitely coming," I said, which sent him into more paroxysms of joy.

Now that Andrew had graduated, his boyfriend Craig was throwing him a launch party at the gallery where he worked. They were going to put up Andrew's paintings and show them off to everyone in Manhattan's high-art network, from the tastemakers to the gallery owners and museum curators. It was perfect timing, because Andrew had recently turned in his notice to Henry. He told me he felt like a quitter.

I told him it was okay, because he'd found something better than escorting. Love.

Yes, Andrew was in love. I'd met Craig and Andrew for dinner a few days ago, and I absolutely approved. They were an amazing couple. Price had come too, to finally meet my friend. It was the first time we'd had a "date" type of dinner with another couple. Andrew had phoned me afterward to swoon repeatedly about Price, at least until Craig called him away into the bedroom. They were already living together, because they were that loved up.

Meanwhile…Price and I…

Ugh. I'd talked the big talk about wanting to be independent, about not wanting to participate in any more relationships, but I was full-on in love with him again, and the sentiment was *not* returned. The most committed thing we'd done since I graduated was exchange test results so we could stop using condoms.

As for my job search, I tweaked my resume and sent it out, but the big houses were looking for on-trend designers, not someone who delighted in the strange and spare. Bulgari offered to bring me on as an unpaid intern, but the last thing I wanted was another internship. My career advisor at Norton called the second week out. Was I finding success in my job search? Had I tapped into my contacts? When I explained my unsuitability for the current market, they advised me to stay in touch with my internship mentor.

"Yeah," I said, rubbing my temples. "I've been doing that."

Price hounded me to strike out on my own. He said I had a vision, something new to offer the world if I'd get my ass in gear and go for it. He told me he'd punish me if I didn't secure my first bespoke customer by August. All I could think was, *why am I in love with you again, after what happened last time? Why am I so fucked up?*

"You'll bring Price to the party, yes? Tell me you'll bring Price," Andrew begged, growing giddy again. "That tall, blond, Scandinavian drink of water. Honey, you're lucky he's not gay, or I'd be all over him."

"I thought you loved Craig."

"I do love Craig, but can't a boy dream? I'm envisioning a Craig and Price sandwich in this mysterious dungeon of his."

I hadn't heard anything more from Price about the dungeon. I suppose I'd stalled in my attempts to become dungeon-worthy. We were having plenty of sex and I was enduring plenty of lessons in surrender, but somehow it wasn't enough.

"How much time do you spend with Craig?" I asked. "Like, in a typical week?"

"All the time I can," he answered dreamily.

"No, I'm talking specifics. How many hours a day?"

"I don't know, babes. As many hours as we can. I love him. I want to be with him."

I thought a moment. "How much of that time are you Dom/sub, or Master/slave, or whatever you're playing around with right now?"

"Hmm. Maybe an hour or two? Long enough for him to fuck me up," he said with a laugh. "Look at this. Freaking look." He drew up the legs of his skater shorts enough to show me a row of lines across his thighs. Cane lines. I shuddered as I recognized them.

"I'm sorry."

"I was sorry too. He didn't even tie me up. He just made me sit on a hard chair and take it. I also had a gargantuan plug in my ass."

I was happy to hear I wasn't the only one being inhumanely tortured by a Dominant partner.

"And look at this." He knelt up on my couch and pulled his waistband down over his cheeks.

"I don't want to see your ass plug," I complained.

"I'm not wearing one now. Look at my ass. Look at my bruises." He waved his butt at me, showing his impressively dark bruises with a proud smile.

I wondered what my bruises looked like. Price had used the Lucite paddle on me again the night before. I yanked my pants down too.

"Wow." Andrew whistled as he looked at my battered cheeks. "I bet that was painful."

I didn't mention that I'd also been wearing a gargantuan ass plug. Showing my naked, bruised butt to my gay friend was pretty much the limit of sharing for me. I pulled my pants back up and looked closer at Andrew's ass, at tiny, clustered patterns of dots.

"How did he do that?" I asked, pointing to the little red pinpricks.

"Something called a vampire paddle. He ordered it from Germany. God, I adore Craig. He's so twisted. He says he's going to put me in chastity soon. You know, the whole cage contraption on my cock, with the lock and key and everything? Just for fun."

I'd learned a little about male chastity during my trips to the BDSM clubs. It didn't seem that "fun," but to each his own. I hoped that Price didn't know anything about vampire paddles.

Andrew talked for a while longer about the depraved things Craig did to him during their play sessions, which made me feel a little better about my own deepening sexual perversity.

"Does Craig ever choke you?" I asked. "Like, with his hand, or a belt?"

"Oh, God, yes," he said, clasping his neck. "I love it."

"Does he do it until you pass out?"

His eyes widened. "Price chokes you out? Isn't that scary? Craig never goes that far."

"It's kind of scary. He only does it every once in a while. When I wake up, he's always kissing me."

"I want him, Chere. For real. I want your man. I'm going to try to turn him gay."

"You know what's funny?" I said, ignoring Andrew's silliness. "We both ended up having inappropriate relationships with our mentors. *Really* inappropriate relationships. What would Norton say if they knew?"

"I know what Cantor would say." Andrew imitated his prickle-inducing gaze. "*I should have been her mentor.*"

He was so spot on with the speech pattern and intonation that I burst out laughing. "I wonder what good old Professor Predator is up to these days."

"I know what he's up to. My friend Tracy sees him at Studio Valiant all the time. He's apparently getting kind of serious with this girl. Woman. An older woman. I mean, you know, not a student. Who would have imagined?"

So even Cantor was having a serious, real relationship outside his wackadoo open marriage. Why was everyone else hooking up so easily and so naturally when I couldn't even qualify for Price's dungeon?

"Good for Cantor," I said glumly.

"Are you jealous? Your thing with Price is way hotter, I'm sure."

"It's hot, but..."

"But what?" he prodded.

"I don't know. I feel like he could leave again tomorrow. I like the rush of being with him, but I feel like all we have is adrenaline, and mystery. There's nothing real between us, and he keeps it that way on purpose."

"Why does he do that?"

"I don't know. It's like, he'll open up to me to a certain point, and I'll think, wow, I'm really seeing him now, and then he'll retreat and get all mean again. It's frustrating. He doesn't talk about his feelings, and he doesn't allow me to talk about mine."

"That's fucking weird."

"But he gives me poetry. He spouts poetry all the time."

He held my hand between his, stroking his thumb over my fingers. "You know what? I think he loves you. I think he's falling for you so hard that he's fighting it. Give him a little more time to open up. He always had his thing about privacy, right?"

"I guess."

"And it's been three years, but it hasn't really been three years, you know? It's been a few weeks since you got back together. You two will figure things out."

"Maybe you're right," I said, leaning into Andrew's hug. "Maybe everything will eventually become clear."

"Probably not. Love is never clear. But if you feel it, you know it."

"I don't trust my love meter at all. I thought I was in love with Simon."

"Simon was a freaky case. How do you feel when you're with Price?"

I didn't even know how to answer that question. Maybe that was answer enough.

PRICE

Chere and I arrived at Andrew's party about an hour after it began. The gallery was packed with students, teachers, and the best of the art world glitterati. It took us a while to hunt down Andrew and his partner Craig. When we finally found them, Andrew threw himself into Chere's arms.

"You came! You're here! I'm so happy to see you. And Mr. Eriksen!"

"Price," I said, shaking his hand. I'd told him five times already to call me Price, but he never listened, maybe because he was half my age. "Congrats on the art degree."

"Thanks."

I turned to greet Craig, who seemed like a stand-up guy. I liked that he was older than Andrew. It made me feel less creepy about being older than Chere.

"Great party," I said. "Very impressive crowd."

Craig gestured toward Andrew, who was whispering in Chere's ear. "Trying to get Andy off to a good start. It's hell out there for a painter."

"Any artist, really. That's why I went back to school for an engineering degree."

Craig laughed. "It was business for me."

"I did that too."

He clapped me on the back. "It's an honor to have you here, and I'm glad you brought Chere. Not sure the two of them would have made it through the last year of art school without each other." He pointed to a swarm of people across the room. "There's tons of food, champagne, you name it. Make yourself at home."

The flat, white gallery walls didn't absorb sound, so the voices in the room rose and fell in sharp tones. There was color everywhere, painted faces looking at painted canvases. We sipped champagne and picked at some appetizers, then walked around the walls looking at Andrew's art. Some of it had already sold, which delighted her. His work contained a bright realism that meshed with his personality, sort of how Chere's work was intricate and elegant, just like her.

After a while, Andrew pulled her away to meet some of his friends. I hung back, content to watch her work the room, smile and offer her card. *Good girl.* This was where she belonged, not selling what she had between her legs, but selling the creative wonderland between her ears.

The party rolled on, a classy, boisterous affair. Even Henry showed up, staying long enough to congratulate Chere and Andrew on their graduation. He shook my hand and, facetiously, congratulated me too. Nice of her pimp to come out, but I had mixed feelings every time I saw him. He'd brought her to me, but he'd used her too, made money off her.

Protected me, Chere told me, the one time we talked about it. *He was good to me.*

Was I good to her? She was getting restless in our sex-only relationship. I enjoyed our sordid assignations and I wanted them to continue, but there was a growing tension between us, some idea that we should be taking a next step. For me the next step was harder sex and deeper pain, and more frequent sessions. It was a collar, and my dungeon. For her, the next step was love and caring, and interconnectedness… She needed to realize I wasn't some fairy tale prince.

While she continued her chat with Henry, I headed to the bar to get something a little stronger than champagne. While I waited for the bartender to pour, I couldn't help hearing a loud conversation behind me.

"I can't believe he's here," said a woman's voice. "And fresh out of fucking rehab. I was counting on his untimely death to drive up the price of his work."

"Glenda! That's awful."

"That's business. I sell on commission. Jesus, he looks great," she drawled, as if this disappointed her.

I turned to look at the two women. One was older, with a pointy nose and big teeth, and the other closer to Andrew's age, in a red, fringed cape. The older one texted furiously on her phone.

"I hardly recognized him, girl," she said, fingers flying. "He looks…human. Apparently the old guy beside him is his 'sober companion.'" She said the last part in a sneer.

"Omigod," said the younger one, giggling. "I give it a couple of weeks."

"I know, right? Two months ago he was mixing heroin and meth. Simon Baldwin hasn't painted sober in ages. I don't know what makes him think he can do it now."

They looked at me then, and I thought, *Simon is here,* and *Chere is here* and *fuck fuck fuck.*

"Here's your drink. Hey, man, here's your vodka tonic."

I turned at the bartender's voice, took my drink, and shoved some money in the tip jar. I scanned the room.

"Oh my God, Mr. Eriksen." Andrew came flying up to me.

"Price," I said between my teeth.

"Price." Andrew tugged on my arm. "Simon is here. I swear to God I didn't invite him."

"As long as he stays the fuck away from Chere."

Andrew turned me around and pointed to the two of them in the middle of a crowd across the room. I could see Simon's face, but not Chere's. He was as dark and ugly as I remembered. His features made me think of a weasel. *Why was she talking to him?*

"Craig says I should leave them alone," Andrew said. "He says it's a big deal that Simon Baldwin showed up here, but after all the shit he did to Chere…" He wrung his hands. "I think I'm going to go over and kick him out."

It was a brave sentiment, but a fledgling painter couldn't confront a living legend in front of this art crowd, and order him to go.

"Don't make a scene at your own party," I said. "I'll take care of it."

I wasn't sure what I meant to "take care of." From Simon's expression, he and Chere were having a normal, cordial conversation. An older man flanked him. His sober companion? Rich, privileged fucks could have something so coddling as a "sober companion," a hired friend to follow them around and encourage them to make good choices. I should have been happy to see Simon cleaned up and sober, but all I felt was rage.

I didn't want him near her. I didn't want him looking at her or breathing the same air. *Asshole. You hurt her.* When he smiled at her, it was a shitty, insincere smile. I didn't care if he was sober now. I'd never forgive him for what he did to Chere, and I wouldn't let her forgive him either. I pushed a group of idiot gawkers out of my way so I could take her arm.

She looked over, and I saw relief in her face. That glimmer of relief calmed some of my riotous anger. She wasn't any happier to see him than I was.

"Who's this?" asked Simon as I glared at him.

"P.T. Eriksen," I replied, shoving out my hand. "I wish I could say it's a pleasure to meet you, but you're an asshole. When you were with my friend here, you treated her like shit."

His hand went limp halfway through our shake. His sober companion seemed flummoxed by this blunt confrontation. I could feel Chere staring at me but I kept my gaze on Simon's face.

After a moment, he shrugged. "Chere and I went through some dark times together."

"You went through them *together*?" I repeated, restraining myself from slugging him. "I think you went through the dark times, and dragged her down with you."

"He's doing better," Chere interjected, her voice high with anxiety. "He went to rehab."

Simon spread his arms with a sigh. "I have a lot to atone for. I was just telling Chere how sorry I was for all the shit I put her through."

He looked sorry as a fucking punk. I glanced at Chere. Was she falling for this bullshit, for his angelic, fake expression?

"So, the Tribeca Train Wreck is sober," I said, turning back to him. "How has it affected your art?"

Simon looked at Chere, like, *who is this guy?* "I'm pretty new out of rehab," he said to me. "So I don't know yet, but I imagine everything will be fine."

"If not, you could always get back into the narcotics. Want a vodka tonic?" I asked, holding out my drink.

"Price," Chere said quietly. She shook her head at me. "Don't."

Don't wasn't going to work for me right now. Everything about him was pushing my buttons. I'd seen Simon in person once, at a gallery show three years ago, but I'd never had the displeasure of standing this close to him. Now that we were face to face, with Chere beside me, I felt dangerously close to losing my shit.

Simon tilted his head at us. "You two are together?"

"We're friends," she said, at the same time I said "Yes."

The last fake drop of pleasantness leached out of Simon's rehabbed features. "I get it," he said. "You're her *customer*."

"He's not a customer," said Chere. "I'm not escorting anymore."

"She graduated from Norton with honors," I added. "She's a designer now. She does amazing work with metals and jewelry."

"I saw your pimp here," Simon said, ignoring me. "I don't care if this dude's your customer, if you're still into your—" He waved a hand. "Your prostitute shit. Whatever."

"My *prostitute shit*?" Chere locked eyes with Simon and took a step in his direction. "My prostitute shit?" she repeated through her teeth. "My prostitute shit paid for your fucking livelihood when no one knew who you were. My prostitute shit kept us in that fucking expensive studio loft and paid for your fucking expensive drugs."

The sober companion held up a hand. "Let's stay civilized, shall we?"

"I don't know if that's possible," said Chere. "Simon and I don't have a very civilized past."

"I said I was sorry." Simon threw up his hands. Conversations were going silent. People were staring. "You never seemed that put out by the work. It was kind of your thing."

"It was my thing because you were putting thousands of dollars up your fucking nose on a weekly basis," said Chere.

"You never tried very hard to stop me," he shot back.

"Wait." I held up a hand. I was so close to beating him. So close. "Are you saying it was *her* fault you were using drugs? Because *she* didn't stop you?"

"She was the reason I started in the first place," he said nastily. "Ask her. Ask her how things were. It's hard to be happy when your girlfriend's a whore."

I felt Chere stiffen beside me. I saw Andrew and Craig pushing forward, their faces pale with concern. But most of all, I saw Simon's lips curl and his eyes rake over Chere in condescending judgment. It was all I could fucking take.

I threw a fist and connected with his face. The sober companion gasped and jumped backward. Andrew screamed. People shouted and glass shattered as a waiter dropped a tray of champagne. I made sure Chere was out of the way and then Simon and I locked in grappling combat. Sober or not, Simon Baldwin had a beating coming and I was more than happy to give it to him.

I only got a punch or two in before he went down like a pansy. I dragged him outside and told him to stay the fuck away from Chere forever, while Andrew's party guests catcalled and shot video. Chere touched my throbbing cheekbone—the one place he'd got me—and cried.

Somewhere along the line, his sober companion called the police. They showed up in a barrage of flashing lights and I got arrested.

It was worth it, one hundred percent.

CHERE

Price had a lawyer on retainer, and lots of money, so he only spent an hour in the holding cell. Once his lawyer bailed him out, he strolled into the common area with his tie, belt, and cufflinks in a manila envelope, and a garish bruise on his cheekbone from his throwdown with Simon. I'd had a bruise in the exact same place during our session at the Four Seasons three years ago, a bruise Simon had given me during one of his rages. Price had been so angry when he noticed it. He'd called me a fucking idiot and told me *Love lies.*

I took in his disarranged hair, his bruised face, and his sullen expression, and I thought, *I love you, you messed-up asshole.*

He was in a prickly mood, but I hugged him anyway and reached to stroke the discoloration on his face. I didn't want to hurt him; I just wanted to acknowledge what he'd done for me. He leaned his head back and halted me with a glare.

"Why are you here?"

"I wanted to be sure you were okay."

"I'm fine." He grimaced at his attorney, then looked back at me. "For the record, it was worth the amount of money I'll have to pay to settle this."

He meant *You were worth it.* His deep blue eyes raked over me before he turned to speak briefly with his lawyer. I waited for their conversation to end, feeling scared and defensive, and a little overwhelmed by everything that had happened at Andrew's party. There were so many emotional words I wanted to say, but I knew he wouldn't accept them. When he turned his attention back to me, I settled for commenting on his appearance.

"You look like a criminal."

That wasn't really true. He looked amazing for someone who'd been in a fight and then spent an hour in jail. "Were you locked up with any thugs?"

"I was locked up with a passed-out drunk guy. Let's go home."

His lawyer, Mr. Dunsingbush of Klein and Dunsingbush, had brought Price some takeout burgers and fries. He took the bag and thanked the man, and promised to call him in the morning.

We got into a cab and shared his late-night meal. Then, instead of parting ways, he invited himself to my apartment to spend the night, and I didn't argue. I knew he needed to blow off some steam and I kind of looked forward to his aggression. As soon as we stepped through the door, he was on me. He grabbed me and kissed me, and traced his fingers up my neck.

"Criminal," I whispered as he stroked my windpipe. "Have sex with me."

"Oh, I'm going to."

I pushed off his suit jacket and worked at his shirt buttons. Before I could finish, he stuck his fingers in the neckline of my silk dress and tore it all the way down the front. *Shit.* I protested between his violent kisses and tried to push him away, but he only finished the job, yanking the scraps of my dress off my shoulders. My bra and panties were tossed on the floor beside the rest of his clothes.

"Be nice," I said. "Don't hurt me."

He laughed and dragged me to the bedroom. I couldn't tell if he was turned on or angry. I tried to catch his gaze. *Look at me. What are you feeling? How can I help you?*

Do you love me?

I think you love me.

He threw me back on the bed and crawled on top of me. "Ready to be fucked?" he asked.

His hands were rough on my skin, stroking and pinching and pulling me toward him when I tried to move away. I was used to Price's violent forms of passion, but this was especially heightened. I fought back because I still hadn't really internalized the thing about surrender. Dungeon-worthy? Not yet. When he pressed me to the bed, I tried to flip over. When he slapped my breasts, I punched his shoulder. When his cock poked between my legs, I scooted back on instinct.

"No," he growled. He grabbed my hips and yanked me back across the sheets. No matter how hard I struggled, I couldn't escape his grasp as he forced me onto his thrusting length. He drove all the way in and I arched up to embrace him, because I was feeling so much and needing so much. He let go of my hips and grabbed my shoulders, and shoved me backward. When I kept surging upward, he grabbed my neck.

"Lay the fuck down," he said. "You belong to me. You're mine."

I couldn't respond to that claim because he was choking me. I moved my hips, not sure if I was trying to evade his thrusts or draw them deeper. I felt locked in high-stakes combat, the battle of protecting my heart and my independence, and yet wanting to give up everything to him.

"Don't," I begged through my teeth as his fingers tightened on my neck.

He didn't like being told what to do, so he choked me harder. I felt buzzing in my ears, in the corners of my brain, and then nothingness washed over me like a black, gauzy shroud. It seemed I slept for hours, but that couldn't have been true, because the first thing I noticed when I returned to awareness was that he was still inside me, still over me. Still fucking me hard.

His fingers loosened, but they remained around my neck. He gazed down at me, blue laser beams permeating my hazy thoughts.

What had he said before I went out? *You're mine.* I murmured words that made no sense, a litany of babble. *You. Mine. Please. Yes. You. You. You. Love. You.*

I reached up to him, ran my fingers over his abs as his muscles worked, as he drove his cock inside me over and over. "I love you," I said.

His lips turned down. He shook his head, a curt motion of disapproval.

"I love you," I repeated, like maybe he hadn't understood me the first time.

"Shut the fuck up." He let go of my neck, grabbed my questing hands and pushed them down on the bed.

Tears rose in my eyes. He didn't understand, or couldn't understand. "I love you," I insisted on the edge of a sob. "I love you. I love you."

"No!"

He pressed a hand over my mouth. I twisted and tried to bite him, and found myself wrestled onto my stomach. I wrapped my fingers in the sheets and held on as he pounded me. I didn't think he'd ever fucked me this hard. He felt so thick and so big, and he was scaring and arousing me at the same time with his frenzied attack. The more I tried to resist him, the harder he drove into me. *Take me, take me, yes. Make me scream. Make me come.*

But you have to let me love you too.

The tears finally spilled over as sobs welled in my throat. I felt his hand at my nape. I tried to struggle to my knees to crawl away but my thighs collapsed before I could get very far. He yanked my hair to signal his displeasure at my "girly shit" and pressed me down like a weight. When I continued to flail, he collected my wrists behind me and held them far up on my back.

"You're hurting me," I bawled.

"Good, I want to."

"Let me see you." I turned my head, straining to look back at him. "I want to see you."

"No."

I stopped trying to turn over and ground my clit against the bed. I heard his lascivious chuckle just before he reached down and clapped his other hand over my pussy. Now I was grinding against his fingers, arching my hips for the fleeting, intermittent contact he allowed.

"Please touch me," I begged.

"You have my cock," he said roughly. "You need your clit stroked too? Spoiled fucking brat."

But he opened his fingers and let me ride him until my pelvis shuddered and my legs jerked at the jolts of delicious sensation. I whined in my throat, animal noises, and the closer he took me to climax, the louder I got. His cock banged over my G-spot while my aching shoulders shook from the strain of having my arms twisted behind me. When the orgasm finally washed over me, I felt pain everywhere, but pleasure too, the kind that left you wrung out and shivering in the aftermath.

He didn't let go of my wrists until he'd groaned through his own orgasm. When he did finally release me, it was a slow, deliberate letting go, like he was freeing me one nerve ending at a time. I shivered and pulled my arms beneath me. They hurt. My heart hurt. Love hurt. *Love me, damn it.*

He withdrew and collapsed next to me on the bed. I turned to him but he was facing away, his hand covering his eyes. It wasn't a welcoming position. I could see the faint shadow of his bruise under his fingertips. After a minute or two of paralyzing silence, I got up to use the bathroom, then went to the kitchen to put some ice in a plastic bag.

I returned and approached his side of the bed. He lay so still he might have been sleeping.

"Do you want ice for your face?" I asked.

"No."

I pressed it to the bruise anyway, very gently.

He sent the ice flying across the room. "I said no. What the fuck is wrong with you?"

I watched the bag of ice hit the wall and slide down to rest in the corner. "I was trying to help you," I said. "Please don't do shit like that. It reminds me of Simon."

"Don't fucking say his name."

I frowned down at him, not that he noticed. "You remind me of him sometimes," I said on a sharp note. "You act like him sometimes. You act worse."

He gave a mirthless laugh. "Well, your loverboy's sober now. If you like him better, maybe he'll take you back."

He was punishing me for saying I loved him. I understood that, but it didn't make his cruelty any easier to bear.

"I love you," I said, just to poke at him.

He pursed his lips. "You loved Simon, so I don't put much stock in your fucking feelings."

"He loved me too, once. We were in love before the drugs. He made a painting about me, called *Heart-Lust.* I cried, because it was the first time anyone had ever done something like that for me, made some grand gesture. It was the first time I felt like I was worth something. The second time…"

I waited until he raised his head to glare at me.

"The second time was at the Mandarin Oriental Hotel, when you gave me the key to this apartment. When you sat and sewed my dress."

He rolled onto his back and covered his eyes again, this time with a muscular forearm. "I sewed your dress because it was ripped."

"You sewed my dress because you cared about me. You gave me this apartment because I meant something to you."

"I gave you this apartment because you were a little too content playing Simon's punching bag."

I gritted my teeth, furious that he'd be the asshole Price now, when I needed him to be the thoughtful, human Price. I needed him to *love me.* "Why are you always like this?" I yelled. I flew at him, trying to pry his arm away from his face.

He came off the bed, grabbing hold of my hands before I could rake my nails over his skin. "What the fuck is the matter with you? What do you fucking want from me?"

"Anything! I want you to just...just..." I grabbed at my chest. "Just give me something of yourself."

"Love?" he scoffed.

"Anything. Simon at least painted something for me. He created something for me. He shared his feelings."

"I share my feelings. You just don't like them. They're not the feelings you want."

"Because they're not your real feelings. Even your poetry was written by someone else, for someone else. What have you ever given me that comes from yourself?"

"I've given you a lot of things, damn it." He stared at me over the space between us. "A lot of helpful things. A lot of expensive things."

"An apartment, a full ride to college? A trip to Oslo?" I wrenched my hands from his grasp. "I never asked for any of that. Why can't you just give me some normal fucking emotions? Why won't you admit you feel something for me? For us?"

I hated that he was making me do this, making me break down and beg him for love while he stood there looking irritated and bored. He had told me, *Love lies.* But it was so, so much more complicated than that.

"You're better off if I don't love you," he said, leaving me to cross the room and pick up the bag of ice from the floor.

"Yes. Same old line. Same old excuses."

"They're not excuses. They're warnings." He leaned against the wall, holding the ice to his cheekbone. "I keep a distance between us for your protection."

"Bullshit. That's a fucking lie. A cop-out. I think you keep a distance between us because there's nothing inside you that can love. There's nothing inside you but selfish emptiness, and money, and violence."

"That's not true."

"You're a cold, selfish, rich, manipulative ass—"

"Chere."

"And you don't love me because it doesn't suit your purposes. You use me for sex the same way Simon used me for money. To get your fix!"

He flung the bag of ice down and stalked toward me. *Shit, shit, shit.* Now I'd pissed him off.

"When did you turn into such a needy, delusional bitch?" he yelled. "I'm sorry if I don't live up to your romantic-fantasy standards. I'm sorry that everything I've done for you is shit. If you don't want the fucking poems, then fucking get rid of them. Burn them, shred them. I don't give a fuck." He caught my elbows, hurting me, digging his fingers into my skin. "If they don't mean anything to you, why have you kept them? Why did you hold onto them all those years?"

I shied back from his angry questions, and gave him my angry reply. "Because they were all I had to remember you by. They're still all I have." I beat my fists against his chest. "When are you going to give me something that's *you*? Where are you? Who are you? What's inside of you? It's been three fucking years, Price, and I still don't know."

"What do you mean, you don't know? I've never hidden my true self from you." He shook me hard, once, and let go. "You're the only one who's ever let me be myself. I'm only sorry—"

He turned away.

"I'm sorry it's not enough," he said roughly. "I guess we were never enough for each other."

He spun on his heel and walked out of my bedroom, his back muscles tense and his jaw clenched. I followed him to the living room, where he snatched up his clothes and began to dress.

Holy shit. I'd wanted to push him to open up to me, to love me. Instead, he seemed poised to break up with me. I started backpedaling, retracting my words in a panic.

"I'm just confused by you," I said. "Maybe I'm asking too much."

"You're not asking too much." In those curt, resigned words, I knew I'd pushed too far, to the point where he'd decided to give up on our entire relationship. He shoved his arms into his shirt sleeves. "You're asking me for things any normal person would want. I'm glad you're normal. Unfortunately, I'm not."

I looked down at the shards of my dress as he scooped up his jacket and started toward the door. I stepped in front of him, hugging my arms over my breasts. "What does that mean?"

He waved a hand for me to move. "It's late. I have to go."

"Now? Can't you stay and talk? What about us?"

He looked down, held my gaze for long seconds. He was gone. There was no more "us" to talk about. He was leaving me a second time, and I knew this time it would be for good.

"I can't do this anymore," he said quietly, without rancor. "I can't be what you want. I don't have it in me." He gave a soft, bitter chuckle. "You're right when you say there's nothing inside me, starshine. Somehow you've always known me better than anyone else."

I blinked at him. "I didn't mean it when I said that."

"I think you did. I care for you, Chere, enough to..." His voice went on, breaking my heart as his fingers slipped around mine for a moment. "Enough to let you go. I think it's best if we parted ways."

"Price—"

"And I'm not going to give you some poem to remember me by, because you're right, that's shitty. It's someone else's words and feelings, not mine." His lips tightened. "I'd give you my words and feelings if I knew what they were. But you're right. I don't fucking know. I don't know what's inside me, especially when it comes to you."

He let go of my hand, kissed my forehead, then opened the door with inexorable words of parting, his own blunt poetry.

"I just know it's not enough to make you happy. And that's not okay."

Price

When I was little, I had all these dreams of power and force and good and evil. I wanted to fight dragons. I wanted to be heroic and save princesses. I pored over the pictures in my fairy tale books, fetishizing the women, so different from my autocratic mother and my nagging nannies. I stared at drawings of lonely Rapunzel locked in her tower, or Cinderella crying by the fire, and my little-boy heart felt full and strong.

When I got a little older, my fairy tale fantasies transformed into superhero daydreams. I wanted to be both the villain and the rescuer to my adolescent crushes. I wanted to hurt women and save them, and be worthy of them. As I aged, I developed very specific fantasies, of towers and dungeons, cages and rope, and tearful, traumatized victims. I masturbated endlessly to imagined scenes of torment and abduction.

Then I grew into an adult, and realized that my needs skirted the edge of what was socially acceptable. Failed relationship followed failed relationship, and I finally gave up. I realized, well, no one will ever allow me to live out these fantasies without coming to hate me. I'll never find a modern woman who'll crave force and slavery, and be willing to surrender to so much pain. I'll never find a woman who will accept this dark, unhinged side of me.

Then I found her.

And then, a few years later, I realized fairy tales rarely came true.

Not that we'd ever been a fairy tale. An insecure ex-hooker and a sadistic commitment-phobe were never the stuff of happily ever after. Still, it hurt to hear her say that I had *nothing inside me.*

Nothing? *Nothing but three years of worry and angst and desire for you, you raving bitch.*

She hadn't just bruised my soul with those words she flung at me. She'd raked her claws over the only part of my psyche that wasn't confident and strong. She'd dug right down to the part of me that wanted to love, but was afraid of being hated again, and again, and again. Yes, I was a fucking coward when it came to love. I didn't need her to point it out to me. I knew.

As she had stood there railing at me, our roles were reversed, and she was the one mindfucking and hurting me, and trying to make me cry, only she wasn't doing it for sexual titillation. She was doing it because she honestly, literally believed I didn't care about her, that I was only interested in using her for sex. *There's nothing inside you but selfish emptiness, and money, and violence.*

Maybe she was right. Maybe beneath my rich, successful outward appearance, there was only a sniveling asshole who needed things his way. Maybe that was all I had to offer her, not love, but jealousy and desperate, pathetic scrabbling.

I'll buy you. I'll pay for you. I'll lock you in my dungeon. That will make you stay.

It didn't escape my notice that I'd spent thousands of dollars outfitting a dungeon I'd never allowed her to see. She needed a happy life, not a slave collar. She needed a good man, not me. I was selfish, empty, violent, and not enough of what she wanted.

Now I didn't know what to do. It wasn't fair to string her along, and I couldn't survive another shakedown like the one she'd subjected me to today. If I didn't walk away from her and eventually manage to forget about her, I'd slog through the rest of my life losing my fucking mind.

I'd just have to distract myself for a while. Block her number, delete her contact information, stay close to home. I had work projects I could concentrate on. Those were great for distraction, and eating up mental energy. I had books for when all else failed.

As for the physical, I could create profiles on BDSM dating sites, and find women to fuck and beat on, women desperate to surrender to men like me. There were plenty of them, the majority willing to subsist without love, only to have some dominant guy's attention.

Or I could try to write poems for Chere, or paint some fucking painting, exposing my soft, cowardly insides to try to win her back.

No. Solitude was so much safer, so much less risky. I went to the guest room closet and dug out the binoculars, and turned out all the lights and prowled to my spot by the window. I trained the lenses on her apartment. All the lights were on, and her drapes were open. There was a rectangle of paper in the center window. I focused on the words.

There's always a way, it read, in her swirly, girly-shit writing.

I put down the binoculars and sat on the couch with my head in my hands. I should never have told her that, because there wasn't a way. My dungeon would remain as empty as my heart. She was right, there was nothing inside me.

Without Chere, there was absolutely nothing at all.

Chere

"Chere, baby. You need to get out of bed." Andrew nudged me, checking for life. I'd been hiding under my covers for about a week now, because I didn't want to face the world.

"Chere," he said again. "You haven't eaten all day. I brought cookies."

"Don't want cookies."

Andrew's eyes widened. "You always want cookies. I'm calling a mental health hotline."

I sat up and tried to hit him with my pillow. And missed. Maybe I did need to eat something. "I don't need a hotline," I said, to make the worried look go away. "I just can't believe..."

I can't believe he left me again.

I'd tried to call. I'd tried to write to him, but my emails bounced back. I shouldn't have been surprised. I'd told him he had *nothing inside him*, which was so awful and wrong. His expression when I said it...

Now I was the one who felt empty inside.

"I have to go apologize," I said to Andrew, huddling deeper in the bedsheets.

"You know what's going to happen if you go to him. More sex. More confusion. From what you've told me... I don't know." He touched my hair, brushing it back on the pillow. "He's warned you he would be bad for you, that he can't give you the relationship you need."

"You're the one who said he loved me."

"But if he can't express that love…" He gave me his worried-best-friend look. "What has he brought to your life besides a bunch of drama?"

Oh, I don't know. Everything. He'd bought me a place to live. He'd supported my dreams and given me the nudge to make them happen. If he hadn't left me the first time, maybe I wouldn't have gone about my coursework with so much focus. Everything he'd done had benefitted me, except this idea that he couldn't give me love.

"He told me that love lies," I said. "That's what he believes. He doesn't know how to trust."

"You didn't know how to trust either, six months ago."

"Yeah, but I still *wanted* to trust at some point in my future. I wanted someone to prove trustworthy."

"You think Price is trustworthy?"

"Maybe," I said weakly.

Andrew frowned at me, but I couldn't stop thinking about what Price had said. *I can't be what you want. I don't have it in me.* If that was true, why had he done so many generous things? Why all the help? Why all the kisses and poetry?

"He doesn't realize he's a good person," I said softly.

"He can be a good person, babes, and still not be right for a committed relationship."

"I think other women have made him believe he's shitty and cruel. But he's not. They didn't understand him."

"And you do? You've been a wreck these past few weeks, feeling freaked out and confused all the time. It shouldn't be that way. Since I've met Craig—"

"Oh, Craig. Perfect, well-adjusted Craig," I snapped. "We can't all be so lucky. Before you had Craig, you used to gush about Price. *Ooh, he loves you so much. Ooh, he's so hot. Ooh, I want that.*"

"That was before I knew how, uh, complicated he really was. And I've changed now. I have higher standards because Craig has changed me for the better. Can you say the same about Price?"

Yes, I could. He'd changed me. He'd made me see the potential in myself. Now I had to do the same for him.

"I need to go see him," I said, throwing back the sheets. "I need to explain that I was wrong, that he has plenty of love inside him, that he's not this monster women have made him out to be."

"Oh, Chere."

I could see Andrew was torn between supporting me and trying to protect me, the same way I'd been torn when he'd decided to start escorting. But in my heart, I knew Price and I were meant to be together. We'd been drawn to each other even when we were apart. He'd said himself that I was the only one who ever understood him, and I understood that he'd run away now because he wasn't okay with himself. He'd held me off all this time because he didn't believe he was good enough. He was afraid because women had lied to him and betrayed his trust. *Love lies.*

My love was no lie, and I had to make him trust me. And somehow, too, I had to let go of my own fears and trust him.

I crawled out of bed and went to the kitchen. I needed some juice and a sandwich, and chocolate to fortify me. I had to make plans. Andrew followed me and watched in consternation as I tore into a bag of chocolate chips, since I didn't have any other chocolate in the house.

"I think he chooses not to do relationships for a reason," he said, leaning on the counter. "Think about what he's into, Chere."

"He's into the same stuff Craig is into. He's a Dominant and a sadist."

"But Craig takes care of me. Price, on the other hand, takes what he wants whether you want it or not. He's very…controlling."

"I like being controlled."

He waved a hand at my cellophane package of chocolate chips. "What if he decides he doesn't want you to have any more chocolate? Ever? Dominance seems oh, so sexy, until he says, 'Oh, by the way, you're never eating chocolate again.'"

I froze with a mouth full of chips. "He wouldn't say that."

"He might say it. Or he might decide you only get chocolate twice a year. Or he might decide you only get chocolate if you let three of his Dom friends stick their huge dicks in you at the same time."

I stopped scarfing the chocolate and wondered if Price had a stable of Dom friends. "You know, that would actually be hot."

"It's a hot *fantasy*," he said. "But you need to think about realities, because if you draw him into a more serious relationship, you're going to be dealing with his controlling shit all the time. Sometimes it might be wonderful and fun, but other times it might be awful and depressing."

"Kind of like my life now?"

"Chere." Andrew refused my proffered handful of chocolate chips. "Listen to me. Really listen. You've just graduated, you're feeling pressure about a job, you ran into Simon again, Price just deserted you for the second freaking time—"

"Because I blew up at him and said a bunch of shit I didn't mean." I put the chocolate chips away and rooted through the refrigerator for something healthier.

"Are you sure you didn't mean it?" asked Andrew. "A few weeks ago, a few months ago, you doubted everything. You've always had doubts about him, and he's always had doubts about you. He had so many doubts, he left you *twice*."

"Fine. Yes, he left me twice. You keep saying that. I know, Andrew. Do you want a sandwich?"

He shook his head. I made a sandwich for myself and then followed him over to the couch. He picked up right where he'd left off.

"I'm just saying that we feel things for a reason," he said. "We feel anxiety and fear for a reason."

"I'm not afraid of him."

"Maybe you should be!"

"He cares about me," I insisted, mostly in an effort to convince myself. "And kink-wise, I don't know anything that could hurt as much as the way I feel right now. I miss him."

A bite of sandwich stuck in my throat as emotion overwhelmed me. "What if he was the one, Andrew? What if he was my happily ever after? If I don't go to him—" I blinked through gathering tears. "If I don't go to him, if I don't give this craziness between us a chance, I'll never know."

Andrew took my sandwich and put it on the table, and pulled me into his arms. "Oh, Chere. I don't know what to say. I don't know what's right."

"I wish he was like Craig. I wish this was easy and civilized, and that I didn't have all these *feelings*."

"I know. It sucks."

"I don't know how to let Price go and wait for someone better, when he's the one who's still consuming all my thoughts. Since I met him, since the beginning, he's consumed me."

"I know, babes. I know."

"So how do I just give all that up? Ugh, this sucks so bad. It's so horrible. And now, after the things I said..." I swallowed hard, feeling panic. "He's blocked me out, my calls and emails. Even if I apologized, I'm not sure he'd take me back. "

Andrew snorted. "He'd take you back. He'd have you back in a heartbeat, because as much as you think you need him, he needs you more. But Chere, honey." He made me sit up, and wiped at my tears. "How much are you going to give him? You need to draw a line before you even consider going back. After Simon…you know what I mean? There has to be a line in your mind that you won't cross. You can't lose track of yourself again, and wind up stuck in another bad relationship you can't extricate yourself from."

"I wouldn't let that happen. I'm different now. I met Simon when I was younger than you, and I'm in my thirties now. I'd recognize the signs."

He arched a brow. "Age does not convey wisdom."

"You're too young to say that."

"And you're not exactly an old hag. Think about it. You'll have other opportunities, other guys you'll meet…"

His voice trailed off as I shook my head. "Not like this guy."

He grimaced. "Yeah, you're probably right."

"I need to go see him. We need to talk things out when we're not all overwrought about running into Simon. I think that's what set everything off, running into Simon at your party, and the fight, and getting hauled off to jail." I shuddered. "But Simon's the past, and maybe…maybe Price is…"

"Your future?"

I let out a breath. "Yes."

We both lay back on the couch under the weight of this decision, this choice that felt like life or death. "You should wait a couple more days," he said. "You should wait until you're feeling a little stronger. I mean, what if it doesn't go well? What if he tells you to get lost?"

"He might. He probably will." I shrugged and twisted my fingers together. "He's probably going to say all kinds of awful things and order me to stay the fuck away from him. I still have to go."

PRICE

My house was quiet, but I liked it quiet. I wasn't a big TV watcher, or a music person. I was a reader, and I was reading a lot to keep thoughts of Chere from crowding my mind. If I thought about her too long, I'd go to her, and I was determined not to. I'd put away the binoculars. No more stalking. No more manipulation. She'd had enough, and I...

Well, I had a stack of books in my living room, and a bottle of wine, and silence to lose myself in the words. I was halfway through Pablo Neruda's *Winter Garden*, a collection of poems I'd read numerous times. It was always a transcendent experience, but I hadn't been able to lose myself in the imagery the way I normally did. Maybe it was too quiet.

In the silence, I heard a footfall outside. The neighbors across the hall? It was late, after ten. I glanced at my watch but didn't go back to the poetry. I had a sense of recognition, of waiting. Then, the knock.

It took just a second, maybe two, for me to realize it had to be Chere. No one else could get by the doorman at this hour, and besides that, I think subconsciously I'd registered the rhythm and weight of her steps. I thought for a moment of not answering. Just a moment, though. If she was here, I was going to see her. Maybe something had happened, some emergency.

I put my wineglass on the side table, and lay the book of poems on top of the others, still opened to my place. I'd go back to reading it shortly. I would not embrace Chere and invite her inside, or kiss her, or fuck her. By her own words, I had nothing to give her.

She knocked again, louder, then rang the doorbell. And rang the doorbell again. She wanted in, the little nutjob. Of course she'd ring the doorbell repeatedly. If I waited a few more seconds, she'd do it again. I pictured her with her finger poised over the button as I threw the lock and opened the door.

And there she was, standing two feet away. She lifted her chin as I stared at her in her pink Lanvin suit, and the black leather mask I'd instructed her to wear to our first meeting three years ago. The air whooshed out of me, taken up by the emotion in my chest. That pert nose, her set mouth, even the tilt of her chin was the same.

"Are you there?" she asked when I couldn't produce any words. She reached out, groping for me, not quite touching me. Then she reached to take off the mask. I almost stopped her but then I remembered, *you can't stop her. She's not yours to control. Don't touch her. Don't look at her.*

She pushed off the mask, blinking at me through a sheen of tears. She held it out to me, and gestured down at her outfit. It hugged her curves as enticingly as it had that day.

"I just thought...remember? The W Hotel?"

"I remember." I drank in the sight of her, trying not to look like I was dying inside. "I remember," I repeated, keeping my tone neutral and civilized. "Why are you here?"

"Well, I thought... I wanted to come back and..." She looked past me. "Can I come in?"

"No."

"Is there someone else here?"

Ha, someone else. Like I would have moved on from her in the space of a week. "No one else is here," I said, "and you shouldn't be here either."

She clutched the mask in front of her, twisting the straps. "I'm here because I need to talk to you. I'm sorry for the crazy shit I said to you, about you being empty inside. I didn't mean it. I was just freaked out from seeing Simon."

"Chere—"

"No, wait. That's not the truth. The truth is, I freaked out on you because I love you. I tried not to fall in love, but I did, and you said—"

"Chere, I need you to go."

She was so sad, and so beautiful. It was so hard to keep my walls up when she looked at me that way, her clear brown eyes full of longing and apology.

But I had to keep my walls up. I nudged her back and shut the door.

The doorbell rang as soon as I threw the lock. I returned to my wine and my book, but my quiet had been shattered. She rang ten more times before I got up and yanked open the door. She was wearing the damn mask again.

"I'm not interested," I said through my teeth. "If I wanted a whore, I'd have called one."

She pitched herself at me, knocking me backward. I tripped and fell and she landed on top of me, a masked pink dragon, breathing fire. Somewhere along the line I'd forgotten she was such a fighter.

"I know you love me," she said, holding me down.

"I don't believe in love."

"Then surrender. You believe in surrender. I tried my best to be the kind of partner you wanted. Why wouldn't you ever let me in your dungeon?"

I glanced at the open door, wondering what the neighbors and their two young children might think of this scene. "You're a fucking pain in the ass," I said, pushing her off me.

She lay back on my floor in her damned designer suit. I remembered it as vividly as I remembered that day we met. The skirt I'd cut off her that day was still in the back of my closet, folded into a pale pink square. She kicked off her shoes.

"I'm not leaving until you talk to me," she said. "Or hurt me. Either one."

"I'm very close to hurting you. Why don't you move on with your life? Why don't you get a fucking job?"

"Because I want to work for you. I want to work at Eriksen."

"You don't have the resume for Eriksen." I took off her mask and flung it across the room so she couldn't put it on again. "I paid for you to go to school so you would make something of yourself. Wasn't that the plan?" Her eyes widened as I yelled at her. "Now you're lying on my fucking floor in the same outfit you wore three years ago—"

"I'll get a job, okay? Is that what I have to do for you to love me?" She crawled over and slammed the door, and leaned back against it, drawing in her knees. I read the body language easily enough: she wasn't leaving. I thought with longing of my wine and Neruda poems. Damn her and her long, brown, curly hair making a halo against the pale wood.

"I'll get a job," she said. "I'll design things. I *want* to design things. Why does that mean I can't have you too?"

"Because I want to put you in a dungeon," I answered in a sharp voice. "It's not about the job, it's about this relationship shit you're looking for. I want sex and slavery. I want you as a toy, not a partner, and it's not fair to draw you into a dynamic like that when you want *love* and *commitment.* Why can't you fucking see this?"

"We can't compromise?" she asked. "There's no way for us to have the sex and slavery and still have love?"

I gave a bitter laugh. "You'd love me for about a week before you tried to run the hell away."

"That's not true. I want your intensity and your roughness. I love to surrender to you."

I got to my feet, waving away her silly declarations. She had no idea what she was volunteering for. "It wouldn't just be sessions," I said. "If I had what I wanted—my ideal relationship—"

Stop. Stop talking, Price. Just stop.

"What? Tell me."

"It would be about more than sex," I said, standing over her. "It would be everything. You wouldn't just be a slave, or a sub. You'd be mine, my possession."

"I want that."

"You think you do, but you don't." I started to pace, desire and angst expended in activity. "I would take everything I wanted from you, everything I needed, no matter what you thought you needed. I'd torment you if I felt like it. An all-encompassing dynamic. That's what I would want." I stopped pacing and turned to her. "You've never been anyone's slave before."

"I've been yours," she said. "For three years."

She looked exhausted, like she hadn't been sleeping well. I hadn't been sleeping well either. Something was missing from my life, a person I needed to make me happy. A person I would end up damaging and hurting.

"Chere," I said, and it was almost a groan. "Why are you putting me through this?"

"Because we belong together."

She was so sure of that, sitting there with her back against my door, and her knees drawn up in her little pink skirt. She was so fucking sure this was possible.

"I'll show you the dungeon," I said. "I'll show you what I want from you, and then…"

I wasn't saying yes. But she realized I wasn't saying no anymore either. I was saying maybe, which was fucking careless of me. She gave me a huge smile as I held out my hand to help her to her feet.

* * * * *

I stuffed down nerves and walked her along the hall to my bedroom, and then to my walk-in closet. She watched as I pushed aside a line of suits, revealing a hidden door.

"That's why I couldn't find it," she said.

I frowned at her. "You tried to find it?"

"Yes. The morning you left me alone."

"If I wanted you to see it, I would have shown it to you."

Her eyes flashed in the harsh closet light. "You've shown it to other women, haven't you?"

It wasn't really a question. It was a reproach. Yes, I'd brought other women here but they meant nothing to me, and Chere meant too much.

"I'll tell you this," I said. "No one I've ever brought here has elected to come back."

With that warning, I turned the knob and walked her inside. On the surface, it was like any other room. It had dark gray walls and a smooth white ceiling, and a polished hardwood floor. But beneath the drywall, I'd had the entire space soundproofed, because I lived for the sound of a woman's screams.

I walked around turning on lights. Lamps, overhead lights, paper lanterns, every kind of light to illuminate this darkly perverse world.

"Wow," she said. "This is…"

It was over the top. I knew. I'd repurposed two good-sized bedrooms to create the space, and furnished it with top-tier BDSM equipment. There was a monster of a bondage rack screwed to the wall, capable of restraining a victim in just about any position. There was a broad, padded leather table for horizontal kink activities, and an adjustable spanking bench for forcing women's asses into the air. There was a sawhorse spreader with interchangeable tops: a flatter, padded one for milder sessions, and a hard, triangular one for punishing a slave who'd been very, very naughty. There was a cage, only one, a low, Chere-sized rectangle with stark metal bars.

Aside from the various kinky structures, there were two tall chests full of thousands of dollars' worth of butt plugs, nipple clamps, sex toys and punishment implements, all collected in the three years since I'd met her. I'd collected them for her, because I'd wanted her even when I shouldn't want her. I'd wanted *this*, a painful, dark, selfish dynamic that could never fulfill her, no matter how sexy and exciting it might seem.

"What do you think?" I asked. From the expression on her face, I thought she was probably soaking her panties.

"So, this is what you want in a relationship? To hurt me here? To keep me locked away in here, all the time?"

"Not all the time. Sometimes. When I feel like cuffing you to one of these structures and doing unconscionable things to your body."

She let out a slow breath. A flush crept up my neck. It had been one thing to admit I had a dungeon. It was another thing to allow her in here to see all the ways I wanted to torture her, to see the sheer magnitude of my perversion in the furniture and equipment I'd bought.

"I'm not afraid of this," she said, a little too loudly. She turned to me and repeated herself. "I'm not afraid of this. If this is what you want, I want it too. I mean, we were always moving toward this, weren't we? You like control…" She gestured around at the racks and chains and leather cuffs. "And I like when you control me. It excites me."

"Will it excite you when you don't like it?" I asked.

"I can't…" She gave me a flash of a smile and twitched self-consciously at her skirt. "I can't imagine not liking it. Am I crazy for wanting this? I'm so turned on right now."

I wanted to fall on her. I wanted to fix her to the bondage rack and do a thousand wretched things to her until she begged for mercy. She'd like it sometimes. She'd hate it sometimes, though. She'd hate *me*.

"You won't always feel turned on." I held out a hand. "Come here."

I hadn't touched her yet, was afraid to let myself touch her, but when she crossed to me I grasped her hand. She was so trusting. I walked her to the far wall of the dungeon, past the solid wood and iron structures I'd use to restrain her.

You think you know rough, starshine. You think you like it rough and hard and violent. You have no idea yet.

I took her to stand in front of the two tall chests of drawers, and I started opening them, showing her what was inside. It was a ridiculously massive and lurid collection. Three years was a long time to fantasize.

There were plugs and vibrators, every kind of nipple clamp, spreaders, and leather gear with clips and O-rings I could use to truss her up however I pleased. I'd accumulated a few serious—and seriously expensive—chastity devices, because I'd imagined her on her knees begging for orgasms. I'd also acquired an ungodly number of punishment implements, because I'd imagined breaking her down into an enslaved puddle of *please-let-me-please-you.* I'm not even sure she knew what the chastity belts and harnesses were for. She knew what the paddles and crops and straps and floggers were for. There was also a whole drawer at the bottom full of canes.

"You see what I mean?" I asked. "You see what I mean when I say you won't always feel turned on? You know I'm a sadist. Sometimes I'll really hurt you. Not injure you, but hurt you until you cry and scream for me to stop. And I won't stop, Chere. That's not how I play. No softness, no safe words. In our relationship, I'll make you miserable on purpose, because it makes me feel powerful and sexually aroused."

She wouldn't look at me. I had to tilt her chin up to focus her gaze.

"Are you listening?" I asked. "This is what I want. Not love. Not dinner and a movie. I want your body and your soul. Over the last few weeks, when I hurt you and fucked you, I let you go home afterward. You had that choice, to end things."

She stared at me, her breathing shallow. "If we started up again, you wouldn't let me end things?"

"No. Not if I didn't want to."

"So if I…" She looked around the silent dungeon. "If I agreed to that level of control… If I let you hurt me and enslave me the way you want, do you think you would ever be able to…to love me in return?"

Jesus Christ, she was killing me.

"You know I already love you," I said, and with those words, my soul went broke. I confessed it. I admitted it. I loved her as I'd never loved anyone, and would never love anyone again. I also had to love her *this way*, or no way, because this was who I was. I took her in my arms and held her against my chest, touching her wild brown hair and her lovely feminine neck.

"Really, you wouldn't let me go, even if I wanted to go?" she asked. "Even if I begged to go?"

"No," I said, because love lies.

"Ever?"

Ever. A fairy-tale word. *Happily ever after.* I wanted us to live happily ever after. I knew I'd never find someone like her again, and if she was willing to put up with me....

"I don't think I'll ever want to let you go," I told her. "If you let me have you, *all* of you, and then you decided you wanted to leave, I don't think I'd be able to let you go. It'd be a really tough thing."

"What if I had to get away?" she asked. "What if you're just too awful? I guess I'd have to escape."

"You could try."

She was so twisted, my kinky girl. She wanted this. She wanted to be my prisoner of love. She wanted me to torment her and challenge her, and make her heart race. At some point, I knew she'd try to run away, just so I'd recapture her and punish her. All these lovely games were ahead of us. All the things in the drawers waited to be used on her body, to make it ache or burn with desire.

She'd cry here, and hate me, and chafe against my will. She'd also cling to me and orgasm. I could become her entire world, and her eyes would come alive each time I brought her into this room to work her over. It could happen.

"So, you want this?" I asked. My smile faded. It was time to be serious. If she wasn't one hundred percent in, I couldn't risk this kind of relationship.

"Do you think you could bear belonging to me?" I pressed. "It's perfectly fine if you want to walk away. It would be better for you to walk away."

She didn't even think before she answered. "I don't want to walk away. We need to be together. We'll figure it out."

Shit. I let go of her and looked down at her pink tailored suit. I'd cut it off her that first day in a frenzy to get at the body underneath, and spent a fortune on a replacement. She was offering me access to that body all the time, along with her smiles and her spirit...

There was so much to figure out, so much to worry about as I brought her into my life, and, of course, into my home. I would need her to live here and be available to me all the time, but she'd want to work too. Maybe I could rent a design space for her in my office building. On the same floor, preferably, so she'd be right there. I'd make her rent out her apartment and invest the money into her fledgling jewelry company. My business mind took over, because my heart was overwhelmed.

There was so much risk, but I'd warned her and rebuffed her, and demonstrated the depth of my perversity, and she was still choosing this. She was choosing me. I didn't know if it would feel like love to her. All I knew was that I hadn't taken a chance like this in years, and that I'd never taken a chance where the stakes were so high.

"Are you okay?" She touched my arm, a light, soothing caress. "I'm the one who's supposed to be scared right now."

"Fuck you," I muttered. "This is all your fault."

"It's going to be okay. Trust me."

Trust me. Women couldn't be trusted, and love couldn't be trusted, but I'd let Chere into my dungeon and into my heart. Any torture that resulted was my own fucking fault, even if I blamed all this on her. I should never have opened the door.

But if I hadn't, I knew she'd still be out there, ringing the bell for the thousandth time.

"Want to try some of the equipment on for size?" I suggested, because if I didn't move around and do something, I was going to die of anticipation. I took her to the spanking bench, bent her over it and swatted her a few times to make her laugh. I showed her the modular parts of it, all the ways it could display her gorgeous ass for punishment or fucking. Next, I fit her wrists into a pair of shackles in the middle of the room. I raised them with a winch until she was on her tiptoes, her shoulders straining in her suit. Practice only. This equipment was made for nakedness.

She couldn't have straddled the sawhorse in her tight-fitting skirt. Instead I showed her how the leather-covered top could be inverted to suit my purposes, so straddling it was either comfortable or torturous for her. I left it in the torturous configuration, so she could imagine how the peaked edge would feel digging into her pussy for some future crime.

And she'd commit crimes, I knew. She'd break rules, push boundaries. She was my fighter, after all.

I led her to the ladder-style bondage rack and made her stand on the lowest bar, and then instructed her to reach up and hold the highest bar she could. Once she obeyed, I went around to the other side, to the space between the rack and the wall.

Since she stood on the bar, her eyes and lips were on a level with mine. I kissed her, a kiss for all the ecstasy she'd brought me, and the agony, and the promise of more. When I opened my eyes, she was staring back at me. I closed my hands over hers.

I'd be able to bind her to this rack whenever I wanted to, with rope or cuffs or leather straps. I'd clamp her tits and loop the chain over the bar above or below, so every time she moved, her nipples would feel it. Then I'd flog her, or hit her with a broad strap or paddle until her ass was scarlet and her legs trembled. Then I'd take her down and carry her to my bed, and fuck her while she was still crying from the pain. Maybe I wouldn't even make it to the bed. Maybe I'd push her down on the floor and fuck her ass, using the absolute minimum amount of lube I needed to get in.

I'd do things like that, and sometimes, more rarely, I'd do gentle things like hold her and stroke her. Maybe I'd write her some poetry. Maybe, finally, I'd be able to find the words.

I kissed her once more and let go of her hands.

"Come on," I said. "Let's see if you fit in the cage. I know you're dying to get in there."

She hopped down off the rack and made for the cage like a kid set loose in a toy store. She was already waiting beside it when I arrived to swing open the door.

"Go on," I prompted. "This will be the one and only time I let you in there with clothes."

I could have made her take off the clothes, but she'd worn them for a reason, and they were special. If she was going to wear clothes her first time in my cage, it was good and right that it would be these.

"Wait," I said. "There's something else for you to try."

She perched just inside the cage's opening, sitting on her knees. It was exactly the right height—tall enough for her to sit comfortably, but not stand. She could stretch her legs out if she raised them in the air. I'd have her try it in a moment, but first I went to the drawers and pulled out a box from the top left one. It contained another relic from our hotel sessions: the supple leather collar I'd bought for her, in the same soft brown color as her eyes.

I brought it over to her, as excited now as she'd been excited over the cage. I didn't stop to show it to her, beyond holding it in front of me for the slightest moment. I wanted it on her. I wanted to see her wearing my collar again. My pet, my toy, my starshine, my pink dragon. *Mine.*

"Let's try it on for size," I said, although I knew the size of her neck like I knew the size of my cock, since I'd grasped both of them plenty of times. I knew it would fit. She'd worn it before, during our last session at the Carlyle Hotel. I held the part with the O-ring against the front of her neck and made her lean down so I could buckle it in the back.

"Oh," she said. "You made it too tight."

"Not tight. Snug." I didn't want a breath of space between that collar and her neck. It symbolized control and surrender, and our history together. Three years. That was a long fucking time.

She sat up and shook her hair back. Holy fuck, she looked magnificent. I'd put the collar on her at the Carlyle, yes, but that meant nothing in comparison to my feelings now. My cock ached, but this moment was more than sex, more than horniness.

This was, finally, her total surrender—and mine. She touched the leather with her delicate fingertips, and gazed at me, her eyes wide. I wouldn't have faulted her for looking around for a mirror, but she only looked at me.

"Do you like it?" she asked.

Jesus. Did I like it? I parted my lips, at a loss for words. I made some motion for her to scoot back, and then I shut her in the cage, locking the door with an audible scratch and click. She stared out between the bars, the same woman who'd come to me, masked and defensive, three years ago, but now she was unmasked, and not defensive at all.

She loved me. She wanted me. She'd asked me to trust her, but I was more amazed by the trust she placed in me.

"Look at what you do for me," I breathed. "You're so beautiful." It was the only poem I'd ever written for her, and the one I fell back on now, when all other words failed. I reached through the bars and touched her face, and skimmed my fingers over the collar.

"Price," she said, her voice high with emotion. "Can I call you Master now? Are you my Master?"

"I'm your everything," I replied, curling my finger in the O-ring. "Owner, Lord, Master. But I'm partial to Sir. It sounds less pompous."

A smile curved the corners of her mouth. "You're never pompous, Sir."

I gave her cheek a little crack for the snarkiness, still holding the O-ring. She gasped, five percent of it dismay and ninety-five percent of it lust. Yes, I was sometimes pompous, and I didn't mind her pointing it out. We could still have jokes and warmth between us. We could have everything now.

I let go of the ring and opened my hand, and wrapped it around her neck, squeezing just enough. "Talk to me, starshine," I said. "Do you want this? Tell me your definitive answer."

I already knew her answer, but I was thrilled to hear it anyway.

"Yes. Yes, Sir, I want this." She swallowed hard against my palm, gazing at me, eyes clear and free of tears. "I belong here in your cage. In your dungeon."

Cages and dungeons weren't the best way to love, but they were necessary between us. They were the best way to make our relationship work. That's what I told myself, anyway.

I grasped her neck tighter, curling my fingers over the elegant brown collar, then pulled her close until our lips met through the cage bars. With a soft growl of contentment, I sealed our covenant with a kiss.

to be continued

Trust Me (Rough Love Part Three)

It's been three years since they first met, and Chere is finally where she wants to be: in Price's dungeon.

Well, she's in his dungeon part of the time. The rest of the time, she's living in his home, eating his food, sleeping in his bed, reading his books, wearing his—well, no, he won't let her wear anything. In fact, there are a lot of things he doesn't allow, more than she ever imagined in her torrid fantasies. Life under Price's control is an adjustment, and sometimes a nightmare.

It's not long before she realizes she's in way over her head…

Don't miss this final book in the Rough Love series. Watch for *Trust Me*'s release in early 2016. And don't forget to subscribe to Annabel's newsletter at Annabeljoseph.com to receive updates about *Trust Me* and her other upcoming work!

Like it Rough?
You may also enjoy these edgy BDSM romances
by Annabel Joseph

The Cirque Masters series

Enter a world where performers' jaw-dropping strength, talent, and creativity is matched only by the decadence of their kinky desires. Cirque du Monde is famous for mounting glittering circus productions, but after the Big Top goes dark, you can find its denizens at *Le Citadel*, a fetish club owned by Cirque CEO Michel Lemaitre—where anything goes. This secret world is ruled by dominance and submission, risk and emotion, and a fearless dedication to carnal pleasure in all its forms. Love in the circus can be as perilous as aerial silks or trapeze, and secrets run deep in this intimate society. Run away to the circus, and soar with the Cirque Masters—a delight for the senses, and for the heart.

The Cirque Masters series is:
#1 *Cirque de Minuit* (Theo's story)
#2 *Bound in Blue* (Jason's story)
#3 *Master's Flame* (Lemaitre's story)

The Club Mephisto series

Club Mephisto... Molly is a 24/7 slave dedicated to serving her Master. When business calls him away on a weeklong trip, he arranges to leave her in the care of Mephisto, the owner of a thriving local BDSM club. Molly is both excited and scared to be given over to Master Mephisto. His power and mysterious intensity have long compelled her from afar.

She finds herself immersed in a world of strict commands, pervasive sex, and creative torments. Over the course of a week, Mephisto strips away privileges Molly took for granted, and forces her to understand and acknowledge the depths to which she can be made to submit. But a surprising conversation the last day threatens Molly's worldview, as does the strange closeness that develops between them. As the time of Master's return draws near, Molly finds herself deeply and inexorably changed.

Note: this BDSM fantasy novella depicts "total power exchange" relationships that some readers may find objectionable. This work contains acts of sadism, objectification, orgasm denial and speech restriction, caging, anal play and double penetration, BDSM punishment and discipline, M/f, M/m/f, M/m, orgy and group sexual encounters, voyeurism, and limited circumstances of dubious consent.

Molly's Lips: Club Mephisto Retold... If you've read *Club Mephisto*, you know the story from Molly's perspective. Now, prepare to relive the experience from Mephisto's point of view in this gripping novella.

When Mephisto's friend Clayton is called out of town on business, he agrees to look after his slave for the week. But Molly isn't your average slave. She and Clayton share a serious, full time dynamic. Mephisto feels a weight of responsibility he isn't used to, and worse, an intense attraction to Molly, the partner of his friend.

Mephisto is determined to sublimate his inappropriate desires and provide a challenging and instructive week for the devoted slave. He subjects Molly to orgasm denial, speech restriction, scenes of erotic torment, even an orgy where she is made to service his friends. Along the way, he experiences unfamiliar jealousy, and deep cravings to possess her himself.

Throughout the week, he is also haunted by persistent questions. Is she happy being a 24/7 slave? Or is there another Molly trapped beneath her submissive, surrendered gaze?

Burn For You... When Molly loses her longtime Master, she feels lost, angry. Confused. She's unsure of her future, even her calling to the BDSM lifestyle. She knows her Master always intended her to go to his friend Mephisto next, but their emotionally—and sexually—fraught history is still a confusion of desire and fear in her mind.

Mephisto wants to help Molly, but he doesn't want to force her into service she's not sure she wants. He owes it to Clayton to help her find happiness, but how? Molly and Mephisto advance and retreat from one another as they try to untangle their complex feelings. More and more it seems their tense standoff will only end one way…

Note: this 63K-word erotic romance novel contains consensual BDSM play, Master/slavery, sado-masochism, anal play, objectification, caging, and other consensual activities which some might find offensive.

The Mephisto series is:
#1 *Club Mephisto* (Molly's POV)
#2 *Molly's Lips* (Mephisto's POV)
#3 *Burn For You* (the romantic conclusion)

THE COMFORT SERIES

Have you ever wondered what goes on in the bedrooms of Hollywood's biggest heartthrobs? In the case of Jeremy Gray, the reality is far more depraved than anyone realizes. Brutal desires, shocking secrets, and a D/s relationship (with a hired submissive "girlfriend") that's based on a contract rather than love. It's just the beginning of a four-book saga following Jeremy and his Hollywood friends as they seek comfort in fake, manufactured relationships. Born of necessity—and public relations—these attachments come to feel more and more real. What does it take to live day-to-day with an A-list celebrity? Patience, fortitude, and a whole lot of heart. Oh, and a *very* good pain tolerance for kinky mayhem.

Comfort series is:
#1 *Comfort Object* (Jeremy's story)
#2 *Caressa's Knees* (Kyle's story)
#3 *Odalisque* (Kai's story)
#4 *Command Performance* (Mason's story)

About the Author

Annabel Joseph is a multi-published BDSM romance author. She writes mainly contemporary romance, although she has been known to dabble in the medieval and Regency eras. She is known for writing emotionally intense BDSM storylines, and strives to create characters that seem real—even flawed—so readers are better able to relate to them. Annabel also writes non-BDSM romance under the pen name Molly Joseph.

You can follow Annabel on Twitter (@annabeljoseph) or Facebook (facebook.com/annabeljosephnovels), or sign up to receive her monthly newsletter at annabeljoseph.com. She also loves to hear from her readers at annabeljosephnovels@gmail.com.

Printed in the USA
CPSIA information can be obtained
at www.ICGtesting.com
CBHW061209010924
13985CB00025B/711

9 780692 573082